# Once in Chicago

## Peter Tiernan

DEEPWOODS BOOKS

*To the people I met
in the summer of 1978
who led me to the person
I've loved ever since.*

# TABLE OF CONTENTS

## PROLOGUE: Three Little Birds

*Don't worry about a thing, 'cause every little thing gonna be alright.*
*- Bob Marley*

"Imagine," May Maloney's husband Owen says. "You're born in the dimple of a giant rock, you live your whole life there, and you die never knowing anything else."

They're driving away from Mesa Verde National Park, having just taken a tour of the cliff dwellings the Pueblos lived in 700 years ago. It's the fifth day of a four-week trip Owen planned from Austin to San Francisco that would go through a dozen national parks and string together six poetry readings. He'd borrowed one of those teardrop camper trailers from a friend, and they were going to rough it across the southwest and up to Northern California.

When Owen first brought up his idea for the trip, May wasn't exactly thrilled. She'd camped out only once in her life, tenting with girlfriends in the Smokies the summer after freshman year. And she hated it. It rained for two days straight, and everything she brought got sopped. When the sun finally came out, so did the mosquitoes. They were so bad, insect repellent couldn't keep them away. Even when they hunkered down in their sleeping bags, they still got bit. Afterwards, her friends counted over 100 bites on May's back.

"Well," Owen said, trying to sell her on the trip. "You won't have to worry about rain or mosquitoes where we're going."

So she agreed to go. Like she agreed to move to Iowa City as soon as they got back from their trip, so Owen could start a new job teaching in their prestigious Creative Writing Program. And like she moved to the Upper Peninsula two years before for Owen's job at Northern Michigan University. And like she agreed to move before that, from Charlotte to Morgantown, also for the sake of Owen's career. She had agreed to all these changes and more, agreed to turn her life upside down over and over, taking whatever nursing jobs she could, because she had faith in Owen, faith that he was doing what was right, not just for his career, but for the family—and now that the kids were gone, for the two of them.

This time, though, she did wonder: was this move really in *their* best interest or just Owen's? Finding out it had been between him and Ada Limón for the title of U.S. poet laureate was a bitter blow. Not that Owen ever showed his disappointment. He laughed it off as a near-miss. "Who needs that sort of pressure?" he told friends. May knew better. She knew how much it hurt Owen to come so close to notoriety. He was 65 years old. He didn't have many books left in him. And here he was, teaching poetry in the hinterlands of the U.P., after a third step-down job in a row. Then this chance to teach at the Iowa Writer's Workshop came along. She couldn't blame him for making one last bid for the limelight he'd always watched from the shadows, one last bold statement before his voice went quiet. Whether it was a selfish impulse or not, they needed the money—more than twice what he was making in Marquette.

She'd be tempted to think of this trip as another ego stroke, too, if he hadn't taken so much time to plot out all the national park visits. May had always wanted to take a family road trip out west, but every year, when they assessed their finances, Owen said it made more sense to teach spring and summer terms and make the extra money. They took the kids to Mammoth Cave once and went to Disneyland. But those were the only long vacations they ever took. So this trip had the feel of a grand gesture, a big blanket apology to May: *I'm sorry we never went anywhere. This is for all the years I never made enough money to make family memories.* Too bad the kids were in their thirties now. And too bad May's idea of a vacation now was a long weekend in Paris or London or, honestly, even Chicago—a little sight-seeing, a few nice meals, some shopping, a spa treatment. But Owen's aversion to cities was a whole other story.

So here was May, five days, two readings, and two national parks into the trip, and she was already sick of climbing into and out of that teardrop camper, dealing with the tiny toilet, drinking bad coffee, being so close to Owen—all the time. How was she ever going to make it another month? How much faith did she really have in him anymore? One thing was for sure: she'd know by the end of this.

"I mean, their whole history, their entire notion of the world, was formed in those caves," Owen tries again to make conversation. These attempts to keep the long drives lively already have a forced air to them. "And then, at some point, the last Pueblo packed up and left. They don't even know why—famine, drought, invaders. It had to be for something terrible. You don't leave your whole life behind when things are good."

"Maybe they were bored," May suggests.

Owen goes quiet. She's looking out her side window, but she can feel his eyes on her. Then he laughs. "Maybe so. It's all a guess. The point is, their reality just slowly disappeared. Dust in the wind…" Owen snaps his fingers and points to May.

Not this again. Not another music quiz. She knows the tune, remembers it from high school, can even hum part of it, but she has no prayer of coming up with the band's name.

"Do we have to do this?"

"This one's for a trip to Iceland."

"I don't know. Journey."

"Good guess, but no. Kansas. Off *Point of No Return*."

"I don't like these music quizzes," May tells him flat-out. "I don't need constant reminders of what I've forgotten or never knew."

"This is what happened to the Pueblos. At some point, people stopped thinking about them. Now, nothing that they cared about matters to us anymore."

Was Owen really equating her resistance to music trivia with the world's ignorance of Pueblo history? "Oh, I don't know," she pushes back. "I bet they cared about the same things we do."

"You know what I mean. I'm talking about their beliefs, their hopes, dreams, fears. They weren't the same as ours."

"Yeah, but they had them." May feels like she's arguing a larger point. "We don't know what they are, but we know they had them."

"So you're saying the particulars don't matter." Owen's voice has a cranky edge to it. "What they felt about their lives, the myths they conceived to make sense of it, the language. None of that matters."

"I didn't say that." Has this become an actual argument? "You said nothing they cared about matters to us, and I'm just saying it's all still the same things—love, family, safety, community. The human condition is the human condition."

"I guess so," Owen concedes glumly, like he knew the answer all along and couldn't bring himself to admit it. "Makes me wonder why I do this," he mutters. It comes out so softly May thinks he didn't mean for her to hear it.

"You do this because you love it."

"Driving around the country, selling books out of the trunk of my car, like some street bum singing a song with a collection hat at his feet, hoping people will take pity and throw a few coins in it."

"That's not what this is at all, and you know it. You were—" She's going to say *almost the poet laureate*, but she catches herself. "You *are* much more talented than that."

"At least seventeen people in Albuquerque thought so."

That's all the books he sold yesterday? May knew the number was low, but she didn't want to ask him. He was barely okay with selling 72 copies of his collected works in Austin. Seventeen? Was this what they had to look forward to at the rest of the readings?

"Barely a hundred bucks," Owen goes on. "That's what my deepest musings are worth. Of course, nobody cares about poetry.

Nobody reads anymore, let alone the most esoteric form of writing. It's all Facebook and podcasts and echo chambers. We're like the Pueblos. Our vanishing has already begun. A hundred years from now, someone's going to say, 'there used to be this thing called books,' and nobody will know where they went because there was nothing written anywhere to tell them."

Okay, now Owen's going too far. Never mind that the notion is absurd; to get rid of writing, you'd have to destroy every single book in the world and punish anyone who took pen to paper—or fingertips to keyboard. It's Owen's outlook that May thinks is so over the top. It wasn't like him to be this gloomy. Yes, he'd had his moments of despair, probably more than usual since missing out on poet laureate. But Owen was generally an upbeat person. He had a way of laughing off disappointment she wished she could adopt. Every time he got down on himself, he'd come right back, sometimes within hours, ready to move forward. That's how she was coming to know when he was sad—not by the sadness, but the rallying from it. Whenever she found a to-do list around the house, she knew Owen had been struggling… and was fighting against it.

A new song comes on. "I know this one," May tries to change the subject. "What's the prize for getting this one right?"

Owen shakes his head. "If you don't get this—"

"'Three Little Birds,' Bob Dylan!" she shouts over him.

"Dylan?! What? No! It's Bob *Marley*." Owen laughs.

"Oh…" May knew that. She just needs to lighten the mood. That's what she does from time to time. Play dumb. Get Owen laughing again. He knows it, yet he lets her get away with it. It's a way she says *I love you*—when he needs to hear it most.

They pass a sign: *MANCOS Colorado City Limits Elev 7000 ft.* May remembers the town's name but can't remember why. "Mancos…" she muses. "Isn't there supposed to be something there?"

"My brother said they had an amazing bakery."

"That's right. Well, we should stop."

Owen groans under his breath. May sees him squint at the clock on the screen between them. She knows what he's going to say. "I don't know, May. We're already an hour behind."

"Come on, Owen. You said you'd stop more if I saw something I like. And Neil was the one saying we should go here."

"Fine," Owen relents. "Neil hasn't steered us wrong yet."

They turn off the highway, right onto Main Street, and drive for a couple blocks without seeing evidence of a downtown.

"Did I go the wrong way?" Owen looks in his rear-view mirror. "Let me check Google Maps."

Up ahead, there's a brick structure jutting up out of the desert shrubland. It looks like a city building from a bygone era, restored and plopped down on the barren plain. On the far wing of the edifice, there's a sign for the Absolute Bakery & Café. He drives past the store and parks a few spots down the street.

The bakery's a big, noisy place with stone walls and wood floors. It's crammed with books, knick-knacks, local artwork, and a long line snaking through the aisles to the counter where everything they sell is on display. "Neil said the cinnamon rolls are the thing to get," Owen mentions, as they file in at the end of the line.

The line's a dozen people deep. When they're in sight of the display counter, May tells Owen, "Get me a coffee and one of those peanut butter cookies." Then she goes to check out a mobile of carved birds hanging at the back of the store. She doesn't want to stray too far from the register; if there's any decision to make, Owen won't do it himself. He'll call to her, and probably too loud.

"Owen?" It's someone else's voice that rises over the chatter. May turns to see a woman behind the counter frozen in front of her husband, face slack with shock.

Owen says something May can't hear. She goes back to him. "My God," he says now. "It's you." The woman doesn't say anything, just goes on staring at Owen. She looks younger than them, but maybe it's because of how thin she is, how smooth the skin is on her face, how her hair isn't grey.

She glances at May, looks back at Owen, then turns to the girl working with her. "Excuse me." She hurries out a side door.

The girl watches her go, shrugs, then gets back to business. "What can I get you?" Owen doesn't answer. May orders for them.

"Who's that?" she asks.

"Tell you outside." Owen whispers.

They get their coffees and treats, then walk back to the car. May asks again, "Owen, who *was* that?"

"The girl from before the summer we met." He stops on the sidewalk and looks down, like he's trying to remember something. *I knew it*, May thinks. She feels a sense of dread confirmed, like this possibility had been hanging over them for a long time. Owen starts walking again. He isn't going to say anything more. But he's going to have to. May isn't about to ignore this for the three-hour drive they have to Black Canyon of the Gunnison. She already knows the basics of the story; there was a girl his freshman year who broke his heart. It was still raw for him the night they met. He cried about it. She helped him through his pain. They never talked about it much after that.

Owen stops again. This time, he's looking back toward the bakery, across a little stream and through a tangle of stunted trees. The woman's there, just outside the door she left, standing beside a dumpster, face in hands, shoulders shaking. "Just a minute." Without any explanation, Owen rushes off to her.

May could spy on them from where she is, but is she really that kind of a person, that watchful over her man, that jealous? No, she isn't. If she bumped into her high school boyfriend nearly 50 years later, there would probably be the same stunned and awkward silence. And if she had the chance to talk to him, she'd be sorry if she didn't take it. Then again, her boyfriend wouldn't rush away from her and hide somewhere to cry.

May goes and sits in the car. Turns out, she can see Owen and the woman anyway. Not as clearly, a few more trees to contend with and greater distance, but enough that she can watch the body language. Why *was* this woman so upset? They're facing each other, talking. She seems to have calmed down. And now she's bowing her head. Suddenly Owen doubles over. The woman puts her hand on his shoulder. Is he crying? Is *she* consoling *him*?

What really happened that summer between the two? When May and Owen first started going out, she used to wonder about that, but she never asked to know more. In fairness, he never asked her about old loves either. There seemed to be an unspoken agreement that the past was the past. Still, now and then he'd write a love poem she didn't recognize as coming from their life together. The lovers were always young, their love always fleeting, the narrator always begging forgiveness. Even his most celebrated poem was foreign to her. "Owl on a Balcony" told the story of an owl perched on the railing of a skyscraper balcony watching two lovers kiss. May asked Owen once what had inspired it. He said a dream. But it was so specific, in a way so few of his other love poems were, that she always wondered: did it really happen? If so, it had to be from Chicago.

Then there was that time when their daughter Maggie went looking through Owen's books to find a good poem for her high school report. She came out into the kitchen holding a copy of Allen Ginsberg's *Howl* in one hand and a Polaroid in the other. "Who's this?" she asked. It was a faded photo of a girl pinning a flower on Owen's suit lapel. Owen took it from Maggie before May could get a good look at it, but she caught enough to see the unguarded joy on Owen's face—and the girl smiling up at him. "Where'd you get this?" He was too bewildered to hide his wonder. "Who is it?" Maggie asked again. "That was my girlfriend before

Mom," he said. Then he tucked the photo in his shirt pocket, walked into the bedroom, and never said another word about it.

God, what she wouldn't give to go back to before she met Owen, to when he and this woman were together, to get inside his head and know what he was really thinking throughout that summer in Chicago and up until the moment they met. But she can't.

May makes a decision then. She gets out, goes around behind the camper, climbs into the driver's seat, and starts up the car. Owen's phone is still plugged into CarPlay. "Three Little Birds" is just fading out—Bob Marley growing quieter, imploring over and over, "Don't worry about a thing, 'cause every little thing gonna be alright."

She manages to turn the car and the camper around—it's her first attempt all trip—and she eases to a stop right across from the path where Owen and the bakery woman are still talking.

*Is* everything going to be alright?

## The Song of Birds

No more sleeping, Owen. Sit up. Stay awake. You have two hours. Then all of this is gone. You head to Chicago, Tara goes to New Jersey, and you won't see each other again until school starts in September.

Wake up, Tara. Turn to me. Smile. Let me kiss you. Please. I need that feeling. I need to hold onto it. It has to last so long.

How long since we met? A month? Why does it feel like forever? Every moment before this has been big and slow and full. Now everything's going too fast.

Birds are singing now, in the little tree outside my dorm room. I get out of bed and go to the window. Are they always so loud this early? How have they never woken me before? They're calling… close, then farther away. Now farther. Three different birds calling. One song.

"What are you doing?"

There you are. There are those soft brown eyes.

"I was looking for the birds. Listen to them. Listen to the singing. How far away it's coming from."

"Come back to bed."

And now you're pushing off the sheet.

And now I'm coming to you.

**Crazy Love**
*I can hear her heartbeat from a thousand miles.*
*- Van Morrison*

Fucking Fitz. We're just pulling away from the dorm, Tara and I are still waving at each other, and he starts in.

"Shit, Maloney. You never said she was a fox."

What a dick. "No, I didn't." You can't let Fitz get to you. Once he knows he's under your skin, he never stops jabbing.

"Now you gotta worry all summer that someone's making the moves on your babe."

"Come on, Fitz." Eddie knows where this is headed. He's sitting next to Fitz up front. I'm behind Eddie in the back, next to Stu, who could give a shit about any of this nonsense. He's got his eyes closed and his head down like he's sleeping. I like Stu. That's why I'm rooming with him next year.

"What does Maloney care anyway? He'll be onto somebody new before you know it. The next pretty girl. Isn't that right, Om?"

They call me Om because of my initials, and they pronounce it like the sacred chant. Fitz is probably too dumb to know that, though. I look out the window. I'm not taking his bait.

"Om, the romantic. Romeo-wen!" He laughs. "Face it: that's your thing. You *love* to be in love."

"This is different." I'm talking to myself more than anything else. But damned if Fitz doesn't hear me.

"Oh, like Ruth was different. Wasn't she your last one?"

"That was a blind date."

"Or who was the one from orientation? Kate?"

"I went out with her for a month."

"Then there was that high school flame that came up a couple times. And the chick you said was your sixth-grade crush. Shit, Maloney. Did you even go a week without a girl this year?"

I'm about to tell Fitz where he can shove it, but Stu pitches forward. It's so sudden, I think he's about to hurl in the front seat.

"Shut the fuck up, Fitz!" He's close enough to Fitz to whisper, only he's barking at him. "Just shut up and drive." Stu's the one person Fitz won't mess with. He's a quiet guy, but he's got a temper. When he loses it, he gets kind of scary.

"I'm just saying," Fitz mutters.

"Well, don't." Stu rocks back in his seat. You gotta love Stu. He's not exactly a barrel of fun, but if you're in trouble, he's the guy you want next to you. "And turn this shit off. I can't fucking hear myself think."

"It isn't shit. It's Bad Company. 'Can't Get Enough.'"

Fitz has awful taste in music. It's all hard rock crap, and not the good stuff—Zeppelin or The Who or Deep Purple. He's into, like, Nazareth and Foghat. Kiss. Shit like that. But don't try telling Fitz his music sucks. He'll take on anyone over that. Even Stu.

"It's shit."

"Well, it's my car. Alright, Stu?"

"It's your dad's car."

Stu's got Fitz there. His dad's some big Chrysler dealer. He's always giving Fitz a new car to drive. This one's a Cordoba. You know, Ricardo Montalban, fine Corinthian leather. That one.

"Can I play something?" Eddie pipes up, all cheery and harmless. That's his way. Nobody can settle Fitz down like Eddie. They've known each other since fourth grade.

"Awright. But none of that mushy Al Green crap."

Eddie's got his box of cassettes right at his feet. He must've known we'd be fighting over the music. "Van Morrison okay?"

"That works."

I laugh. One, because Fitz is so wigged out about anything related to love. And two, because he's letting Eddie play Van Morrison. Like, really? Van's on a whole other plane when it comes to love.

"That's funny?" Fitz glares at me in the rear-view mirror.

"You just can't handle anything romantic, can you?"

"What? I got plenty this year." Fitz totally misses the point.

"I'm not talking about sex, Fitz."

"Well that's what you *should* be talking about. You're nineteen years old, Om. You don't even know who you are yet."

"I know how I feel."

"You *think* you know how you feel. Then you don't feel it anymore. Then you move on to a new girl. Never mind who gets hurt."

"One girlfriend for a month," I fire back. "An old flame for a weekend. A drunken one-night stand with a sixth-grade crush. And a blind date. Nobody got hurt."

"What about Julie?"

The car goes silent. Such a low fucking blow. "Julie was a friend."

"Try telling *her* that."

"What do you know about it?"

Eddie makes a squeak. He didn't mean to. But it's out there now. And I can't B.S. my way around it. Eddie went out with Julie's friend. He knows the whole story. Even if he told Fitz a tenth of it…

"All right. So I didn't see that one coming."

"You didn't see that she was falling for you?"

Stu growls. "Turn up the music. I can't listen to this."

"No. I didn't."

"You were too busy doing your thing, and she took you seriously."

"Let it go," Eddie says to Fitz.

Now I'm pissed. "My *thing*?!"

"Getting girls to like you, then ending it," Fitz says. "That's what you like best. The beginnings and endings. Especially the endings, when you can be sad. And go back to pining."

"Fuck you."

"You're always pining, Om. Pining after pining."

"I am going to lose my fucking mind," Stu snaps. "Cut with the pop psychology bullshit and just drive."

"Am I wrong? Tell me I'm wrong."

I can't believe he brought up Julie. She's a whole other thing. I never loved her. Sure, we got along, spent a ton of time together, had a lot of laughs. But as friends. *Friends.* "I kissed Julie one time."

"That's all it took, Casanova." Fitz laughs. "She got all hopeful. You finally realized what was going on. Then you got scared. Because you don't really want love. You *want* to want it."

Eddie turns all the way around to make sure I see his big sad eyes. "There's nothing wrong with that, Om." What he should say is, *I'm sorry I blabbed to a dick like Fitz.* But I can tell he's sorry. And Eddie's such a good guy, it's hard to be mad at him.

"I already said I fucked that one up. Okay? I feel bad about it."

There. That's what Fitz wants to hear. He wants to know the knife he's twisting hurts. So maybe he's right about Julie. I don't know why I didn't love her. But he's not right about Tara. Tara's different. I know what I feel.

"That wasn't so hard was it?" Fitz says with that cocksure I'm-better-than-you giggle of his.

"You really are an asshole, Fitz, you know that?" Stu kicks his seat. "I don't know why the hell we even hang out with you."

"Well, at the moment, it's because you're in my car."

"Your *dad's* car."

"That you're sitting in. Bitching."

*Whoa.* Not a smart move. Stu doesn't say anything for a while. *He's letting it go*, I think. Then Stu grabs Fitz's headrest and gives it a hard shake. "You like being a cabby, then act like one. Just fucking drive. We don't need to listen to your shit."

"You can get out any time you want, Stu."

"How's it feel to know the only reason your friends hang out with you is so you can drive them around?"

Fitz doesn't say anything to that. But he isn't quiet either. He goes on huffing and puffing like he's psyching up to lift some heavy barbell. Stu turns away, forehead to the window. Eddie puts a hand on Fitz's knee. "That's not true."

We sit with the music after that. *Can I just have one more moondance with you…my-y-y love.* The song ends. Now it's "Crazy Love." After Van repeats "love" about ten times, Fitz pops out the cassette and throws it over to Eddie. "Find something else."

"Aw." Eddie loves Van.

"Aw what? We don't always have to listen to your shitty music."

That does it. I gotta get out of here. I don't care how I get home. Fitz, picking on Eddie, his only real friend. What a jerk.

"I gotta get some gas." Fitz cuts off a guy to get to the exit. We pull into a Shell station and next to the gas pump. Fitz turns off the car and looks back at Stu and me. "I'm not paying for this."

All I have is a ten and two twenties. But I just want to be done with Fitz's bullshit. I don't know how far we are from Chicago. And I don't even know where Wheaton is. My parents moved there from Cleveland when I was in school. All I know is we're in Bumfuck, Michigan. But I can talk to the guy at the counter, get directions. It's not like I've never hitchhiked before. I give Fitz the ten, Stu comes up with three singles, and Eddie has a five. Fitz gets out of the car and starts pumping gas.

"I'm out of here. I'd rather hitchhike than put up with Fitz's shit."

"Come on, Om, don't do that. Fitz'll be cool. I'll get him to be cool." Poor Eddie, always having to make peace.

"Bringing up Julie. It's too far."

"I'd go with you if my parents weren't having a dinner," Stu says.

"Can you take my stuff? I'll get it tomorrow." Stu lives right by Wheaton, in Glen Ellyn. Fitz and Eddie are further away, in Oak

Park. Stu says okay. I get out of the car. Fitz has his head down, filling up his precious Cordoba. I don't even bother to say goodbye.

"Where are you going?"

"Getting another ride."

"Come on! You're not gonna do that. Get in the car."

"I can't take your shit anymore, Fitz. I can't."

"I'm an asshole," he says. Like that's supposed to make it all okay.

"Well, I'm tired of dealing with it."

Fitz finishes gassing up and comes around the car toward me. "I'm sorry, okay? Maybe I'm jealous. Ever think of that? Maybe I wish I was more like you. That I could feel that way."

"The Julie stuff. That's just off limits, man."

Fitz puts his hands up. "I hear you. I'm sorry. That was wrong. And this new girl. Tara. I'm sure it *is* different. I mean, you care for her. With Julie…"

He trails off. That's Fitz. That's the best he can do to smooth things over. If he kept going on about Julie, I'd be walking. And, anyway, what he stopped himself from saying is probably right. The difference is, I feel something for Tara. I didn't for Julie. Don't ask why. So I cut him a break. "Well, I've got a whole summer to try to forget about that stuff."

Fitz grins and wags a finger at me. "That's what I'm talking about! Just because you're gonna miss Tara doesn't mean we can't have fun. I'm telling you, Om." Now he's slapping me on the back. "You are going to *love* Chicago. It's one big party. You catch a train, jump on the El, take a cab, and you can be anywhere you want to be."

Fitz slings his arm across my shoulders, like we're best pals. He walks me back to my door. I let him do it. He has a point. I can't spend my whole summer not having fun. I have figure out what I want to do. Where I want to be, as Fitz says.

Problem is, right now, the only place I want to be is where I was when I woke up.

## For What It's Worth

*There's something happening here. What it is ain't exactly clear.*
*- Buffalo Springfield*

I told Mom I wouldn't be home until after dinner. I didn't want her making a big deal out of my first day back. Fat chance. Seeing as how it was the first time I ever set foot in this house, she was going to do that no matter what. Now here I am, lugging my duffel bag up the front walk, and it's just after four o'clock. I didn't know you could get from Ann Arbor to Chicago in five hours. And that was with our gas station fight and lunch thrown in. Mom's going to freak when she sees me.

Should I ring the doorbell, or just waltz in? It's weird either way. I'm a stranger here, but not really. Might as well go right in— Wouldn't you know? The door's locked. I ring the doorbell. And wait. And wait. Mom's probably at the store. And Dad's still working. Am I locked out? I go around to the side of the house. The garage is way in the back. There's a door into it that's unlocked. Two cars are inside, Dad's Audi and my brother Neil's beat-up VW van.

What's he doing here? I haven't seen Neil in five years. He's 25, six years older than me. Last time he was home, he'd just dropped out of Oberlin, and all I remember is trying to hide from the yelling. Then he was gone. Mom said he was in the Outer Banks, working on a boat. I never got the full story. Neil and I used to be close, up until he went to high school. Then he grew his hair to the middle of his back and went all freaky on us. Hey, it was 1969. You can't blame him. He lived in a different world than I do—had a draft card, went to protests, bitched about "the establishment." All things I don't think about. After he dropped out and left home, Dad referred to him as The Last of the Great Hippies. He meant it as a put-down. I don't think Neil would've minded.

The door inside the garage opens into the kitchen. It's a mess. Mom wouldn't have left it like this. It isn't just a day's neglect either. Glasses and dishes everywhere; the garbage can overflowing; food not put away—a carton of eggs, an open jar of peanut butter, a half-filled bottle of Jack Daniels. I call out. No one answers. I walk into the living room off the kitchen. I hear talking up by the front door. The TV's on in a side room. A baseball game's playing. That's what I notice first. Then I see Dad. He's lying on the couch, tie tugged loose, shirt untucked, a cocktail cradled on his stomach.

"I'm home." He must've heard the doorbell from there. Did he just decide to ignore it?

He looks at me, raises his eyebrows, and shakes his head. "Shit. Not you too. Aren't you supposed to be in school?"

What does he think? That I dropped out like Neil? "School's over. I told Mom a week ago. She knows I'm coming home."

"Your mom isn't here." He takes a drink. "She's up at the cottage."

"The cottage?" We have a place on the Canadian side of Lake Huron. But Mom usually doesn't open it up until June.

Dad puts his glass on the table beside him and pushes upright, groaning. "She wanted some time alone. Whaddaya gonna do? Her choice, not mine."

The last time I saw my parents was Christmas break. They seemed fine. Not exactly lovey-dovey, but that wasn't their way. Sure, there was the usual bickering, but they were laughing too, doing puzzles together, playing gin rummy.

"Short day at work?"

"Short day," he mutters, then turns to the TV. It's the Cubs. Dad loves the Cubs. I want to ask him how work's going, but I don't think I'll get a straight answer. Anyway, judging from the fact that he's home drinking on a Thursday, I pretty much know where things stand. "There you go!" Dad points at the TV. "Two men on. Tying run at the plate. Come on, Kingman!"

Coming to Chicago had been a big career move for Dad. After working for a bunch of little ad agencies in Philly and Cleveland, he finally landed his dream job in the city where he grew up. He was head of accounts, third in line to run the agency, he told me. And he had this sweet office in the Wrigley Building. He was so proud of that. He mailed me a photo looking out his office down on the Chicago River. And all he wrote on the back was, "I made it!"

"Have a seat." He slurps his drink. "Bottom of the ninth. Last chance." Come to think of it, that's the only photo he ever sent me after the move to Chicago. I didn't even get one of the house. But they were excited to move here, both he and Mom. He let her find the place to live, hire a decorator, redo the kitchen. Every time I talked to them, they seemed hopeful. Happy.

"Fucking Kingman! Two men on. Nobody out, and this knucklehead's swinging for the fences. Just put a bat on the goddamned ball." Dad's waving his drink around, ice clattering. He looks up at me. "Sit down. *Sit!* We still got chances."

I must be staring at him funny, because he gives me this offended pout, raises his glass to the light, and looks at it like he's checking for a crack. "Hey, this is my first one. Lay off, alright?"

I put my hands up in surrender.

"A pop up? Are you kidding me? Who the hell is Larry Biittner?"

"Is Neil here? I saw his van—"

"Not for long," Dad says. I wait for him to go on, but he doesn't.

"Well… I better go get moved in. Where am I staying?"

"Damnit! Who are these bozos we've got pinch hitting?

"Upstairs?" I try again.

Dad lurches up, sways on his feet, then goes and turns off the TV. When he swings around to me, he rocks back and shudders like it's a shock that I'm there. One drink, my ass.

"Take any open room." He waves his hand. "Neil's somewhere."

I get my duffel bag and go upstairs. There's a long hallway, and all the doors are shut. Music's coming from the far one. I drop my stuff, go down there, and listen. Neil's singing along to whatever's playing. I knock. Last time I saw Neil, I was in junior high. You don't barge in on someone if you're not sure they'll recognize you.

The music gets low. "Yeah?"

I open the door. Neil's sitting on the floor, surrounded by towers of eight-track tapes. He looks up at me like my presence doesn't compute. "Holy shit," he finally says. "Look at my little brother! All Joe College and everything." Painter's pants and a rugby shirt—not even maize and blue. How's this college? "Last time I saw you, you were hoping for pubes."

"No I wasn't. I was fourteen."

He laughs, gets up, gives me a bear hug, and thumps me on the back like he used to when we were kids. He looks so different. For one thing, he's shorter than me now. And he's skinnier than I remember, not in a spindly way; more wiry, like a wild cat. His hair's still long, but it isn't straight anymore; it's frizzy and flying all over the place. Plus, he's got a beard, a damn good one too, better than Dad can grow. It's the tan, though, that's so surprising. Us Maloneys don't tan. We burn and molt like snakes. But here's Neil, all brown and leathery, like one of those bums I saw in Florida on spring break.

"What're you doing here?"

"I'm home from college. I told Mom. Didn't she tell anyone?"

"Mom's not here."

"Dad told me."

"He actually talked to you?" He turns the music up. One of his hippie protest bands. *There's something happening here.*

"He didn't say much. He was too busy bitching about the Cubs."

"And drinking." Neil sits back down with his tape towers.

"That too. Since when did he start drinking in the daytime?"

"Every day that I've been home."

"Maybe that's why Mom left."

"I don't know." Neil picks a tape off one stack, studies it, and puts it on another. "I got here five days ago, and they weren't talking then. She's the one who asked me to come home too. She wanted me to look through my stuff and decide if I wanted any of it."

"And that's all it took to get you home?"

Neil laughs. "Well, no. The guilt-tripping did that. That's what's so strange about her leaving. She begs me to come home, barely spends a day with me, then up and takes off for the cottage."

"Something's weird."

"Dad's been a mess since she left."

"Why's he home so early? Work can't be going great."

"I didn't ask. We don't talk." Neil starts a new tower. "Anyway, I don't care. I'm outta here tomorrow. You want any of this shit?"

"Those?" I don't have an eight-track player. Plus, I wouldn't want them, anyway. You can't rewind them. They always jam. "No."

"I'm talking about all of it. The tapes, the player, the receiver, speakers. Everything. I got no room for it. My van's full."

When Neil was in high school, I'd sneak into his room and listen to his stereo. He was into the Columbia Record Club. You know, get 15 tapes for a $1.99, then buy so many a year. That's how I learned what kind of music big kids thought was cool. I didn't know then that Neil's tastes were so obscure. Like I say, he was big into folky stuff. Not just Dylan, but no-names like Fairport Convention, Phil Ochs, Leonard Cohen, a bunch of others. "Sure, I'll take it." I don't want Neil feeling bad about his collection. "Where you going?"

He looks at me like he's deciding whether to answer. What's wrong with everybody? I'm not here 10 minutes, and the whole family seems to have secrets. "I don't know. Somewhere west. The mountains. Colorado. So how much money do you have?"

"What?"

"For all this stuff. Anything you got is fine."

*Shit.* I didn't know I had to pay. "I have a twenty." Actually I have two, but I'm not going broke for a bunch of crappy eight-tracks.

"Good enough. You're getting a sweet deal."

He's right. But I can't help feeling like I got suckered into it. I get a twenty out of my wallet and hand it to him.

He pockets it. "So… you gonna stick with school?"

Just because he didn't, he thinks I *won't?* "Yeah."

"You know what you wanna do?"

"Not yet." Who figures out what they want to do their first year? I know some things now that I *don't* want to do, like being a dentist. Taking all those boring, hyper-competitive science classes. Why did I ever think I wanted that in the first place? "I did meet a girl."

He stops sorting tapes and looks up at me with a big gawping grin. "Fantastic! Does she live in Chicago?"

"New Jersey."

"Then what are you doing here?"

I'm not sure what he means. "I'm home."

"Go out there! Get a job. Stay close." I never thought of that. Would Tara even want me there? "Where in Jersey?"

"This place on the shore."

"She's on the Jersey shore?" He throws up his hands, like this is a no-brainer. "Owen. Come on! You know how easy it is to get a job and find a place to live in a tourist town?"

"I don't know. We didn't talk about that."

"Well, then talk about it, if it means that much to you," Neil's suddenly all worked up. "Don't just let her go. I made *that* mistake."

"Oh yeah?"

I expect him to say more, but he doesn't. He gets up and goes over to a bunch of boxes in the corner. "Well… I better go through these. I'll just leave the stereo and tapes right where they are."

"Did you say you're going tomorrow?"

"Yeah."

"What time?" Geez. My brother's finally home after four years, and I'll barely see him for a day.

"I'm in no hurry." Neil digs into a box. I wait again. Nothing.

"Well, I better get unpacked. Great to see you again."

"Yeah. Great."

I take the room at the head of the stairs. It's the closest to Dad, but there's a phone on the wall right outside my door. The cord's long enough that when I call Tara, I can pull the receiver all the way to my bed. By the time I get settled and head downstairs to eat, the house is all shadows. I check in on Dad. He's snoring away on the couch, the bottle of Jack on the floor beside him, drunk down to a couple inches. I just want the day to be done. I scarf down a bowl of Cheerios. With all the dirty dishes in the sink, I'm tempted to pile mine on. But I can't stand the mess. Funny thing is, the dishwasher's empty when I open it. It's like Dad's trying to trash the place. Making a point. To Mom? She isn't even here.

I go to my room. It's still light outside. I pull the drapes across the window that looks into the backyard. They're too flimsy to make it dark. It reminds me of when I was a kid, and I got sent to bed before sunset. Only now, instead of wanting more of the day, I wish it would hurry up and be over. I get into bed; the same one I've slept in for years. Same pillows too. It feels familiar, but it's not comforting. Maybe Neil's right. Maybe I *should* go to New Jersey. Why wouldn't Tara want me there? So what would I do? Is there a train that goes that way? How much would it cost? And how much more money would I need to rent a place and get by until I found a job?

Neil would know these things. He's been doing whatever he wanted for years. First thing in the morning, I'll ask him how to go about it. He's right. I'm 19. I'm too old not to do what I want.

## Over My Head

*I'm over my head, oh but it sure feels nice.*
*- Fleetwood Mac*

I wake up before eight and go downstairs. Nobody's around. I check the garage. Neil's van is gone. The kitchen's cleaned up; that's one good thing. And there's a note on the breakfast table. It must be from Neil. When I get close enough to read it, though, I see it's from Dad: *MOW THE LAWN.* Red pen. Inch-high letters. Double-lined.

Welcome to summer.

I start to crumple it up, then notice there's writing on the back— *Had to go*—with a big red X over it. *Had to go.* That's all Neil wrote. No reason. No apology. No goodbye. Why even write it? Then Dad crosses it out and just turns it over. It's like he wants me to find it— *See what a turd your brother is?*

I switch it up for breakfast, Raisin Bran instead of Cheerios. I'm pouring milk on my cereal when the phone rings. I'm not getting it. Soggy Raisin Bran's terrible. It rings seven times then goes dead. Now it's starting again. Is it Neil? Dad? I look for the phone. It's on the wall going into the living room.

"Owen." It's Mom. And that's all she says. Like I'm the one who needs to talk first. I wait her out. "I'm sorry. There was no time to tell you. It's been hard with your father. I couldn't take it anymore."

"You couldn't wait a couple days?"

"No. I couldn't."

That took the fight out of me. I don't know why. Maybe because she didn't try to make an excuse. "Is it the drinking?"

"That's part of it."

"Are you guys talking?"

"I've tried to call. He won't answer."

"Call him at work."

Mom sighs. "He definitely won't talk there. Look: things aren't good, Owen. I'd tell you more, but I'm on the beach payphone. Let's just say, I can't give your dad what he wants. And I don't know what I want. So I need some time."

"Are you staying there all summer?"

"I think so." *Then why did I need to come home?* "You're welcome up here. The Pace girl, Marla, she was asking about you."

"I'm not coming to the beach. I guess I'll do what *I* want too." I don't mean to backtalk. I'm just trying to be real.

"I don't blame you."

"So we're all just doing what we want."

"What's wrong with that?"

"I don't know." Maybe I expected us to still want to be together. Is it asking too much to have your family *want* to be a family?

"If we don't," she says, "nobody's going to be happy."

It suddenly starts pouring outside. "I gotta go."

"Then go. This is the summer of getting what you want." Before I can figure out what to say to that, she says, "I love you, Owen."

"Love you too." I sound like I'm bummed about it. "Really." She hangs up.

The rain's coming down hard. There's ticking on the window. Hail. Bouncing on the driveway. So much for lawnmowing. So: what *do* I want to do? I walk around the house. I never got a chance to take it in last night. It's bigger than our place in Cleveland. Newer and more polished, with fancy baseboards and carved wood around the ceilings. Our living room furniture looks brand new, but that's just because we never use it; it's the kind that's for show. Even the TV room Dad was in feels like a place where you shouldn't relax.

I go back upstairs. Neil's door's open. This really is the best room. It's farthest from Dad. The stereo's all set up. And you don't have to hide from the sunset. It takes 10 minutes to move everything out of the other room. Before I put things away, I check out Neil's tapes. There's a small stack off to the side. I shuffle through it. Softer stuff— Joni Mitchell, James Taylor, Elton John, Carly Simon. No way Neil bought these. Maybe they were a girl's he knew, the "mistake" he mentioned last night. I find a Fleetwood Mac album—not *Rumours*; the one before with "Over My Head." I push the tape into the player.

There really isn't much to put away. Nearly everything I brought home is laundry. The rest is books and papers and pens and shoes and toiletries. A couple of the books are gifts from Tara. I turned 19 a week after we met. She already decided I wasn't a dentist or a lawyer or a businessman. I was poet. That came as news to me. I don't even get poetry. That's why she gave me the books. She said I had a way with words, and I should see what others did with them. One was a flimsy little book called *Howl* by some guy named Allen Ginsberg. The other was as thick and heavy as a dictionary. *The Norton Anthology of Poetry.*

I haven't looked at either—until now. I start with the little one. Easier to get through, I figure. But am I ever wrong. It's just one long sentence about this guy's friend and how tortured they were by the world. And it goes on for, like, 20 pages. I flip through the anthology. It feels like I'm in church, trying to find my place in the Bible. I stop at Robert Frost—there's a name I know—and read "To Earthward":

> *Love at the lips was touch*
> *As sweet as I could bear;*
> *And once that seemed too much;*
> *I lived on air.*

What would *I* live on now? I skim to the end, like the answer might be there. A short one catches my eye. "The Red Wheelbarrow."

*so much depends*
*upon*

*a red wheel*
*barrow*

*glazed with rain*
*water*

*beside the white*
*chickens.*

I like that one. It's simple, but it seems important. I can see that wheelbarrow and those chickens. I could do that. What would I write about? I don't think the same way when I'm not with Tara. I don't care what Fitz says, being with her makes me feel different than I did with any other girl. Why? What was different? What do I see in Tara that I didn't in other girls? Like Julie.

I have a photo of Tara. Somewhere. It's from a sorority dance we went to. Her roommate must've taken it when I wasn't looking. We're in Tara's dorm room, and she's pinning a flower on my suit coat. *Where did I put that?* I start looking through the folder I brought home. It's mostly course packets, papers I wrote, random notes. But then there it is. Tara's got the little white flower in her hand, and she's holding it between us, inches from my chest. She's looking up into my eyes and smiling. It isn't a smile for the camera. It's a small smile, just for me. A knowing smile. A smile of unguarded affection. And the way I'm looking back at her… I've never seen myself so dazed by wonder.

There's a nightstand next to the mattress Neil threw on the floor. I open the drawer. All that's in it are four joints. Well, look at that! *Thanks, Neil.* I'm not a pothead, but I definitely smoked my share at school. Most of the time, it was with Julie. She always had pot. Funny. Tara and I only did it once. Yet being with her was so much more… meaningful. What does that tell you? I take out a joint, push the other three to the back of the drawer, then put the books Tara gave me in front to hide what's behind them. What to do with Tara's photo? I slide it into the little *Howl* book.

Now, to find some matches. Dad's a smoker. He always says he's going to quit, but he never does. I don't feel too bad going into his room. It's only when I'm already in there that I wonder if I should be. The things I see tell me more than I wanted to know. Two beds separated by a space you couldn't reach across. Mom's closet open with a big gap in the hung-up clothes. A green whiskey bottle on Dad's nightstand. I check the drawer. There are a bunch of matchboxes in there, the fancy kind, actual boxes with wooden matches inside. Dad isn't going to miss one of these.

I'm just going to have a couple hits. I don't want to get blitzed or anything. Just a nice, mellow buzz. I cough up the first hit, then take it too easy on the second, so I do another. I hold it deep and calm, then let it leak out… *There.*

I could write something like that wheelbarrow poem. Something clear like that, so anyone who reads it can see and feel exactly what I can. Something small. A moment… yesterday morning, lying next to Tara. With those birds singing, and the sun reaching into my dorm room. The way my heart inflated with waiting for her to wake up. How precious the seconds were.

I find a pad of paper and a pen. I write, *you lie beside me.* Then I'm stuck. I start doodling faces in the margin. I'm a little bit high, but nothing crazy. Maybe I'm just not in the right mood.

Tara gave me her number. She wanted me to call her. But how soon? It's barely been a day. I take the scrap of paper with her number out of my wallet. If she doesn't want to talk to me, she doesn't have to answer…

"Hello?" Great. Her dad.

"Is Tara there?"

"Who's calling, please?" All stiff and cold.

"It's Owen."

He muffles his voice. Other voices hiss back at him. It's like my calling started a spat. Finally, it's her. "Hello?"

"Tara. It's me. I was just—"

"I can't talk right now. Can I call you back later?"

I bet her dad's right there. "Sure. You've got my number, right?"

"I do."

"I miss you."

"Me too," she says. Then she hangs up.

It's still raining. I take another hit. Then I put the joint back in the drawer. I lie down on the mattress. What am I going to do with the summer? I don't even know where to go around here. This might as *well* be Jersey. What if I did go out there? Just showed up at Tara's door? Calling caused enough of a stir. What would her dad do if we were face to face? Maybe Tara was like me. Maybe she didn't want to be where she was either. Maybe all she wanted was to be together. I close my eyes and try to imagine where that might be. I can't get out of Ann Arbor. I see us in the Diag where we met. I see us walking on campus, throwing a frisbee in the Arb, lying in the sunlight. Why didn't we stay in town? Tara's roommate did. She said it was easy to get a job and find a place to stay. Why didn't we even talk about that? Imagine us being there now.

*Imagine…*

The room's too bright. The overhead light's blaring in my face. Dad's staring down on me. How long have I been asleep?

"Is this it? Is this all you did with your day?"

"No…"

"So you were too busy to mow the lawn."

He's coming at me so fast. "It was raining."

"Well, it isn't anymore."

"What time is it?"

"Almost three."

"Why are *you* home?"

"Because I want to be." Dad takes offense.

I must've closed my eyes. "Hey!" Dad barks.

"Sorry."

"There's still plenty of time to cut the grass." He backs away. "You can't do nothing all day."

I get up and mow the lawn. When I come back in, Dad's right there in the kitchen, shaping a burger patty in his hands. "I figured we'd cook out." I look around for a bottle. I don't see one.

After I take a shower and change, we go out on the porch, and Dad fires up the grill. It's gas-powered, connected right to the house. Pretty slick. Dad's got the patties cooking in a minute. Then he turns to me. I'm sitting in a lounge chair. "Want a beer?"

"Um." It feels wrong to drink with Dad boozing it up.

"You drank beer at school, right?"

"Yeah."

"Okay. Then I'm going to get us a couple beers. Keep an eye on those patties, will you?"

I get up and grab the flipper thing. Sometimes burgers just catch on fire; you've got to be ready. Dad comes back with some beer called Old Style. It goes down pretty easy.

"What are you going to do with yourself?" Dad asks out of the blue. I want to say something, but nothing comes out. I end up shrugging. "You can't do nothing all summer."

"I was going to look for a job," I recover. "But I didn't know if I could use your car."

"You want to use the Audi? Fine. You can do the shopping too."

Great. I can just see it now. Every day a to-do list. Mow the lawn. Get the food. Clean the clothes. Do the shit. Dad must see the disappointment on my face. "Let me talk to someone," he says. "See what I can do. Hell, you don't need me climbing up your ass every day." It's the nicest thing he's said to me since I got home.

We watch the grill and drink our beers, then Dad gets two more when we bring the burgers inside. He's pacing me. I can tell by the way he eyes me when I drink. So I go slow. And I don't know if that's the reason or not, but Dad keeps things pretty pleasant.

"I hear you talked to Mom," Dad says while we're eating.

"Yeah." I'll be damned. She took my advice and called his office.

"She's not happy with the move," he says. "There's a lot of pressure at work. A lot of demands. And late nights."

"I can imagine," I say, though I haven't seen any of that yet. *And what about the drinking?* I want to ask.

"You might find yourself alone some of these nights." He downs the rest of his beer and looks at mine.

I pick up the bottle, then put it back down. As soon as I'm done, he's going to get another. "That's fine."

Dad drums on the table. "Just so you know, I don't support what your brother's up to."

"I know." He hadn't since Neil dropped out; why would that change now?

"I hope you're finding more purpose in school."

"I am." I wasn't, but I can't tell Dad that. He's footing the bill.

"And your grades? You keeping them up?"

"Three A's and a B."

"The B. What was that in?"

"Biology."

Dad takes a deep breath. Here comes the lecture. "There's no shame in not wanting to be a dentist." That surprises me; it sounds like he's letting me off the hook. But the very next thing he says is: "That's why we got you into those pre-business school classes. There are a lot of ways to go with that." I'd totally forgotten: the two of us spent an hour on the phone a few weeks ago, plotting out my courses for next year. I just signed up for what he told me to take. I didn't know they were pre-business. In my defense, I wasn't listening very closely. Tara was waiting for me to go out.

I get up from the table. "That's what I need," I say to appease him. "A lot of ways to go."

For the second night in a row, I'm in bed before the sun goes down. But it's darker in Neil's room, so it's harder to tell.

My days have to get better. I didn't go anywhere. I got high and slept all afternoon. And the one thing I actually wanted to do—writing that poem—I thought about for all of a minute.

Worst of all, Tara never called back.

## With a Little Luck
*We can make this whole damn thing work out.*
*- Paul McCartney and Wings*

Dad's standing over me again. It doesn't feel like it should be morning yet, but there he is, fresh shaven, hair slicked back, with a sky-blue polo shirt and matching blue, green, and yellow plaid pants. Oh, and the whitest shoes I've ever seen.

"I've got a client meeting in the city," he says. "PAM Cooking Oil. They're buying a measly fifteen-second spot, and for that, I have to take them golfing all day and partying all night. On a Saturday. Can you believe that shit?" I'm not ready to talk. It can't even be seven o'clock. "I thought we'd go out for breakfast," Dad goes on, more chipper than he's been since I got home. "I'll show you around Wheaton before I catch my train."

What are you gonna do? I'd rather stay in bed, but when Dad gets something into his head, you don't have much of a choice. We drive the way Dad walks to the train station. "You can do this in twenty minutes," he says. "Less if you hurry." He points out the station, but we drive past it, across the tracks and a few blocks further to a big road named Roosevelt. Around the corner, there's this cheesy sign for the Seven Dwarfs Restaurant.

"You know John Belushi?" Dad asks as he's parking the car.

"Yeah, I know John Belushi."

"He worked here. Can you believe it?"

No. I can't. The place is like some Snow White nightmare acid trip. Eddie told me that MacDonald's and Burger King do studies to figure out what colors and designs get your appetite going. This place must've decided to do the opposite.

I just want fried eggs and bacon, but Dad makes me get a side of French Toast. He says it's the best he's ever had. Meanwhile, he just gets coffee. "I'm going to be eating and drinking all day."

The French toast is good. But it's so much, I can't eat it all. Dad leans in, cuts himself a wedge, and takes his time chewing it, eyes closed, nodding. "What did I tell you?"

"It's good."

He puts his hand on my arm. "If somebody offers you a job today, don't take it just yet, alright? I've got an idea. Something that'll look good on a resume." I smile. For Dad's sake. But it sounds like the kind of job Stu told me his dad got for him, toiling away in the back office of some Podunk bank. Don't get me wrong. I'm okay with work. But I'd rather do fun work than, you know, *work* work.

When we're leaving, Dad says, "Oh. I almost forgot. Some girl named Tara called last night. Woke me up." Talk about a jolt. Dad's watching me over the roof of the car. "A gal from school?"

"Yeah."

"Well… good. Just tell her to call before ten."

So Tara called back. At least I know now that she wasn't trying to dodge me. Now I can call *her* back.

On the way to the station, Dad turns up the radio and starts singing to some Paul McCartney tune I never heard before. The only song I ever remember him singing to was "Bad, Bad Leroy Brown." He'd actually hunt for that song on the radio. What gives? He seems all keyed up, like Fitz gets when we're headed out to the bar, dancing in front of the mirror, singing like nobody else is around.

Dad leaves the car running when we get to the station, whistles to the rest of the tune, then gets right out and starts walking away. It's only when I go around to the driver's side that he stops and turns around. He looks so ridiculous standing there in the middle of that parking lot, with those loud plaid pants, bright white loafers, and his little gym bag, like some pro golfer on the lam.

"Don't wait up," he calls out.

I stay until the train comes then drive off. A minute later, I stumble across Main Street. There have to be some jobs down here. I park and walk around for 20 minutes without finding a single place where I'd want to work. Then, I see Rave-On Records. I cross the street and go inside. It reminds me of Schoolkids in Ann Arbor. I could see myself working here. There's a slinky Stones tune playing that I never heard before. I ask the guy at the counter what album it's from.

"It's not out yet," he says. "This is just a single. 'Miss You.'"

It bounces along like some dance tune. You wouldn't think I'd like it. But Jagger does this catchy doo-wop moaning thing I can't get out of my head. I don't even have a record player, but I buy the single anyway. Then I ask the guy, "Are you looking for summer help?"

"The owner was talking about it," he says. "If you come back on Monday, he'll be in."

How cool would it be to work here? Who cares what it pays. I bet I'd get records on discount. I go back to the car. I'm done looking for jobs. Everywhere else will be a downer compared to this.

First thing I do when I get home is call Tara. A little girl answers. "Is this Owen?" she asks, a high voice, all hushed and hurried.

"Yes it is."

"She can't talk now."

"Okay. Well…" The way she said it. I can't tell: is she unable or not allowed? "Tell her I'll be here all day."

"Where's here?" She whispers like we're passing a secret.

Now I'm whispering. "I just meant at this phone number."

"Oh."

"So she can call."

"Ah," she finally gets it. "I'll tell her. Promise."

So: more waiting. Only now, it's different. The way that girl whispered, someone doesn't want me calling. Probably her dad. Why would he have his hackles up? The girl gave me hope, though.

She was on my side. And she probably knew Tara's feelings better than her parents.

I decide to work on the poem. On the porch in the backyard. It's windy out there, bulging grey clouds moving fast. I bring along Neil's joint and take a few hits just outside the sliding glass door. The sky's getting darker. It's going to storm soon. It feels nice.

*So, you wake up. Tara's next to you. You see the sun. You hear the birds. They're calling to you. Your heart rises. Gets full. And you know; you know it's love.*

I try out a couple lines. They're okay. But the words don't hold enough back. I don't know how to explain it. I want that slow-growing emotion I felt, that drowsy wonder. And you can't beat someone over the head with it.

It starts to rain, big blobby drops. The wind kicks up. I get inside just before it starts really coming down. I try to write more, but nothing comes. What am I going to do with the rest of the day? I turn on the TV, crank around the channels. It's Saturday morning stuff—*Fat Albert*, *The Pink Panther*, *American Bandstand*. I turn off the TV. There's a stack of *People* magazines on a table next to Mom's chair. Steve Martin's on the cover of the top one. That wild and crazy guy. I flip through. It's all ads for cars and booze and cigarettes and gadgets. I wonder if Dad's agency did any. There sure are some weird ones. A Citizen watch ad that looks like a *Playboy* photo. One that advertises U.S. savings bonds as "more dependable than a man." A Canadian whiskey ad with this rugged Mountie spooning some total babe in the woods, playing up the whole "smooth" angle. Geez. They might as well have them screwing. In the back, there's a blurb about Paul McCartney, who has to pitch in at home and bake bread because they only have one servant. Life must be rough.

Dad singing to McCartney… Can you believe that? And dressing like some extra from *The Love Boat*. I guess when you're an adman, you can start to believe the bullshit you dish up. Is this what Mom was dealing with every day? Or is Dad just cutting loose now that she's gone? What is he—47? It's weird.

I toss the magazine aside and go upstairs. Back into my room. I put in another one of Neil's mystery girlfriend's tapes on low— Eagles, *Hotel California*. Then I try again to write my poem for Tara. But I can't get past the few lines I already wrote. It's the music. The competing words. I can't think over them. *New kid in town. Everybody loves you. Life in the fast lane.*

The hell with it. The joint I took downstairs is in my front pocket. There's not much left. I smoke what I can, hide the roach in the nightstand, and put the notebook in there too. Can't leave this sitting around. I'd get all types of shit from Dad for writing poetry.

There are books on the shelf of the nightstand. Some are definitely Neil's—Kerouac's *Dharma Bums*, *Ariel* by Sylvia Plath. There are a couple trashy romances too. Then, an odd ball: *The Family*, about Charles Manson and what the cover calls, "HIS ZOMBIE-LIKE DISCIPLES!" It's creepy to know the book's there by my bed, with a black-and-white stencil of Manson's face and those crazy eyes glaring at the room. Still, it's the one I pick up. And I can't put down. I read for a couple hours. They hook you right in with all the criminal shit Manson did before he really got dangerous. Stealing cars. Pimping out girls. Forging checks. Going in and out of jail. But he kept getting let go. He kept getting more twisted. And he kept sucking more people into his cult. The author calls it *the vortex of evil…*

I'm not sure where I am when I wake up. Then it comes back: I'm alone. In this house. In this town I don't know. I'm waiting for Tara to call. And I'm worried she won't. It's early still. Just after five. Time's going so slow. I'm not hungry, even though I haven't eaten since the Seven Dwarfs. Still, I know I'm going to have to eat some time. Might as well get it over with—something to do. I find a packet of hotdogs in the fridge, take out two, and fry them in a pan. There aren't any buns, so I wrap each in a slice of Wonder

Bread covered with mustard. And I eat them over the sink so there's nothing to clean up.

Now what? I've got to get out of this house. It's stopped raining. I could take my bike out, check out the neighborhood. I go into the garage. My bike's nowhere to be found. Did they sell it? Without asking me? Okay, so it was a yellow Yamaha Moto-bike with a banana seat. More for a kid than a 19-year-old. But I was riding it just last summer. What made them decide I was done with it?

I go out on the sidewalk and look the way I haven't been yet, up Summit, the road that forms a corner with Prairie. The houses are older there and smaller. Music's playing somewhere. "Love Her Madly" by The Doors. Sounds like a party. I go looking for it. The place is hidden behind a bunch of overgrown bushes. The driveway's cracked and weedy, and what little I can see of the house is covered in vines. There's a boarded-up window up near the roof. The house is pulsing with music. All at once, though, it stops. That's when I realize I've gone a few steps down the driveway. I back away. The music starts up again. Were they watching me? Can they see me *now*? I want to run, but I don't. What is there to be scared of? It's that damn book. It's got me all creeped out.

When I'm coming back inside, I hear the phone. I rush over and answer it. No one's there. *Shit.* Should I just call Tara now? If it was her, then she'd answer right away. If it wasn't, I could say I've been out a while and was expecting her call… or might've missed her call. No. Too desperate. I have to stay here and wait. I go back up to my room. It's so dark. I pull up the blinds. All the way. For the first time. *There.* Light. Not bright or sharp. But enough to fill the room.

I pick up the Manson book and go sit in the chair. It's one of those folding metal ones. I don't want to lie down in bed. I don't want to fall asleep again to this book, slurring it into my dreams. But I *do* want to know what drew people to this psycho. I just want to be alert when I do it. I read as long as I can, until the words start sliding by and I have to circle back to stop them. As soon as that happens, I'm up, washing my face, brushing my teeth, in bed, and ready to face sleep. No more thinking about Manson.

Tara didn't call. It's morning, and she didn't call. Oh well. If she didn't, then she couldn't. I take a shower and shave—not that I need to. I get my book and go downstairs. It's eight o'clock. I don't expect Dad to be up. But what's weird is everything's clean. Just like I left it. It hits me right then. He's not here. I go back upstairs and look in his room. Nope. Never came home. This is probably the shit that pissed off Mom.

I have some Cheerios and toast. When I'm done, I stay in the nook and read. Half an hour later, I look outside and here comes Dad in a jogging suit and sweatshirt, carrying his gym bag, probably with those country club duds inside. He looks like hell. If I were a cop, I'd stop and see what his deal was. When he comes in from the garage, he gives me this stupefied look, like he's surprised I'm awake. Doesn't say anything. Just nods. Then he goes to the refrigerator and takes out a carton of orange juice. He opens it and drinks straight from of the spout. Mom would've lost her mind.

"So how were the PAM guys?"

"Who?"

"Your clients."

"Oh. Yeah." He gives me a weak smile. "It was a good night. Maybe a little *too* good. But, hey, that happens in this business."

I have nothing to say. His thing is his thing. I'm not Mom. I give him a tiny *hmm*, then go back to reading. He stands there a while. I can feel his stillness, and I want it to stop. But when he starts moving again, I wish he hadn't. He's rushing around too fast. And all chipper, like it's a happy new day. I get up and head for my room.

"Hey!" We're on opposite sides of the living room. He holds out both hands, like he's getting ready to explain himself. I'm bracing. "I talked to a guy at my agency. He's got a summer opening. We'll be working together." He spreads his arms out wide.

Does he want me to hug him? I don't know what to say. I'm not even sure how I feel. "Doing advertising?"

"Part of it, yeah." He starts coming toward me, hands waving around, putting on a sales pitch. "It's not the glamorous part. It's research. But that's what gets turned into the good stuff."

It sounds like Stu's bank job to me. "Is this for sure? I mean, is it a done deal?" What I really want to say is, *do I have to do this?*

"Well… you've got an interview with a buddy of mine, but it's just a formality. Chris Negroponte's his name. Monday morning at nine. So we'll take the seven o'clock train in. You got a suit?" I'm speechless. "Don't worry. I got one that'll fit you." He breezes past me and heads for the stairs. "You coming?"

"Where?"

He laughs. "Upstairs. We gotta try this on. Dress to impress!"

I follow him. He starts whistling. We're heading into his room when it hits me: it's that fucking McCartney song.

## It's Alright, Ma (I'm Only Bleeding)
*It's easy to see without looking too far that not much is really sacred.*
*- Bob Dylan*

We sit next to each other on the train. It's either that or cram in with a stranger. That's how crowded it is. I should've sat with a stranger. Dad goes on and on with interview advice. *Look him in the eye. Be confident. Speak up. Stay positive. Don't make that face. Don't fake your way through anything. Wear your ignorance on your sleeve—* one of Dad's favorite sayings. I know, I know. It's the easiest place to brush it off from. "Oh," he adds, "and have some questions ready."

*Have some questions.* Okay, here's a few. *What the hell will I be doing? And what if I don't like it? When do I have to get there—and how long do I have to stay? How much am I getting paid?* I don't say any of that out loud. I just nod at Dad, then lean my head against the window. It's not like other trains I've taken, those ones we took out west when I was a kid. There's barely any countryside. It's just town after town, station after station. The first few nice, but then shadier and shadier. More concrete, more blight, more abandonment. No wonder no one else looks outside.

I think about Tara. How I'll be away from the phone all day. She could call, and there's nothing I can do about it. I tried reaching her after Dad sprung the interview on me. But it just rang and rang. Hey, it was Sunday. Maybe she went to church. I never asked her opinion on religion. At that point, I should've worked on my poem for her. But I didn't even try. It was easier wallowing in self-pity. No wonder she hadn't called. I didn't deserve it.

"Do you have a pen?" I ask Dad.

"What for?"

"I just want to write down some questions to ask."

I spend the next 10 minutes coming up with lines for the poem. When I hand back his pen, Dad's smiling at me, all proud, like, *look at my boy. Look at the wheels turning.*

"Keep it," he says.

North Western is the biggest train station I've ever seen. We rush out onto the sidewalk, practically shoulder to shoulder with all the other people trying to get to work. I see beggars lurking in doorways, bums sitting on curbs, and then, right in front of me, a businessman peeing against a wall, oblivious to everyone.

"Don't stare," Dad says. "Don't make eye contact with anyone." Why? What are they going to do? Punch me if I look at them?

We cross a river, filing over a narrow bridge. "Chicago River," Dad mutters, like saying it too loud would blow my cover as a go-getter hustling to work. I can't help rubbernecking, though. Skyscrapers are all around me. Cars speed every which way. People stream by. I catch an eye and look away. Another for longer, until I get a glare. I see Dad's point now. People don't like you looking at them. But it's hard to find somewhere for your eyes to go. We turn left. Dad nods over his shoulder. "Sears Tower. Tallest building in the world." I look back. An icy black monolith looms above us, two white pillars spearing the clouds. "Don't stop." *Then why the hell point it out?*

Somehow, the river's in front of us now. We turn right before we get to it. And there, in front of me, are two of the coolest buildings I've ever seen; huge cylinders with concrete petals climbing all the way to the top. Perfectly aligned. Cone-shaped flowers stacked to the sky. They're balconies. I can see lounge chairs on them. "Marina City," Dad says.

The sky starts opening up. "Is that the lake?"

"Don't worry about that." Geez, I was just asking. It's not like I wanted to go for a swim. We cross the river on a busy bridge. "There it is." Dad points to a cockeyed cream-colored building with a clock tower in the middle. "The Wrigley Building."

We go through its revolving doors. It's almost as big and busy inside as the train station. There are all sorts of stores and people selling stuff—coffee, newspapers, shoeshines. Dad says hi to a few people before we veer off into a hallway lined with more elevators than I've ever seen for one building. Then, we're going up. And any second, the doors will open. And I'll walk out into an office. And people will look at me and think, *here's the boss's kid, just waltzing into a job he doesn't deserve.*

Only when the doors open, no one's around. There's this long marble counter facing us with the agency's logo behind it. *CCGO.* And on either side, there are these uncomfortable looking benches. It feels like a museum with no exhibits. Dad tells me to wait here. Then he goes over to one side of the counter and disappears through some side door. More people come out of the elevator. Some look at me. Some don't. They all go through that door. One guy smirks at me just before he heads inside. Like, *ah, another poor sucker.* He might as well have whispered *run.*

Dad comes breezing out seconds later, and there's a woman with him. She's not much older than me. "This is Denise," Dad says. "She's our receptionist. She'll let you know when Chris is ready."

"Chris?"

Dad's annoyed. "Negroponte. The man you're interviewing with."

"Ah, yes." I nod like he's just imparted some great wisdom.

"I've got a meeting. I'll be back around eleven. Then we'll go to lunch." He goes over to the elevator and hits the button. It's quiet. Dad gets antsy. He turns to us. "But you're in good hands here." He points at Denise. The elevator dings. Dad gets on, turns, realizes we're still watching him, and gives a sheepish wave. I look at Denise. It's everything I can do not to laugh. Why's he acting so weird? She just gives me this fakey smile and goes behind the counter.

"Would you like some coffee?"

"No, thanks."

"You can sit anywhere," she says. I take a seat opposite the side door. Whenever it opens, I can see inside. There's a glass room not too far off. A guy goes into it. Then an older woman comes out and whispers something to Denise. She freezes, leans in, and whispers back. They go back and forth with snippy hisses, like they're trying to keep down an argument. The woman leaves abruptly. Denise gets up from her seat, comes around the counter, and walks over to me.

"So..." She claps her hands together. "Mister Negroponte couldn't make it today. But he's arranged for you to meet with... *John Francis*." The catch in her voice; I'm supposed to be impressed.

"Oh. Okay."

"Mister Francis is the vice president of the creative team."

"Great."

She motions me to follow her through the door. I see the guy who went into the glass room. He's sitting at the end of a long table. Denise holds out one hand, like Carol Merrill presenting door number two on *Let's Make a Deal*. Next thing I know, I'm standing in front of this guy, Denise is gone, and we're in some sort of weird standoff. He's leaning back, hands behind his head, and he's got this silky flowered shirt on, unbuttoned so you can see his chest hair and the thick gold chain around his neck. He looks like Burt Reynolds. It feels like he should talk first, like opening my mouth is a trap. What would Dad say to do?

"You got something for me?" he says finally, pushing his chair forward and pointing to the leather folder I'm holding.

"Yes." I take out the resume I typed last night and hand it to him.

He skims it then looks at me like he's confused. "Sit," he says. I already don't like this. I sit down and cup my hands on the table. He keeps looking at my resume. After a good minute, he humphs and tosses my resume aside. "Honor boy."

Would he rather I *didn't* make the honor roll? Would a C average make him happier? "Yes sir," I say, as in *fuck you*.

"So…" He fondles his gold chain. "What is it you can do for us?"

I thought that's what they were going to tell me. Does this guy even know who I am? Did he even get the message that Dad set this up? He had to. He's a VP, one of three. "I can do anything you want. I'm a very quick learner." *Be confident.*

"Accounts? Creative? Operations?"

Are those my only choices? I don't even know what they mean. I know Dad's head of accounts, and I don't want to work for him. Operations sounds technical. "Creative, I guess." How's that for assertive? I want to say that Dad mentioned something about research, but I don't want to bring up Dad to this guy. It's weak.

"That's my territory. You got some samples in there?"

I crack open my folder and make a show of thinking about it. What I have in there is two blank sheets of paper and one with the lines of Tara's poem. "Um… No."

"No writing? No drawings. Nothing?"

I shake my head. I wish I had the balls to read my poem to this guy. The illustrious Sir Disco Francis. He heaves a big sigh. "You seem like a good kid. Let me explain how this works. I don't hire people for what college they went to or what grades they got. I hire people for ideas." He stops so I can take that all in. Like it's this super complicated point. "So I need to see something. And people know that. They show me ads they wrote or designed. And if they're just breaking in, they make up ads for made-up products. All to convince me they can do the job. You understand?"

"You want a fake ad?" I'm sort of serious, but a little smartass too.

Disco Francis stares at me stone-faced. Then he bursts out laughing. "You're a funny one. I'll give you that."

He gets up and holds out his hand. When I shake it, he looks away. Big strike in Dad's book. You look people in the eye when you're shaking their hand. And just like that, not five minutes in, he walks out of the room. What the hell? What am I supposed to do now? I'm just standing there in the middle of that fishbowl. I don't want to go out to the reception area so soon. How humiliating is that? But I don't want anybody to see me standing here either. I go back to the lobby. Denise gives me a quick glance, then looks down at her desk.

"I'll take that coffee now."

She looks flustered, caught off guard. *Good.* I'm done acting like some meek nobody who doesn't deserve to be taken seriously. Denise hurries to the side door. I head for a bench where I *can't* see the door this time. I don't want to have anything to do with what's behind it. I sit down and put my folder on the floor. Denise comes back carrying this fancy tray, with a tiny sugar bowl and mini pitcher of cream. She leans down and presents it to me. I take the cup and wave her away. She's hiding her eyes from me. She's upset. *Shit.* Why am I acting like such an ass? "Sorry."

"No!" She acts surprised. "It's no trouble."

I lower my voice. "I shouldn't be a jerk. But this kind of sucks."

"Yeah, it does," she says, looking square at me.

"Nobody likes the kid whose dad gets him the job."

She glances back at the door. "That's not what's going on." The elevator dings. A group of men get off, chattering away. "It's just office B.S.," she whispers, then goes to welcome the visitors.

So there I am in the corner with my coffee and nothing to do but avoid people. I start thinking about the ads I saw in *People* magazine. The smoking ones hyping taste over cancer. The liquor ones promising sex over alcoholism. The smooth Canadian. Why would I want to write that shit? I open the folder to the page where I wrote the new lines of Tara's poem. I get the pen out of my coat pocket and rewrite the whole poem in my neatest cursive.

I'm going to call Tara tonight. Right when I get home. And if I can't get a hold of her, I'll call again. And again. All night, until she answers the phone. I'm done sitting around, waiting for things to happen to me. Hoping they'll be what I want. Hope is worthless.

I haven't looked Denise's way in about an hour. She's been busy, what with people coming and going, and the phone ringing off the hook. When I glance over, though, she's eyeing me. What are the odds? Anywhere else, and I would've gone and talked to her. What was this office B.S. she mentioned?

Dad gets back around 11. He makes a beeline for Denise. He doesn't see me in the corner. "How's everything going?" Denise cocks her head my way. Dad looks over and waves. Then he leans in to whisper. When he comes walking over, he's got this fake grin plastered on his face. "I understand there was a little switch-up, eh?"

"Yeah…"

"But you got to talk with Mister Francis. That's a big deal." Dad's expecting me to say something. All I can think is what a colossal ass-hole the guy is. "How'd it go?"

"Quick."

"What do you mean?"

I tell him what happened. That it was five minutes. That he thought I'd have a fake ad. "I don't think he knew why I was here."

The fake grin's gone. Dad's pissed. "Give me a sec." He marches over to the side door and disappears. Denise and I eye each other with *oh-shit* looks on our faces. I wonder if I'm going to hear yelling on the other side of the museum walls. Whatever Dad did, though, it was quick. In just a couple minutes, he's standing back in front of me. He's breathing heavy and his face is red, but he's smiling. "Okay! Let's go get something to eat."

We leave the building some way that drops us onto a lower road, under a run of rusty girders that hold up train tracks. "The El." Dad points above me as we go. He's walking really fast now, faster than this morning, and he doesn't seem to care if I keep up. Fine by me. I don't want to rehash what happened with the interview.

We go to a place called Gene & Georgetti. It's this dark little house in the middle of all these buildings. Inside, though, it seems bigger and swanky. "You know who's been here…" Dad says, like it's not a question. If I had to guess, I'd say Al Capone. It's that kind of a place. But I don't want to say that, so I just shrug. "Frank Sinatra!"

He expects me to be impressed, but it's like me telling him that Bob Dylan had a cup of coffee here. The waiter comes, dressed better than both of us, with a crisp white shirt and a black bow tie. Dad gets a martini and orders me a beer; doesn't even ask if I want it. Then he orders his food too. Linguine. I haven't even cracked the menu. "Do you have a hamburger?"

Dad laughs. "Get the linguine." I don't even know what linguine is, but the waiter's all poised to write something, and I don't want to slow things down. So I get the linguine. When our drinks come, Dad huddles over his like he's praying. He takes the first couple sips without picking up the glass, just slurps right off the rim. Then he pinches the stem in his fingers, leans back in his chair, and props it on his chest. "I am *so* sorry about this morning."

"It's okay. It's probably for the best." I need to figure out a way to tell him; I don't want to be the boss's kid.

"Denise said you were pretty upset."

"Just surprised."

"You *should* be upset." Dad thunders, way too loud for a place like this. "I am! That was a *fuck-you* from Francis. Or Negroponte. Or both of them." Dad downs the rest of his martini. "But don't you worry. You're getting a new interview."

"Maybe we should just let it go."

Dad glares at me like I'm a traitor. "No way." He waves down the waiter and orders another martini. One more word about the interview, I'm going to say something I shouldn't, and Dad's going to explode, right in the middle of all these people. This isn't about my interview anymore. It's about Dad's pride. I can't argue against that.

The linguine comes. It's got clams in it and tons of garlic. I don't think I'm going to like it, but I do. The noodles are flat and soft, but not sticky. I'm having a helluva time twirling them into a bite on my fork; that's the only bad thing.

When Dad starts again, it's not about the interview—thank God; it's about what to do next. Walking the Miracle Mile, going up on something called the sky deck, seeing the Water Tower, whatever that is. If it were up to me, I'd go home and call Tara.

Dad gets martini number three, we finish the meal, he pays, and then we start walking out. All of a sudden, this fat guy swivels in his bar stool and clamps onto Dad's arm. Dad swings around like he's going to deck the guy. "Maloney!"

"Bud…" Dad looks down at where the guy grabbed him.

"Man, he was going to lay me out," the guy says to me. "Wasn't he?" He holds out his hand. "I'm Bud. Bud McGee."

We shake. He's got a big soft palm, and he doesn't squeeze too hard, just hard enough. "You must be Bowen, the Michigan man."

"Owen," I say. Bowen's my real name, but no one calls me that. Bud breaks out laughing, like I said the funniest thing in the world.

"I get it. I'm Bud. Not Bo. And definitely not Bowen. They used to call me Blowin' McGee in junior high."

"You two have the same name," Dad states the obvious.

"He named you *after* me!" Bud twists back to get his beer.

"I went by Bo until I was ten," I find myself telling the guy. "Then people started calling me Mo Baloney."

Bud throws his head back and howls. I like this guy. "I'm a Michigan man myself, you know. Class of fifty-three. Same as your dad."

Dad looks uptight about all this—even after three martinis. "Mister McGee and I roomed together in college."

"Wild times, eh Mikey?" I've never heard anyone call Dad *Mikey* before. "I see they've already fit you in a monkey suit." Bud sweeps his hand at my clothes.

"He had an interview." Now Dad's just full-on peeved.

"Well, if he's looking for a job, Mikey, he's got one."

"Thanks, Bud, but—"

"You're a young man," he says to me. "You should be kicking back, grabbing life by the balls."

Dad claps his hands. "We gotta go."

Bud hoists his mug. "The offer's there."

Dad wheels around and hurries for the door. I give Mr. McGee a little nod. He winks at me.

"What's *he* do?" I ask when we're back out on the street.

"Don't worry about that. You're not working for him." Dad's walking super fast again. And weaving. I'm worried he's going to plough into somebody, but he sails past everyone without a problem. I guess he's had practice. When we get to Michigan Avenue, he puffs out a big mouthful of air. "Okay if we do this another day? I gotta go straighten out this interview B.S."

Here's another chance to speak up. *Let it go, Dad.* But I don't do it. Again. I tell him okay and hurry off to catch the train. By the time I get home, it's after three. I've got my coat slung over my shoulder and I've pitted out my shirt. Mr. Businessman comes home. I call Tara right away. No more waiting. No more helpless hoping. Call. And call. And keep calling.

Tara's mom answers. I hang up. I was ready for her dad. I was hoping for the little girl. I never fathomed her mom. Why? I don't know. It must say something. Gutless: that's what it says. I have to call back. See it through. No matter who answers. I just—just—need to think. What would a mother want to hear from a boy? If her daughter said she loved him? If her husband had a problem with it…

I go upstairs and change clothes. I put on some music, a Dylan tape. Then I get a joint out of my nightstand. I light it, lie back on my bed, and smoke it down. It's decent weed, but I'm not going to lose my mind on this. I start drifting off. The joint's still lit. I put it out, lurch out of bed, and go get the folder Dad gave me. I left it downstairs. I'm going to read Tara that poem. I'm going to tell her that I want to come out there. Stay the summer. Be close.

What do I say? *Remember how you said I should write? Well, I wrote something for you…* I play it over and over in my head. Rehearse it. Get it sounding natural. Then I head back upstairs.

The phone rings. I grab the receiver. It's Dad. "Good news. It was all a big misunderstanding. The job's yours."

"What is it?"

"What's what?"

"The job. What am I doing?"

"What are you *doing?* What does it matter? You're making money. You're getting experience." I don't say anything. "Look: you're not going to freeload all summer."

"I wasn't going to."

"I'm sticking my neck out here, you know."

"Okay, I get it." I hang up on him. What's the use of arguing? The phone rings again. Here it comes: the ass-chewing.

"Sorry…"

"Owen?" It's Tara.

"Tara." I'm rattled. I'm not ready.

"Everything okay?"

"Yeah… yeah… I just—I wasn't expecting you. I didn't know if you were getting my messages."

"I was."

It goes quiet. She wants me to talk. "I didn't want you to think I stopped thinking about you."

"Owen, I have something I need to tell you—"

"I wrote something. A poem. About us."

"Owen. I'm not going back to Michigan." *Smack.* Like running into a wall. I can't breathe. "This isn't about you. You were the only good thing. It was everything else. I never knew why I was there."

"No one knows why they're there," I find my voice.

"Well, I *have* to. I can't waste money. So I'm gonna take a year off, stay with my sister in Colorado, and figure out what I want."

"Maybe *I* should take a year off. I don't know what I want either. I can come out to Colorado."

This time, it isn't the silence that hurts. It's the waiting. The dread… "I need the time alone."

"So you're saying we're done?"

"If I don't do this, I'll always wonder."

"You'll wonder either way."

"I'm sorry, Owen. Please. Try to understand."

She says goodbye. So I say it back. And then we hang up. And she's gone. I walk into my room. Dylan's griping on and on. *There is no sense in trying… he not busy born is busy dying… not much is really sacred… it is not he or she or them or it that you belong to…* I go back into the hall, pick up the folder, and open it. There, staring me in the face, is the poem I never read to Tara.

> *You lie beside me, sleeping still.*
> *Birds sing the sun into the room.*
>
> *Their calls reach here from distant hills.*
> *Now one so close it wakens you.*
>
> *They sing this song for you and me,*
> *The song of us about to be.*

The page has Dad's agency name at the top. The poem comes off like the fake ad that asshole Francis wanted me to write. A fake ad for love. Isn't that what all love poems are anyway? I pick up the phone. I dial the number on the sheet.

"This is CCGO. How may I help you?"

"Is this Denise?"

"Yes, it is." She's all perky.

"This is Owen Maloney. Can I talk to my dad?"

There's a pause. "I'll connect you." She sounds sadder than Tara did.

Dad gets on the phone right away. "What's wrong?"

"I don't want the job. I'm not going to do it."

"Owen, this is all set. You can't back out now."

"Well, I am."

"We'll talk about this tonight."

"No, we won't."

He lowers his voice. "Now, you listen to me—"

"No. I'm not doing it. If you keep pushing me, I'll just leave. Like Neil." Screw it. He needs to know I'm not fucking around.

"Awright! Just calm down. We'll figure out something else."

"*I'll* figure it out," I say. Then I hang up.

It's four o'clock. In less than an hour, my whole life has blown up. All the time Tara and I spent together; the things we said to each other; the plans I was making; the hope I felt. All gone. The Dylan tape starts over. I lie down. I try to sleep for about an hour. I get up. Look out window. Watch a robin make a nest by the front door, a neighbor mow his lawn. *Meantime, life outside goes on all around you…*

I wonder if it's too late to go ask about a job at Rave-On Records. I think about that overgrown house, the people hiding inside it. I wonder if they're still playing music. I go get the poem. It all sounds like something that never happened now. Some bullshit dream. I wad it up into a ball and burn it over the kitchen sink.

The phone rings. My heart leaps. Maybe it's Tara. Maybe she's changed her mind.

It's Dad. He's shouting. "Hey Owen! Got another idea!" It sounds like he's at a party. "Remember Bud from lunch?"

"Yeah…"

"Well, he's my best friend. I named you after him."

"Yeah, and he hates his name."

"Maybe you *should* work for him."

"I thought you said you didn't want me to." Hell, he wouldn't even tell me what the guy did.

"I changed my mind." He says something else, but the chatter overtakes him. The next thing I hear is, "—but only if you want to."

"What does he do?"

"I just told you. He owns a bar."

"I couldn't hear you."

"It's a pretty swinging place," he yells.

It hits me. He's there, right now. "What would I do?"

"I don't know. We can talk to Bud. You can come here and check it out. He'll probably give you a job on the spot."

Here's Dad again. Telling me what to do. A *swinging* place, he says. I can just feel the lounge lizards slithering around.

"But listen, Owen. This is only if you want to. Really. I don't want to pressure you."

I don't know. Working in a bar. In downtown Chicago. This wasn't what I wanted. It's something Fitz would do.

"But I *do* have to give Bud an answer."

"I'll do it."

## Paint it Black

*It's not easy facing up when your whole world is black.*
*- Rolling Stones*

Everything's happening so fast. Here I am, the next day, sitting in Bud McGee's Saloon. It's on a street near the end of Rush in the middle of a bunch of other bars. It reminds me of Dooley's in Ann Arbor. All the dark wood and green stuff. A leprechaun. We're crammed around this table just off the bar—me, Dad, and Bud. A waitress has just brought a round of beers, we've barely started talking, and Bud has already decided I'm working for him.

"Susie, meet Owen," Bud says. "You'll be showing him the ropes."

"Great." She strikes a tone that's right on the edge of genuine and sarcastic. She's pretty, but—I don't know—she's got this bored look like she's trying to disguise it. *Bedroom eyes*, Fitz would probably say, only not seductive so much as sleepy.

Bud points out the other workers. Garrett, this short, sour-faced bartender. Bob, the doorman—Moose, they call him, because his last name's Moss and he's a giant, maybe even seven feet, with a big mane of curly hair and a handle-bar mustache. Bud says he was an offensive tackle for Wisconsin. A couple other servers rush past, Nick and Donna. Then there's Dan. Dan Kretchmer. "Kretch'll be your boss," Bud says. "Listen to him and you'll be fine."

He calls him over. "Kretch, this is Owen, the kid I was telling you about. What do we have for him this week?" Dan's a bear of a man, not as tall as me, but maybe twice as heavy. He isn't fat so much as burly, massive shoulders, a huge barrel chest. His face is all red, and he's got this wide-eyed look like he's on his way to put out a fire.

"I got him on the day shift. Training the next three days."

"No nights?"

He glances at me, like who the hell is this snot? "It'll be easier to fit him in next week."

"See if you can get him a night this week. Anything but Friday. Just to give him a taste." Dan nods and charges off to his next problem. A night? I start thinking about logistics. "Don't worry," Bud reads my face. "It can be crazy, but you'll get used to it. Then you'll want it to be crazy, because that's where the money is."

"How late do the trains go?"

"Shit. Not very late," Dad says. Bud sighs. His stomach dimples around the table. "I could drive in the days he's got a late shift."

Bud waves him off. "You don't want to do that." Then he aims a finger at me. "Tell you what, you can stay in my basement. I had another guy do it. It's got everything you need—bathroom, kitchenette, queen-sized bed. Your dad's been there."

Dad sounds like a balloon deflating. "I don't know, Bud. Walking around Chicago after two a.m."

"You know where I am, Mikey. Just three blocks up Dearborn."

Dad looks at me. "What do you think?"

The alternative? Sitting alone in my room in Wheaton with nothing to do but think about Tara. "Sounds good."

Kretch takes me downstairs to his office to fill out paperwork, get my schedule, and go over a few things, like what I'm supposed to wear (white shirt, black pants, black shoes); where the guy's locker room is if I'm getting changed there; how a 10 a.m. shift means on the floor and ready at 10, not just breezing in the door.

"We like to be clean cut too," Kretch says. "A good shave. Hair not too long." He points at my head. My hair's longer than his, but it's not *that* long.

Oh, well. "I'll get it cut."

"Next week's fine." He opens a desk drawer, pulls out what looks like a ball of green socks, and throws it at me. "Welcome to Bud's."

I unfurl the ball. It's a tie. There's a white stencil on it—a cartoon leprechaun that looks like Bud grinning at me. "One more thing," Kretch says. "People are gonna find out how you got the job. You'll probably get shit about it." That catches me off guard. I was worried about having an in at the agency. I never thought it would be a problem at a bar. "You'll have to handle that yourself. If I step in, it's only going to make things worse."

When I go back upstairs and sit down again with Bud and Dad, he takes a key off his key ring, and hands it to me. "All you gotta do is take the steps, open the door, and the basement's right there."

The plan is that I'll work the next day, spend the night in Bud's basement, maybe work a double shift on Thursday to get the night experience, then do the lunch shift again on Friday.

At home, I iron the only other white shirt I own, take the black pants from Dad's suit, get another change of clothes, and put it all in a gym bag. I get my toiletries, too, and throw in a jacket. Dad offers to cut my hair. I don't want him anywhere near me. He's had a few more drinks since he's been home. "Get it out of your face at least," he says. Fair enough. My bangs are so long they fall over my eyes, and I'm always swinging my head so I can see. I get the sharpest scissors I can find, the little ones in Mom's sewing box. I wet my bangs, comb them down, and cut off an inch. Then I blow-dry my hair. Maybe I should've let Dad do it. He probably knew the bangs would ride up higher after they dried. At least it's out of my face. I'll find a barber on the weekend.

I get up early and take the eight o'clock train into the city. I'm thinking I'll go to the apartment first, check it out, and get dressed for work there. I didn't realize how long the walk was, though; we took the El to Bud's yesterday. Now it's nine-thirty, I'm still going up Rush Street, and I have to be dressed and ready in half an hour.

When I open the door to Bud's, Moose is blocking my way. "We open at ten-thirty," he barks down at me.

Kretch comes bustling up behind him. "This is Owen. It's his first day. Owen, Moose." Moose gives me a nod, but he's still scowling. God, the guy's scary. Kretch checks his watch. "Cutting it close."

I've got 10 minutes to get dressed and on the floor. Everything's going fine until I have to tie my tie. The white ink of the leprechaun makes it really thick, and the knot keeps coming out huge. I'm starting to panic.

"Need help with that?" A guy pokes his face into my mirror. His tie looks perfect. Hell, *he* looks perfect. Hollywood handsome. His hair looks like he got it done by some celebrity stylist. It's feathered and lying perfectly in place, long but clean, effortlessly sharp.

"I can't get it any smaller."

"You can't tie these like that. Here." He reaches for the two ends I'm holding. "Turn to me." Our faces are inches away. The guy's older than me, mid-twenties, I guess, so maybe he's out of the zit stage. Still, I've never seen skin so clear. And, shit, he smells good too. Why didn't I think of cologne? I'm already pitting out and I've barely moved. "There." He backs away.

I turn to the mirror. Damned if the knot isn't just like his. "You're going to have to show me how to do that."

The guy taps on his watch. "Not now. We're on." I follow him up the stairs. Just before he opens the door to the bar, he turns to me. "I'm Terry Stratton, by the way."

"Owen Maloney."

He smiles. "I know who you are." Then he pushes the door open and struts out onto the floor like he owns the place.

The waitress from yesterday is standing next to Kretch when I go to the front door. "You're going to shadow Susie for the first few shifts," he tells me. Then he says to her, "Make sure he gets a couple tables to himself after the rush."

Susie's closest in age to me of anyone I've met so far. She's short, with straight blonde hair in a thick bob. Like I said, you can tell she's pretty, but it's almost like she doesn't want to be. She's got those hooded eyes, like she's trying to hide how big they are. It's her mouth, though, that gives her away. Her lips are full and shaped the way women try to fake with lipstick.

"I'm Susie Starling." She thrusts out her hand and shakes mine tighter than Bud did. "And you're Owen. Mike's son."

"You know my dad?"

"Everyone knows your dad."

She walks me around the bar, shows me where the kitchen is, how to put in an order, how the bar's broken up into sections, the plusses and minuses of each. She starts in the side room, where the kitchen is. "This is the best place to be whenever we serve food, or if it's backgammon night. Any other time, and it's a crapshoot. If we're not busy, Kretch sometimes closes this room down early."

In the main bar, Susie says, "Section one here by the front door is great on night shifts. It's like one big party. You can hit people up right when they walk in. And sometimes they never go any further. It's awful for lunch, though. There's nowhere to sit except those four stools at the window." We walk along the bar toward the back. "We'll be working sections two and three today. Two's my favorite. You got those two tables there." She points over where I sat with Bud and Dad yesterday. "But you also got this whole area where people stand. Plus, you're right near the bartender, so you don't have to schlep drinks very far. Quick turnover."

Susie stops next to a jukebox by the men's room. "Everything from here back is section three. It's got the six-top and that railing. So it's okay for lunch, but death at night. Only tourists and people from the burbs hang out here. That means shitty tips."

Susie slaps the top of the jukebox where all the songs are lit up. "You wanna get in good with Kretch? If it's quiet, play songs from these last two rows. These are the ones he picked. They've been here forever. Don't play these." She waves her hand at the rest of the rows. "It's all the new crap people begged Bud to get. You know, disco and pop. Kretch hates that shit. Puts him in a bad mood."

"So it takes quarters?" I point to the coin slot.

"No, Bud set it up so it's all free. Watch this." Susie punches in a letter and a number. "Paint it Black" by the Stones starts playing. Susie cocks her head toward the door. Kretch is already bobbing to the drumbeat and the droning sitar. He looks back, sees us watching, points our way with both hands, and gives us a little clap.

Susie smiles. "It's good to keep Kretch happy."

"Awright, ladies and gentlemen, we're on!" Kretch calls out. Moose unlocks the door—and all hell breaks loose. In minutes, the bar's filled. That's how it seems, anyway. "This is nothing," Susie says over her shoulder, as I fight through the crowd to keep up with her. Our two tables get seated right away. We haven't even taken their drink orders, and Kretch is leading a group back to the six-top. Meanwhile, a few clusters of people mill around in our section. I help get waters. I take some tickets back to the kitchen. Susie's explaining everything she's doing, but we're moving so fast, most of it's going right by me. And this goes on and on for four straight hours. I'm wrung out. I just want to sit down. Finally, the crowd thins out enough so you can hear yourself think. Then we've only got the two tables. Susie leans an elbow against the bar. She puffs a loose strand of hair out of her face. She's always doing that. There's something endearing about it. "Okay, got all that?"

Does she really expect me to remember everything? "I guess so."

She laughs. "I'm messing with you. It's a lot, I know. Why don't you take over, and I'll shadow you, tell you what you need to do?"

Sounds simple enough, but I run into trouble on my very first order. Four businessmen are standing in the back. One wants a Guinness, one a Tom Collins, another a Harvey Wallbanger, and the last a Jack and coke. I go to the railed-off part of the bar where you order your drinks. Garrett stares at me. "I have an order."

"No shit."

I tell him the drinks: "A Guinness, a Tom Collins, a Harvey Wallbanger, and a Jack and coke."

"Make that."

"Make that what?"

"Sorry, Garrett. I forgot to cover this." Susie turns to me. "The bartenders want you to say the drinks in a certain order, so they can make them as fast as possible. If you don't get the order right, they say, 'make that,' like 'do it again.'"

"Okay…"

"You ask for your call drinks first, well drinks second, wine, then bottled beer, then tap beer."

"What's a call drink and a well drink?"

"A call drink's a certain brand of liquor. Like Jameson. A well drink's generic—whiskey, vodka, gin." I don't know my liquors. I've only really drank beer since high school, aside from one rough bout with Boone's Farm Strawberry Hill. "Try again," Susie says.

I know the Guinness comes last. "Okay. A Tom Collins, a Harvey Wallbanger, a Jack and Coke, and a Guinness."

"Make that." Garrett looks off toward the front of the bar.

I look at Susie. "Tom Collins is a well drink. It's just any old gin."

Awright. I got it now. "Harvey Wallbanger, Tom Collins, Jack and Coke, and a Guinness."

"Make that."

Susie sighs. "Man, you got a hard first order. So… the Jack and Coke—that's a call drink."

"Like Harvey Wallbanger."

"That's the name of the drink. Jack Daniels is a brand of liquor."

I give Garrett the right order. "Jack and coke, Tom Collins, Harvey Wallbanger, and a Guinness."

"Make that."

Now Susie's frustrated. "Garrett…"

"Just give him the fucking order," someone barks behind me. It's Terry. Air spurts out of Garrett's mouth. His head wobbles like a loose balloon. But he finally starts the drinks. I give Terry a nod of thanks. The way he got Garrett to move, he's someone important around here, I can already tell.

"Technically," Garrett mutters, "a Harvey Wallbanger is a call drink because of the Galliano."

"And how the fuck's he supposed to know that?"

"That's why I'm telling him."

"Well, don't." Terry strides away.

Susie raises her eyebrows. Garrett takes care of all the drinks. Then he leans over the bar. "You better have your orders right for the night bartenders. They'll walk away from you if you don't."

Everything after that goes smoothly. All the rest of my orders are for draft beer. The only challenge is how to carry so many glasses. Susie shows me how to balance three in each hand and squeeze three more between your forearms. I could do it just standing there, but walking? And snaking through a crowd? No way.

Soon enough, there's no one in our section. Kretch comes back and lets us go. Susie shows me how to close out and how much of her tips to give the bartender and doorman. Then she hands me $27.

"What's this for?"

"That's half the tips. You earned it."

I didn't think I'd get anything, but no way I deserved half of Susie's money. "I can't take all this." I hand the twenty back to her.

She waves it off. "You can buy me a drink."

Like when? Now? I'm about to ask her, but Kretch comes barreling over. "What do you got going on tonight?" He's looking at me.

All I know is that I've got to find Bud's house on Dearborn and get settled in his basement. "Nothing."

"Great. Clancy just called in sick, and you need night experience. So you're flying solo in section three." With that, he wheels around and rumbles away. Susie must see the shock on my face, because she's looking at me with pity.

The next hour goes by easy. But then the 5:00 p.m. shift comes in. A new set of waiters and bartenders take the floor. The bartender up front is some old guy. The one taking over for Garrett's a girl— well, a woman really, not so much by age, which could be just a few years older than me, but by the way she looks. To say she's pretty is too sweet. There's an intimidating edge to her. Her eyes are cold and lively. And she has an angular, wolfish face that makes her hard to see straight on. Maybe that's why she seems so unapproachable. I'm afraid of what she'll do when I screw up my first order. She doesn't scare Terry, though. There he is with here, leaning in close, like he's telling her a secret. And she's nodding, carving the blade of her face like a wielded knife, those sharp eyes glinting everywhere.

My first order's easy. Two Guinness and a Pabst. I go to the service rails. She's busy washing glasses. So I wait. I wish Terry was still here to introduce us. I wish I had Terry's swagger. I'd lean out over the bar and call to her. Finally, she comes over, glancing everywhere but at me—up and down the bar, over to the front door, across the swelling crowd. "Two Guinness and a Pabst," I say right off. She has no time for introductions.

But I'm wrong. "You're Owen," she declares, doing the job for me. "I'm Jill Tanner." She holds out her hand. And there's her face straight on, for just a flash. Softer than I would've thought. "That order needs to be a Pabst and two Guinness. Pabst isn't on tap."

Great. My first order with Jill, and I messed it up. At least she didn't snap at me like Garrett. And it goes on like this all through the night, me fumbling through my orders, Jill patiently correcting me. In a way, her quiet guidance is even worse than the constant *make-that* barking. I feel like I'm letting her down. Eventually, I get the hang of it and nail a couple of long orders. "Very good," Jill praises me like I'm some sort of dimwit.

Before long, ordering's no big deal, especially compared to fighting through the crowd. I can't carry as many drinks as Susie did, so sometimes I have to make two trips to get an order done. Plus, I go a lot slower, because I'm worried about spilling. Still, nobody seems to mind, and the tips keep flowing in. Kretch is the only other person remaining from the day shift besides me. The bar doesn't thin out until after 11. All the stools are still taken, and there are a few clusters of people here and there. But it's quieter, the conversations hushed, customers slouching back, waiters hanging out with them. These must be the regulars.

I'm starting to wonder when I'll get let go. I'm tired, and I still need to find Bud's basement and see what I'm up against there. My last table pays the bill and gets up to leave. I follow them to the front door. Maybe I should ask Kretch if I can go. Just then, one of my customers wheels around and comes staggering back my way. He's got his shirt untucked and his tie tugged loose. He's drunk, drunker than the three beers I served him. How did I not notice that? At the table, he looked like any of the other hotshots I served through the night. But now, he looks like some desperate frat boy, taking one last lurching lap through the party. He bumps me on the way past and careens into the bar, down where I pick up drinks. Jill hurries over. They talk quietly like friends, but then the guy yells out, "Bullshit!" and swipes to grab Jill's arm. She backs away. There's more swearing, and Jill's looking off to the front door.

I rush over. "Is there a problem?"

"It's okay, Owen."

"Who the fuck are you?"

It's not okay, no matter what Jill says. And the guy's got his finger in my face now. I knock it away. "You oughta leave."

"I'll leave when I fucking want." He shoves me. I stumble back. A glass goes crashing behind the bar. I come back at the guy. He grabs my collar. I grab his. We twist and shove. Then his head snaps back and he's sliding away, clawing at the air. Kretch has the guy in a headlock, and he's dragging him to the door.

"Shit." Jill's looking down at the broken glass. It didn't make it to the floor. Shards sparkle on the back bar next to the ice bin. Glass and ice; not a good combo. "We've gotta throw all this out," she says. Then she looks up to the front of the bar. "Uh-oh. Let me talk."

Kretch is charging at us. "What the hell happened?"

"Just another drunk. Grabbed Owen out of the blue."

Kretch folds his arms. "He was getting after Jill." We have to tell him something. He probably heard the guy yelling.

Kretch glares at me, then Jill, then me again. "Listen to me." His voice is low, anger contained. "You have a problem with a customer, you bring it to the front door. We take care of that; you don't. We don't need any heroes here. You got it?"

"Yessir." Kretch squints at me like he's trying to decide if I'm being a smartass with the sir stuff. I'm not. That's what I'd say to Dad.

"The guy knocked a drink into the ice," Jill says.

"Shit. Okay, you: take the ice bin into the alley and dump it. Make sure all the glass is out. Then you're cut." He lumbers away.

*Did I just get fired?* Jill sees the worry on my face. "That just means he's closing your section, and you're done for the night. It's a good thing. This is when you *want* to get cut. There's no more money to be made."

I'm sure she's being straight, but still, Kretch was *not* happy with me. Jill shows me how to pry the ice bin out of its metal hole in the back bar. It's heavy. She asks if I need help carrying it. "No, I got it." I swing around to go.

"Hey," Jill says. "I can take care of myself. But thanks anyway."

"Okay."

Jill points to the door for the back alley. It's just a long crack between buildings, no wider than a sidewalk. It's dirty and oily, and it smells like beer and trash and a dead animal. There's a dim yellow bulb above our door, and down at the Dearborn end a blue light flickers. I dump the ice. Then, when I'm going back in, I hear voices at the dark end of the alley. There's enough light to see who it is: Terry and Moose talking to a couple other guys. Terry gives a little tilt of his chin, like he doesn't want anyone else to see. I do the same. Then I go back inside.

I work the ice bin back into the hole, and Jill wipes it down with a paper cloth, just to make sure no glass is there.

"First night," I say, "and already Kretch doesn't like me."

"Kretch just wants everyone to be safe. He'd never say it, but he's probably happy to know you'll stand up if you need to."

I look over at Kretch. He's got his hands on his hips and he's scanning the bar. I go to the jukebox. I punch the buttons. "Paint it Black" starts up. Kretch's head snaps my way. He squints to make eye contact. Then he cocks his head, like he's weighing a heavy decision. Finally, he shoots out both hands and points at me with an approving grin.

**I'm So Lonesome I Could Cry**
*I've never seen a night so long, and time goes crawling by…*
*- Hank Williams*


It takes me a while to cash out by myself. By the time I get down to the locker room and out of my work clothes, it's after 1:30. Right when I'm about to head out, Terry comes in and straddles the bench beside me. "How'd you make out on your first day?"

"Twenty-seven at lunch, fifty-six tonight."

Terry nods slowly. "You'll do better."

"What's good for a night like this?"

"I never like walking out of here with less than a hundred." Shit. Was I *that* slow? "You did have the worst section," he reassures me. "But you'll learn how to push."

"I'll get faster."

"Speed helps. But it's really about getting closer to people, having them give you more money." Doing the math, I made nearly 15%, yet Terry's saying I should make almost twice that. "You'll get there. A couple weeks, a few changes, and you'll be raking it in."

Changes? What does *that* mean? I'm not going to ask. It's late. I get up to leave. Terry gets up with me. "Hey," he puts his hand on my shoulder. "Don't say anything seeing us in the alley, alright?"

"Sure." I'd forgotten all about it.

"A lot of us go back there for a smoke break. It's no big deal, really, but Kretch doesn't like it."

"I get it."

"I want to stay on his good side." Terry lowers his voice. "One of these days, he's going to be looking for someone to take over for him. And I want to make sure it's me."

"Okay." Now he's got me wondering, though. What I saw wasn't a smoke break. For one thing, he and Moose had been off work for hours. For another, the guys they were with didn't work at Bud's.

Terry keeps eyeing me. "Did you get something to eat?"

I *am* hungry. "I haven't eaten all day."

"Shit, Owen. Not even at lunch?"

"When were we supposed to get that?"

"You just ask the kitchen whenever. They'll take care of you."

"That would've been nice to know."

Terry laughs. "I bet someone's still there. Hang on." He hurries upstairs. Crap. At this point, I'd rather just go to bed. Terry's back before I know it, though. "Someone left half a Reuben." He hands me a sandwich basket. There's a pickle in there too. I sit down again. Food isn't a bad idea after all.

Terry watches me eat. "Good?"

"Yeah, thanks."

Maybe that's all he wanted, a little gratitude, because now he's headed out. "I'm here tomorrow. If you need anything, just ask."

After he's gone, I wolf down the rest of the food. All in all, a pretty damn good day. The money's great, but getting in good with a guy like Terry, that's even better.

When I go back upstairs, Kretch is there by the basement door. "See you at nine-thirty," he says.

Shit, that's less than eight hours away. "Nine-thirty."

"And you know how to get to Bud's?"

"Over to Dearborn and turn right."

"That's it. If you get to North Boulevard, you've gone too far."

I nod and head out. Does he think I'm an idiot? Maybe that's how Kretch is when everybody walks out the door. Jill said he worried about our safety. And he knows that Dad's friends with Bud. Plus, it's my first night. I guess it makes sense that he'd be a little overprotective. Hell, with the craziness on Division, can you blame him?

Gangs of people are weaving along the sidewalks. Cabs are swarming all over the place. It's what—quarter to two now? You'd think things would be dead.

Thankfully, it takes less than 10 minutes to get to Bud's. It's a super-narrow place, the width of a garage, and it's wedged in between a bunch of other thin buildings. A townhouse, Bud called it. There are some steps up to the front door, and there's light in the windows on either side of it. Bud must've left them on for me. He said to open the door, and the basement would be right there. I can see another door inside; that's got to be it. I get the key out and put it in the lock. It goes in but won't turn. I turn it the other way. That doesn't work either. I jiggle the key and try again. Still, no go. I turn the key over. Maybe it's upside down. No… What the hell? I go back out in the street to see if any lights are on in the high windows. The whole place is dark except for the light Bud left on in his hallway. I can't ring the doorbell this late. I can't wake up Bud and his family. *Shit.*

I head back to the bar. Maybe Kretch can tell me what I'm doing wrong. It's only been a half hour, but Division's quieter now, still a few people prowling the street, but nothing like when I left. The door to Bud's is locked. It can't be much later than two; somebody's gotta be inside. I knock. Nobody comes. They're probably in the basement. Even if I pounded on the door, they wouldn't hear me. I look around for something open. Susie said there were a few four o'clock bars nearby. They're nowhere I can see. But across Dearborn, there's a little diner that still has its lights on. Maybe they have a payphone. I really don't want to, but I'm going to have to call Dad. What else can I do?

I can tell as I'm crossing the street that this isn't going to be a nice place. Its outside lights are weak and yellowed, and I realize the blinking neon "Bill's Diner" sign is what made the blue color I saw down the alley behind Bud's. The windows are covered with clouds of soapy film, and the rest of the place is wrapped with dented sheet metal. Even as I open the door, I'm thinking maybe I should find another place. But now everyone's looking at me, a line of down-and-outers at the long counter, swiveling in their stools to size me up. The guy behind the counter is eyeing me too.

"Do you have a payphone?"

"We got a phone, but it's for paying customers."

I see one of those glass cake stands on the counter. It's got a couple donuts in it. "How much for one of those?"

"That'll set you back five bucks." I hear cackling at the end of the counter. There's a card taped to the cake stand with "$2" written on it.

"This says two."

The worker ignores me. What can I do? I buy the donut. He hands it to me with a napkin, then takes a phone out from under the counter. A couple old buzzards are still watching me, so after I dial, I pull the phone with its long cord over to the front door where they can't hear. Problem is, there's a cheap speaker above my head, squawking out hillbilly music. *I'm so lonesome, I could cry.* No way I'm going to ask the guy to turn it down. I huddle against the corner. The phone rings and rings. Finally, Dad answers. He's groggy, confused. Probably drunk. I explain the problem. "Wai-wai-wait. What?" I'm not sure he can hear me over the hillbilly warbling. I repeat what I said, slower. "You must've done something wrong."

"I didn't do anything wrong, Dad!" All the creepy vulture heads snap my way. I lower my voice. "I don't know what to do."

"Where are you? I'll come get you."

"I don't want to stay here," I whisper now.

"Okay, I'll pick you up at the bar."

"No, not there." The thought of standing alone out on Division, this big defenseless target, feels as scary as sweating it out here.

"Then where?"

It comes to me suddenly. "How about the train station?"

"All that way?"

"How long will it take you to drive there?"

"Less than an hour."

"That's okay."

"Take a cab," Dad tells me. Then he hangs up. I bring the phone back and get the hell out of there. I hadn't thought of taking a cab. But I don't see one anywhere. I head toward Rush Street, and I start eating the donut as I go. That's what changes my mind. I just wasted five bucks on the stalest, shittiest donut I've ever had. Now I'm going to let some cabby fleece me too? Fuck it. I'll walk.

Rush is lit up like a technicolor fire, car lights sparking red and yellow down the street, huge signs flaring up out of the inferno—*SINGAPORE Exotic Dancers, CARNEGIE, MOULIN ROUGE, FACES.* People gather in the entryways, all ablaze themselves, in bright disco clothes and glittering chains, out for dancing, for mingling, for cutting loose. Above it all, a glittering building says *PLAYBOY.*

After a few blocks, Rush dies down. Thankfully. Another block, though, and it's darker. I'm just as afraid as when I was in those flames of light. Every block I get past brings relief, then it's the next block, and there's a whole new threat to reckon with—two shadowy figures across the street, dead silent, facing me as I go… a car blocking my sidewalk, lights off, music throbbing… someone yelling, "Hey! Hey! Hey!" Are they calling *me?*

I go on and on. Five blocks, ten, more. Then I see the spire-like top of the Wrigley Building, and I know I'm close to somewhere I've been. But the last block slopes down and ends abruptly. I'm beneath the El, in the city's underworld. Either way I look, a tunnel of dim lights trails off into echoing darkness. And it smells like garbage. In front of me, there's a crack of light, buildings in the distance, on the other side of a wasteland. The piles of garbage at the sides of the tunnel start moving. They're people, curled up and sleeping. And it isn't a wasteland in front of me; it's the river. *The river…* How did I forget that?

Well, thank God for it, because now I know where to go. I walk beside it towards what I can see is a bridge. I take the staircase at the end, and I'm out of the netherworld and up on a high road again. Wabash. I remember this. Now Wacker. And there are those two towers with the perfect flowers stacked to the sky, only now, with so few lights on, they're like skeletons of those flowers. Where the river splits, I go left, and then Randolph is there, and I cross the bridge I took with Dad two days ago. Another block, and I'm finally at the train station. I look down to where Dad and I came out of the station to a riot of color and bustle and noise. No one's here, and there's hardly any light. Just a series of arched doorways to darkness. I don't want to get anywhere near them. I don't want to push my luck. So I stand. And I look around.

I turn, slowly… slow enough that you'd have to focus on me for a while to know I was making a circle. I wonder where the headlights will come from and when I'll see them. I count down from 100. It goes too fast. I start to pray. I pray for the headlights to come. I pray no one will attack me. I pray and pray, shuffling around in my secret circle. And just like that, headlights are floating down Randolph and swinging across me. Now Dad's car is there at the curb, waiting—the only miracle of this wretched night.

I get in. Dad puts his hand on my knee. "You okay?"

I let out nearly all the air I have. "Yeah."

"I'd be scared too," he says as we drive off. The car lights sweep along those dark doorways. People are curled up in every one, backs to us, turned to the comfort of the shadows.

"We'll find a job in Wheaton. If it takes a while, so be it."

I don't say anything. I think about those bodies huddling in the shadows. Where would I be if I didn't have someone to call?

## The Passenger

*We'll ride through the city tonight, see the city's ripped backsides.*
*- Iggy Pop*

I wake at 7:12 with a start. Dad's gone, and here I am, alone again in this sad house. I take a shower and have a bowl of cereal. I look out the nook, straight up the road to where it turns toward town. I think of Tara. For the first time in what seems like forever. It amazes me that I ever *stopped* thinking about her. I know I have to. I have to move on. If I don't, it'll tear me up inside. But some warped part of me *wants* that, the part that needs to believe it was love…

Suddenly, I'm rushing upstairs. I open the bag I took to the city and take out my white shirt. Too wrinkled. I go into Dad's closet, get a fresh shirt, fold it, and lay it flat in my bag. Then I rumble back downstairs and write Dad a note: *GONE TO BUD'S*. I have no idea if I'll get there in time. Twenty minutes to the station, that's eight; an hour into the city, nine; so half an hour to get to Bud's. This time, I have no choice but to take a cab.

Turns out, it's just a $6.90 fare. I give the cabbie eight, get out, and knock on the bar door. Moose opens it. For a second, he looks surprised, then his eyes settle into that dead glare. He calls out over his shoulder, "Look who's here."

Kretch bustles up to the door. He stops when he sees me. "Bud said you weren't coming in. Said you had some trouble last night."

I shrug. "Well, I'm here."

"Yes, you are." Kretch cocks the side of his mouth and nods. Proudly, I think. And I'm glad to think it.

They team me up with Susie again, only this time, we're in the side room where there are more tables, and Susie's letting me lead.

I'm running back and forth to the bar a lot more and losing sight of my section. One customer asks for a soup spoon, so I race off to get it. Another asks for Dijon mustard right when I get back. It's hectic and stressful, and I can tell people are getting pissed.

"One thing you've got to learn," Susie says. "Every time you come into your section, check on every table." You'd think taking care of five four-tops wouldn't be hard, but I keep finding ways to screw up—bringing the wrong order to a table, forgetting one guy's drink, letting dishes sit uncleared. Susie lets me make every mistake. "Shit happens. It's the way you deal with it that matters." I tell the guy whose drink I forgot it's my first day. "Don't do that," Susie says. "Just own up to the mistake, apologize, and move on."

The rush seems to go on forever. Then, just like that, it's over. "This is the best thing about this section," Susie says. "You work your ass off for four hours, then you're done. Nobody hangs out and has drinks over here during the day. We're usually the first cut."

We're back by the kitchen, watching over the one table we have left, and there's nothing to do but talk. "I have to remember to eat today," I say, not meaning anything by it, just filling the silence.

"Oh, shit. I forgot to tell you about that, didn't I?

"It's okay. Terry brought me a sandwich after work last night."

"Terry? Brought you a sandwich?"

"Highlight of the night." I told Susie I got locked out. But does she know about my run-in with the drunk or the broken glass in the ice?

"Bud called before you got in this morning. You could tell he was chewing out Kretch."

"About me? Kretch didn't have anything to do with it."

"All I know is Kretch doesn't smile much, but after you went down to dress, he had the biggest grin I've ever seen. Whatever Bud was mad about, Kretch was damned happy to see you."

Probably because Dad called Bud and told him what happened. Then Bud called Kretch to let him know I wasn't coming in, that I got left on my own the night before. Bud's best friend's kid, out on the streets, with all the bums. Maybe Bud expected Kretch to make sure I got to his house safely and blamed him for my quitting.

"I'm not a quitter," I say out loud. It sounds brave, but it's not the real reason I'm here. Being here is more an act of cowardice. If I was honest with Susie, I'd say that I came to work because I couldn't stand the thought of sitting around stewing over Tara.

"So what are you going to do tonight? Susie asks.

"I don't know. Go back to Wheaton, I guess."

"Well, that's a giant pain in the ass. I bet they'll find a place for you. If not, you can stay with me. I'm just a few blocks that way." She points towards Bud's but further from the lake.

"I don't want to put you out." I'm just being polite. Truth is, the offer comes as a huge relief.

"I've got a little rehearsing to do, but that's just a couple hours. Then we can find somewhere to eat, and I'll show you around."

"Rehearsing? Are you in a play or something?"

"It's just this dumb comedy thing I'm doing."

"Like stand-up?" Susie doesn't strike me as funny.

"Sort of. But don't tell anybody that."

Kretch comes barreling our way. "You guys are cut," he tells us. "Owen, got a minute?" I glance at Susie. She raises her eyebrows then hurries off. I never told her if I'd stay with her or not. I wish I had. Who knows what Kretch has planned?

"Let's find somewhere quiet." He leads me over to section three, back by the alley door. On the way there, I notice Terry sitting at the front window. "You got that key to Bud's?" Kretch asks. It's on a ring with the Wheaton house key. I start taking it off. "That's okay." Kretch holds out his hand. I give him the whole ring. He pulls a loop of keys out of his pocket. They're chained to his belt. He finds a key and compares it to mine. "Looks the same." He hands back my key ring. "And you saw where the basement was?"

"It was right there."

"Down the steps."

"Yeah." Where else would a basement be?

Kretch stares me down like he doesn't believe me. "Alright. Terry's going to take you over to Bud's, and we're going to figure out what the problem is. If we can't, we'll go from there. Okay?"

So that's why Terry's here. "Okay."

I wait for Kretch to hurry away like always. But he just stays there, looking at me. So I turn to go. "One more thing." He's taking his wallet out of his back pocket now. "If you ever run into trouble downtown—day, night, I don't care when—you call me first. Not your dad. Not Bud. Me." It feels like I'm getting chewed out. He hands me a business card. All it says is "Dan Kretchmer, Manager, Bud McGee's," then a phone number.

"Any problems at all, that's the number, got it?"

"I got it." I look him in the eye, and I harden my jaw to show him how serious I am. I don't want Kretch mad at me, or disappointed, or upset. He throws out his arm like a roundhouse punch and lands it across my shoulders. "You had yourself quite a first day." He laughs. "It's a story for the ages." He's got me in a walking bear hug now. I feel like if I picked up my feet, he'd carry me along. "But you came back. So it's a good story. One you'll be laughing about by the end of the summer."

Kretch gives me one last squeeze, stops in front of the jukebox, then tees up—what else?—"Paint it Black." "I don't know why I love this song so much. It's sad. As sad as it gets. But I put myself in that guy's shoes—not that that's the way I feel—but I think, how brave is that? Here's someone who had happiness, lost it, and now doesn't want it. Can't bear it. So what does he do? He doesn't give up. He throws himself into—not unhappiness—but nothingness, blackness. It's an anthem. For stoics."

I don't really follow, but I'm not about to tell him that. "I get it."

Kretch wraps his knuckles on the top of the jukebox. "Sometimes, songs aren't what they seem. Neither are people. Every day, someone surprises me. Today it was you."

As soon as Kretch walks away, Terry gets off his stool and comes over, intercepting me before I go down to the locker room. He's got his hands out like I could use a hug. "Not your fault, man. I told Kretch, that key was a problem back when I lived there."

Just then, the door swings open. Susie steps between us. She doesn't say anything. Neither does Terry. I have to—for Susie's sake. "I've gotta go do this," I tell her.

Her eyes shift to Terry, then back to me "Oh. Yeah. Sure."

"Bye, Susie," Terry says before she even leaves. I thought maybe she could come along. But I can tell by their body language neither of them wants that.


When we leave the bar, Terry starts walking toward the lake, the wrong direction entirely. "Aren't we going to Bud's?"

"We're getting my car."

He turns into the alley on the other side of Marlarkey's, and there, parked so you can barely get around it, is a little red sportscar. It's as shiny as new, not a scratch on it. It has a "TR6" on the grille and a British flag on the back side.

"This is your car?"

"It appears so." He opens his door without unlocking it. The black soft top's down.

"You left it here a while."

"I'm not worried. I've got nothing worth taking." He gets in, starts it up, and pulls up to the sidewalk, so I can get in.

"That tape player's pretty damn sweet." I point at the dashboard like he wasn't aware it was there.

"Our thieves aren't that ambitious. They want to grab and go. Groceries, jewelry, wallets, purses—that kind of stuff." He takes a purple box out from under his seat, picks out a cassette, and puts it in the tape player. The traffic crawls along Division. "And they're principled too. They want to rob you, sure, but it's nothing personal. If you make it easy for them, they won't trash your shit."

The music starts bouncing along, a driving drumbeat, a snarling guitar. No singing, just that propulsive beat. I can see the spine of the cassette on top of the dashboard. Iggy Pop, *Lust for Life*.

"I guess they don't steal cassettes."

"No, they do," Terry says. "They just don't bother to look in my car. They figure, *this guy isn't going to have anything; if he did, he'd lock it up.*"

"Sounds like the thieves are more trusting than they ought to be," I say. He laughs. We turn up Dearborn. No other cars are on the street as far as I can see. Terry sails along, wind riffling through that perfect hair of his, music blaring, people watching us pass. Last night, I couldn't see how ritzy this stretch is—gated entryways to high-rise luxury condos, stately townhouses with beautiful brickwork and stained-glass windows, manicured plant boxes flowering all along the sidewalks.

"This place reeks of money."

"Gold Coast, baby!" Terry downshifts to a quick stop to let two women cross the street. One gives him an eye and smiles. He sweeps his hand like he's opened a door for them.

How did he get here? So polished, so cool... so regal. "You bought this car from bar tips?"

Terry looks at me like he's disappointed I don't know the answer. "You're going to make a lot of money, Owen. A lot. Either you'll save it or you won't. You'll go home and get a good night's sleep or you'll go out after work and drink away your hard-earned dough. I saved, and now I'm investing."

*Investing in what?* I want to ask, but he lurches off the line and revs away. We find a parking spot a few houses past Bud's and walk back to his door. I start up the stairs. "Where are you going?" Terry's on the sidewalk, and he's pointing down. I look that way. There, off to the side, a small, purple-flowered bush hides a narrow stairwell. I can't see where it leads; it's under where I'm standing. Terry heads down there. "I knew this was the problem," he says, when I'm beside him. "When Kretch told me you were locked out, I thought, *he doesn't know the basement door's outside.* 'Course, I didn't tell him that." Terry asks for my key, turns it in the lock, and opens the door. Just that easy. Man, do I feel dumb.

We go inside. Terry flips on a light. We're in a room crowded with curiosities. A couch with three glass chandeliers sitting on it. A huddle of pinball machines covered with skimpy sheets. Dozens of age-old paintings in thick wood frames, lined up along the wall and leaning against each other, all sorts of other stuff. "Don't touch anything in here," Terry says. "These are some of Bud's antiques." He wends his way across the room to a shadowy hallway. There, he flips on another light. The hall isn't that long. At the end of it, there's a closed door. Before we get there, a staircase comes into view on the left. It probably leads to the door I thought I got locked out of last night.

Terry pushes open the door. And now we're in my apartment. It isn't much: a counter with a sink, a mini-fridge, and a toaster oven; a bed in the same room—a big one, at least; and a closet-sized bathroom. There's a nightstand by the bed and a metal chair in the corner. That's about it. Terry's looking around like it's the most amazing apartment he's ever seen. "I bet no one's been in here since me."

I drop my gym bag and sit down on the bed. I'm tired.

"What have you got in here?" Terry kicks the bag.

"My work clothes, toiletries, some books."

"You got a new shirt for tomorrow?"

"No."

"You need one. You had a ketchup stain on your pocket."

Man, nothing gets past Terry. "I can wash it off."

"Fuck that," he says, loud enough that I bet someone could hear upstairs. "You're gonna need at least three shirts and a couple pairs of pants. Let's go buy some shit."

"Now?"

"Are you busy?" You'd think he's saying that in a mocking way. But he's absolutely sincere, waiting for my answer like I might actually have plans.

"Let's go," I say.

Terry watches me lock up, then we get in his car. It's a Triumph, I notice for the first time, only because the name's in the middle of the steering wheel. "Ever been to Water Tower Place?" Terry asks.

"I've never been anywhere."

It takes 15 minutes to get there, even though it's not too far away from Bud's. We park on a side street and start walking toward the lake. Waiting at Michigan Avenue for a light, I look to the right, and suddenly I'm facing a miniature limestone castle with towers everywhere and a vaulting lighthouse-like steeple in the center.

"That's the Chicago Water Tower. It's the only building that survived the Great Fire."

Dad was going to show me this. "When was that?"

"I don't know. You'd have to ask Kretch or Bud. They're into the city's past. I'm more into its future."

The Hancock Building looms over us, black steel girders crisscrossing tighter and tighter into the sky. Terry stops before we get there. "Here we are." We walk into this boxy, marbled grey building, and we're facing the longest escalator I've ever seen. We ride it up, and when we get to the top, we're under a succession of glass floors, clear golden octagons encircling a see-through elevator, climbing one after another, all the way out of sight.

Terry knows right where to go. We take the elevator a few floors up and make a beeline for this store that looks like a place where jungle tourists stock up. Banana Safari. Something like that. He picks a short-sleeve shirt off a rack and holds it in front of me. "You're a large," he declares. Sometimes I am; sometimes, if I want it tight, I'm a medium. But I just agree with him. This is his world. The shirt's tan and soft and slinky, not smooth like silk, but gauzy like lace. "Gabardine," Terry says. "Loose, comfortable, never wrinkles."

I try it on. Terry's right. It's unlike anything I own. It's got big chest pockets and those buttoned straps on the shoulders. What are they called? Epaulettes. I look older, more relaxed, worldly.

"Yes!" Terry approves. We head to another rack. "What about these?" They're super soft V-neck t-shirts. I check a price tag. Nearly 25 bucks. Terry's already got me up to $40, and I haven't even gotten what I need for work. "I have a bunch of clothes at home."

"Yeah—but it's probably all Joe College shit, the kind of threads that scream out, *I don't belong here*."

"I don't have the money for these."

"Fuck the money. This is my treat. Well, mine and Kretch's. He gave me a hundred bucks to set you up."

"I don't know." I'm starting to hate all the special attention.

Terry reads my mind. "I get that you don't want charity. But we're here now, you're with me, and I know what I'm talking about."

"Okay." We get two of the pricey t-shirts—blue and tan. Then we get a pair of white shorts, the kind where you need a thin belt. So, the belt too. We go downstairs to Marshall Fields and get two white shirts, another pair of black pants, socks, and underwear. I can barely carry all the bags we have. It all comes out to over $200. "I'm going to pay you back," I tell Terry as we get to the car. We've got so many bags and boxes, they barely fit in the Triumph's little trunk.

"We can worry about that later. Let's go get something to eat."

"Okay. But it's on me."

Terry knows a place around the corner that's on the sidewalk. Great for people-watching. He orders some kind of white wine, so that's what I get. "They got a great scampi," he says.

"Okay." I close my menu. I have no idea what scampi is.

When the wine comes, Terry holds his glass up to me. I clink it. "So. You got into your place, you got some threads, and you got a little money. Watch out Chicago! Here comes Owen Maloney." I laugh. We drink. "One more thing, and you'll be dangerous."

"What's that?"

"You gotta fix that hair. No offense, but it looks like you got earmuffs." I swipe my hair off my ears. "Don't get me wrong. It isn't horrible. It's not Garrett's punk cut or Moose's furry Prince Valiant. But you can do better. What're you doing tomorrow?"

"I gotta be on the floor at ten."

"I'll see if I can get you set up with Wendy. She's the one who cuts my hair. Sometimes she squeezes me in first thing in the morning."

The scampi comes. It's a shrimp dish with thin noodles and buttery, garlicky sauce like the linguine Dad got me—again, nothing I'd order on my own, but it's good. Really good. Terry orders a second glass of wine, and now I'm sweating the money again. The waitress asks if I'd like another. I say no. "Yes he does," Terry tells her.

We're almost done eating when a guy walks up behind Terry, hesitates like he's going to turn around, then comes up to our table. "Mister Stratton!"

Terry looks up with a sort of dread. The guy's got round wire-rimmed glasses and a blue blazer over his white polo shirt. He carries himself in this composed, sophisticated way, like some debonair fifties type. I must be wrong about the dread, though, because Terry recovers and breaks into a wide smile. "Hadley!"

He stands up, and the two of them slap each other on the back. "This is Owen Maloney." Terry points to me. "He's Mike's kid. He just started at Bud's. Hadley's a regular."

"I'm headed there this very moment." Hadley flutters his hand like an actor on stage. "One cannot be late to backgammon night." He's got this high-flown way of talking; you can tell he's cultured.

"No, one cannot." Terry laughs. "Too bad you didn't have your section tonight," he says to me. "You missed our biggest tipper."

Hadley blushes. "Worth every penny to have my cocktails delivered when I require them."

"Vodka gimlet, Rose's, a dash of lemon juice, sugar, and a sprig of mint," Terry rattles off.

"Preferably three leaves," Hadley says under his breath.

"Just tell the bartenders a Hadley special. They all know."

"I'm also in on Saturdays. For hot dog night." He doesn't seem like the kind of guy who'd go for hot dogs. But I guess he does have a rakish edge to him. Who's that actor? Peter O'Toole. That's who he reminds me of. He almost sounds British.

"And Sunday morning for eggs benedict," Terry says. "And Tuesdays in the front window with the regulars."

"A man needs a home away from home," Hadley appeals to me, almost sheepishly. Then he turns to Terry. "So… is hot dog night ever going to resume?"

"Probably next week. We're still looking for someone to do it."

"Excellent to hear." Hadley pats Terry's back. "So nice to meet you, Mister Maloney." Then he ambles away.

"We got a lot of characters at Bud's," Terry says. "Hadley's one of the biggest. He's what people mean when they say eccentric."

In the end, Terry and I split the bill. Then we walk to the car with the shadows of the setting sun reaching out in front of us. "You wondered how you can make money here," Terry says as he starts the Triumph. "Let me show you something."

We cross Michigan Avenue and head down a quiet lane, trees arcing above us, people sitting on stoops. We could be in a small town. Then everything peels away. The sky opens above a line of streaming cars. And there's the lake. Finally, I see it, for the first time. The only other Great Lake I've seen is Huron, where Mom is. This is nothing like that. It's all concrete where the cottages would be, and you can't hear waves or see the shore. I don't know if there's even sand. A cement barrier rims the water. White boats spread across the horizon, stock still like they're in a postcard.

Terry turns right. We're confronted by a shimmering monolith marooned in the lake; a rounded triangle springing into the sky, burnished in bronze, sunshine swerving in and out from smoothed corner to corner. "Lake Point Tower," Terry announces. "Very exclusive. I'm on a wait list to get in. Forty-eighth floor. That side there, looking straight up the Gold Coast." We turn around within a couple blocks. Is that all he wanted to show me? How did that explain the money Terry makes? We're headed back north. A wall of high-rises blocks the setting sun on Terry's side. They drop their jagged shadows all the way across the road.

The oncoming car lights seem to glide through Terry, trailing off the back of his head like some electric headdress. He turns up the music. *I am the passenger. And I ride and I ride...* We come up to a bend, and suddenly there's a deep stretch of sand spread out beneath a dozen high-rises. The shadows of the buildings are just starting to jut into the lake. People are scattered within them. Most are walking back into the city, as if they'd been waiting for the gloom to guide the way. Night people on shadow bridges. "Oak Street Beach," Terry says. "Great for girl-watching." He points into the city. "That's Division. Bud's is four blocks away. We come here all the time. Now," Terry glances over his shoulder, "look back."

The Hancock Building looms over us, its black face tapering high above everything else. Down by its side, the *PLAYBOY* sign I saw last night shines dimly. I imagine bunnies in bikinis. I bet that's what Terry meant by girl-watching. We take an exit and swing back into the city. Now we're in a wide-open space. "Lincoln Park," Terry says. "You gotta see the zoo. The monkeys are my heroes. They fly around their cages, do whatever they want, fling crap at each other." He points off to his side. "Bud's house is right across there."

I figure that's where we're going, but he turns away from Bud's. "You can drop me off here if it's easy."

"I haven't even shown you how I make money."

We go another block away from the lake, and it's all two-story buildings now. You wouldn't know we're crawling across a giant city. Another zigzag, we turn down a narrow lane, and suddenly it's darker, as if night fell all at once. I know why: no streetlights. Hardly any lights in the houses either. Ahead of us, the scaffolding for the El is silhouetted against a high grey wall. Terry drives under the tracks and turns left just on the other side. Then he stops in front of an iron gate. He presses a button on his visor, and the gate slides open. We follow the El down a block, then turn into a parking space beneath it. Terry turns off the car.

"Here's what makes me the serious money." I go with him to the back entry of a stark brick building—just three cement steps and a dented green door. "Wait here a minute." Terry keys into the door and starts up a stairwell. Then the door shuts.

I turn and there's the El, floating tracks of steel, darker than the night, stitching together some unseen gash across the city. I think about going back to the car. But Terry wanted me to wait here. The wall's hooded in darkness now, so I can't see what's at the base. But there's a line of graffiti all along where the tracks are. I can't decipher the jagged markings; they must be a warning or some threat. *Stay out. You don't belong here.* Someone took a big risk perching up there to paint those symbols. More night people. A different breed than the beach walkers at sunset or the alley sleepers last night. Where did they come from, these brazen vandals, so daring, so desperate that they'd face the dangers of the train to mark their territory?

The door wrenches open. Terry bounds down the steps, shaking something in his hand. I hurry to catch up. Terry stops in front of his car and looks all the way up the height of the wall, like he only just noticed it. "You know what's on the other side of this?"

"I was wondering."

"Cabrini Green."

"What's that?"

"The projects. Rough place."

"What's with all the graffiti?"

"Gang signs. One group claiming these streets as theirs."

"But it's on this side."

"That doesn't stop them from climbing over and taking what they can. So they're telling rivals, *we steal here; go somewhere else*."

We get in the car. Terry unrolls what I see now is a brown lunch bag. He pulls out a stack of bills and fans it open. They're all twenties—at least 100 of them. Terry puts the bills back, rolls up the bag, then tucks it under his seat. He starts up the Triumph and we pull out. While we're waiting for the gate to slide open, he says, "If Cabrini Green weren't so scary, I wouldn't have all this money."

"What do you mean?"

"Since this place is so close to the projects, I was able to buy four units for nothing. And I rent 'em for twice my mortgage. Every month, I make six grand, just for having the balls to do it." We leave the lightless roads and drive back into archways of glittering light. "Pretty soon, all the beautiful people will run out of places to live by the lake, so they'll start moving this way. Then I'll be able to sell my units for ten times what I paid for them." Terry wags his finger. "Property. *That's* how you make money down here."

When we get to Bud's house, Terry helps me take the shopping bags inside. "Okay," he says, "I'll go tell Kretch you're settled in."

"Thanks, Terry. Really." I can't remember the last time anyone did so much for me, besides my family. Maybe never. I'm getting choked up thinking about it. "I'll pay you back."

Terry brushes me off. "We still got work to do."

After he leaves, I find a closet and a couple drawers for my new clothes, take a shower, and get in bed. It isn't even 10 yet, but it feels later than the night before. I don't know what Terry meant—that there was still work to do—but I'm not taking any more charity. I'll get my schedule for next week, take the train home after work, and pack some clothes that look more like what Terry got me. The only way to blend in is to do everything yourself…

Something's buzzing. A fire alarm? I lurch out of bed, look around the room, head down the hall. No smoke anywhere. It's morning. There's daylight in the windowpanes of the basement door. And a shadow too. That's what's ringing: a doorbell. I unlock the door and open it. Terry's there.

"Hurry up and get ready. We're cutting it close."

"Where are we going?"

"You need a haircut, I got you a haircut."

What did I decide last night? *Do everything yourself.* "That's okay. I can get one later."

"Bullshit. You'll go to some crappy barber in the burbs, and your hair'll get even more fucked up. Come on."

I head back to get dressed. Here I am again, going along.

"Might as well get ready for work," Terry calls out. "You won't have much time after. And you don't want to rush Wendy."

Terry's so right. Wendy takes her time with everything. It starts even before the haircut. She washes my hair and rinses it real slow. She combs it out and blow-dries it ever so gently. Then she gives me a neck and head rub. I've never had a barber do any of that. Afterwards, she pulls up a chair in front of me, scootches in close, and asks, "What do you want to do?"

The most I ever told a barber was "not too short." This time, though, I think about what Terry said, how I looked like I was wearing earmuffs. "Maybe a little shorter on the sides?"

Terry's shaking his head over Wendy's shoulder. He puts a finger to his lips to hush me. "Do what you think's best," he tells her.

She swings me around in the chair. Now I'm facing the full display of her tools—little scissors, big scissors, scissors with metal teeth, electric clippers, countless attachments, brushes and combs, three different hair blowers. She cuts. She trims. She feathers. She snips and scrapes and shaves. And when she's done, she swings me back toward Terry and hands me a mirror to check her handiwork.

I look like I've never looked before—older, sharper, neater. No, not as cool as Terry, but more with-it than ever. My hair isn't parted on the side and swinging across my forehead anymore. It's closer to the middle, falling more naturally, flowing away from my face. Gone are those furry muffs. For the first time since before high school, I can see my ears, at least the lower part of them.

"*There's* someone who's going somewhere," Terry points at me with a smile. "There's Owen Maloney."

He peels three twenties off a big roll that probably came from the money in the paper bag and hands them to Wendy. More for me to pay back. I thank her up and down; it's all I have to offer. Then we hurry out of there.

Terry drops me off with 10 minutes to spare. Moose cocks his head at the sight of my hair and scowls. Kretch just checks his watch. Susie comes up from the back of the bar, gets one look at me, and shakes her head. "I knew it."

## Stayin' Alive

*Feel the city breakin' and everybody shakin'.*
*- Bee Gees*

After work, Kretch gives me my schedule for the summer—Thursday night, Friday night, Saturday day, and Sunday brunch. Terry says I couldn't have hoped for better shifts. "The only one that sucks is Saturday. You'd think it would be good because it's on the weekend, but nobody's working so there's hardly any lunch rush. What you want to do," he tells me, "is ask Kretch to be the hot dog guy. You walk around with one of those big cookers you see guys carrying at Cubs games, and you sell dogs for ten cents. Sounds like a shitty deal, but you get to keep everything you make, and the tips are always great. Everyone gives you a buck and tells you to keep the change, they're so happy to be getting a dog on the cheap."

When Susie hears my schedule, she says not to mention it to anyone. "It took me three months to get on Sunday brunch. People are gonna be pissed. They'll think you got special treatment." By the look on Susie's face, she's one of those people. Heck, maybe I am. Kretch also set me up in the side room on backgammon nights.

It takes two full weeks to fall into a good rhythm. I take the train from Wheaton on Wednesday, work Thursday through Sunday, then go back to the burbs Sunday afternoon or Monday morning. In my spare time downtown, I pretty much stay to myself. I brought this crappy recorder with me, and I've got a shoebox of my old cassettes, so I can listen to music. I keep it turned down low; I don't know what Bud and his family can hear through the floor. A couple times, I've pulled that one folding chair out in front of the basement door, sat there, and read—mostly the Manson book. I tried to read the poetry Tara gave me, but I can't do it. It just makes me think of her.

It still hurts that whatever we had wasn't enough to make Tara want to stay in Ann Arbor. I'm not really sad about it anymore so much as angry. Not at Tara. I know it's not her fault. But at the world, at how fleeting love is, how it can be so overpowering one minute, then gone the next. That is, if what I was feeling ever really *was* love. I don't know. Maybe I'm just mad at myself. Maybe I'm mad that I still haven't figured out what love is.

The other thing I do in Bud's basement is work out. I'm one of the scrawniest guys at the bar. Terry goes to the gym three times a week, and it shows. His biceps almost burst out of his sleeves. He invited me once to go swimming at the beach, but I made up some excuse. I didn't want him to see me with my shirt off. So I'm using Neil's Bullworker every day now. It's this isometric exercise gizmo that's the size of a baseball bat. It's basically two metal cylinders with big springs inside them. It's got handles on each end and cables on the sides. You can squeeze the thing together or pull it apart a bunch of different ways. I take it wherever I go—downtown then back to Wheaton. The thing barely fits in my gym bag. If I don't put it in just right, the bag won't zip up. It looks like I'm carrying a rifle. And I'm fine with that. The odds of a cop stopping me to check are a lot lower than the odds of scaring someone away from accosting me. I do the same 15 exercises every day. They take half an hour.

As far as money goes, I don't need any gauge to tell me I'm getting richer. In my first two weeks alone, I pocketed nearly $1,000. I asked Kretch if I could do the hot dog deal, and he said he'd think about it. I'm also picking up extra shifts. People are always looking for someone to work for them. My goal is to get to $10,000; that's what Terry said I should be able to make in a summer.

Making money's the easy part. Holding onto it's another story. Terry wasn't kidding about how fast it goes. After every shift, there's someone who wants to unwind with a few rounds. Bud's stays open until two, but there are bars all around where you can get a drink up to five a.m. On Thursday and Friday nights, I work the same shift as Terry, so I always get roped into going out. Friday to Sunday, Susie and I work together. Susie doesn't like going out on Fridays, when Bud's people party the hardest, but we usually catch a bite to eat after the Saturday and Sunday day shifts.

All that translates into cash flying out of my pocket. And those are just the nights. Bud has season tickets for the Cubs, four box seats in the first row along third base, right where the Cubs' on-deck circle is. Bud rarely uses them, so he makes them available to whoever's first to ask Kretch. Turns out, there aren't a lot of Cubs fans working at Bud's. Terry gets the tickets whenever he wants. And he just so happens to like going on Thursdays and Fridays before our shift. I've gone with him, as well as Moose, Jill, and those two guys I saw in the alley with Terry. He didn't bother to introduce them beyond *Owen; Carl and Jimmy. Carl and Jimmy; Owen.* We catch the El around noon, party a little by the stadium, then games start at 1:30 and last about three hours. Most of the time, we miss the last couple innings so we can catch the train back, hurry to Bud's, dress, and be on the floor by five.

I've seen three games now, and they're a blast. The first one I went to, in the very first inning, Manny Trillo, the Cubs' second baseman, pulled a ground ball right at me. It took two big hops, and I snatched it out of the air like it was nothing. Everybody was impressed; Terry and Moose and Jill were there that day. I shrugged it off and gave the ball to Jill. Terry leaned over on the other side of me and whispered, "Very smooth."

Another time, Terry got talking to Kong talking in the on-deck circle. That's Dave Kingman; everyone calls him Kong because he's big, strong, and a little Cro-Magnon looking. He plays like that, too, lashing at the ball with animal fury and either belting it a mile or whiffing. Kong's a grumpy, standoffish guy. Terry started joking with him about his batting average, and Kong grumbled, "They don't pay me to hit singles." "No," Terry fired back. "They pay you to be a circus act." Kong glared at Terry, waggling that big bat 10 feet away. I thought, shit, he's going to bash Terry over the head with that thing. But then he snuck out a smirk and nodded, like, *this guy knows the score*. I'm telling you; everybody listens to Terry.

Like I say, the games are a blast. But I can't keep doing this every week. Go to a ball game, get to work, rush around non-stop for eight hours, get drunk fast, stumble home, collapse in bed. Then do it all over again. Susie even says something to me about it when I take the floor after another Cubs game. "I don't know how you do it."

I just shrug. Hey, it's the price of having fun.

"You're not staying out late tonight, too, are you?"

"I hope not," I say.

"You hope?" She laughs that tough but tender laugh of hers. "You're the one in control of that, you know."

She's right, of course. I don't have to stay out if I don't want to. The thought of that sticks with me as I work, the comfort of it, of just stopping and doing nothing. But now, as it's closing in on one a.m., and the bar's thinning out, everyone's watching Kretch, wondering who he's going to cut. Usually, there's logic to the way he lets people go. But Kretch doesn't always follow reason. So everyone starts to get anxious. And that gets me amped up. I'm feeling like maybe I got a second wind.

Rumors are, Terry knows a guy at Faces, and he'll let us bypass the line at two. Faces is this hot disco on Rush. I passed it that night I walked to the train station; all those glittering people dressed like *Saturday Night Fever* extras. Getting into Faces is a big deal. Everyone at Bud's has been talking about wanting to go. So when Terry gets cut first, I'm not surprised. Kretch isn't the type to let someone's after-hours plans affect his floor decisions, but this time those plans involve everyone. Whatever the case, Terry's getting cut puts every-one on edge. People are saying they're only going to let in the people who are with Terry when he gets to Faces.

Even Susie's excited. "I gotta go for at least one drink," she says, when I ask if she wants to go. Then Kretch cuts *her*.

Off-work employees start huddling up by the front of the bar. I keep getting tables. At around 1:30, there's just me and this waiter named Fuzzy who's been working at Bud's since it opened in the Sixties. The crowd around Terry starts moving to the door. Jill's there. So is Garrett and a couple guys who got hired after me. Susie gives me a little wave. Terry sees me too. He stops next to Kretch. And he's saying something to him. The Faces pilgrimage leaves the bar. But Terry stays. Now Kretch is barreling my way.

"Maloney. You're gone. Give Fuzzy your tickets."

Terry intercepts me on the way to the locker room. "Hurry up. I'll cash you out." That's not exactly in the Bud's employee hand-book, but you owe the bar what you sold. There's no way around that. It's just a question of whether I get all my tips. And what does Terry care about a few bucks here and there?

I'm back upstairs in minutes, dressed in the shorts and safari shirt Terry got me. He gives me my money right away. I knew I had a good night. Over $100. But I don't want to count it right then; it seems petty. Terry's the one who brings it up. "You had a nice night."

"Yeah?" I look at the wedge of folded bills.

"Two hundred twenty. You beat me."

Over $200? "It didn't seem like that much," I say. Did Terry mess with my tips the other way? Did he *give* me money?

There must be 15 of us bypassing the line and strutting up to the bouncer at Faces. Some guy waiting there says, "What the fuck?"

"Private party," the bouncer grumbles. He's a huge guy, not as tall as Moose, but wider. Nobody's going to argue with him. We go through a long tunnel of neon-blue hoops. They've reserved a table for us just off the dance floor, which has lights pulsating in it too. Reds, oranges, and yellows. Then blues, greens, and purples. And there's a fog machine, and soap bubbles are floating everywhere.

I recognize most everyone in our group, but there's a guy dressed up slicker than John Travolta, and he's in between two girls in halter tops and short skirts. I ask Garrett who they are. "Part of Terry's entourage," he shouts over the head-splitting music. I keep looking over that way. I can't help it. One of the girls, the blonde to the right of Travolta-man, has the prettiest face I've ever seen. Not beautiful; not like Tara. Sunny. Serene. Pure. Her eyes catch the light, sparkle, and swirl. And now and then, they freeze on me.

Terry taps my shoulder. "I want you to meet someone." I'm sitting next to Susie. "Unless I'm interrupting something." He looks back and forth between us. We both laugh. Then, as if he knew what I was wishing, Terry takes me over to that pretty girl with the twinkling eyes. "Astrid. This is Owen. Owen, Astrid's an au pair for one of our regulars. You waited on the Professor yet?"

I know who Terry's talking about. He's the guy who sits on the rail up front reading books. I ran a sandwich order for him back to the kitchen, but he usually gets everything from the bartenders.

Terry pulls up a chair for me. "Astrid wanted to meet you." He swings his arm with an exaggerated flourish, like this was some sort of introduction at a fancy ball. Then he promptly leaves us.

I didn't catch what Astrid did for the Professor, so I ask her. "I'm an au pair." She has a heavy accent. I'm still not getting it.

"What is that?"

"I live with a family and take care of their children."

"Ah. Sort of like Mary Poppins."

"Mary who?"

"Never mind." She laughs. The first round of drinks comes. I'm having a beer. She's having something with a tiny umbrella in it. We watch the dancers. I think of what to say to keep the conversation from dying. "Where are you from?" I shout over the music.

"Sweden."

"Astrid the au pair from Sweden."

She smiles. "And you are Owen the bartender from Bud's."

"Pretty much." Why correct her? Bartender's cooler than waiter.

"Terry says you are someone to know." I laugh. "He says I should be nice to you." She puts her hand on my knee.

It takes a second to collect myself. "Then I should be nice to you."

She takes a long drink then stares into my eyes, like she's trying to decide something. "I think you are too young."

"No…" Who is she to be calling me young? With that sweet face of hers and those gleaming eyes, she could be in high school.

A mischievous smirk crinkles one side of Astrid's mouth. She leans in and whispers, "Prove it." Then she puts her hand over mine, guides it under the table, and sets it on the inside of her thigh. We touch foreheads. I kiss her. When I stop, she hums like she wished for more. I look around the table. They're all watching the dancers, that riotous spectacle of sleazy glamour. She puts her hand between my legs. "Where can we go?"

Nowhere in here if I don't want Bud's people watching. "Let me think." It's 15 minutes back to my apartment. I drink my beer. Travolta-man says something to Astrid, and she moves her hand off my leg. I don't see Terry anywhere.

Now Susie's getting up, and she's waving at people like she's about to go. She glances at me but doesn't wave. When she disappears into that blue tunnel of lights, I make a snap decision.

"Sorry," I tell Astrid. Then I hurry to catch up with Susie.

Terry comes out of nowhere. "Where are *you* going?"

"I gotta get up early."

"Man, Astrid's hanging all over you. Who cares about sleep?"

Jill comes up to us. "Which one of you has the balls to dance?"

Terry ignores her. "Come on, Owen. You gotta stay."

"No, I'm gonna go."

"So… nobody, I guess," Jill says.

I hurry away. I catch up with Susie about a block up Rush Street, under the Carnegie Theater marquee, blaring *GREASE*. Susie's surprised. "Well, look who's taking control of things," she says as I fall into step with her.

"I don't want to be dragging ass tomorrow."

"So you passed on the pretty au pair."

"Do you know Astrid?"

"She hangs out with Terry." I stew on that for a while. "She *is* pretty." Susie doesn't want to drop the subject.

"I don't know. It just hit me. Suddenly, I wanted out of there."

"All a little too fast and easy, eh?" Susie gives me a side eye.

Was that it? Was I afraid of Astrid coming on to me, her guiding my hand up her thigh—and then that long soft kiss? No. That wasn't it. Not at all. I left because I saw Susie leaving. But now that I know Astrid hangs out with Terry so much that Bud's people know her… "She said Terry told her I was nice."

"And that's all it took," Susie says under her breath.

"He was kind of pissed I was leaving."

"I'm sure he was."

I can't take it anymore. "What have you got against him?"

"Terry? Nothing. He just always wants to be the ringleader," Susie says. "And I don't want to be in his circus."

"Circuses are fun." I'm just joking.

"They're fun until the elephant stomps on you."

Terry doesn't talk to me for a week. He takes other people to the Cubs games and doesn't wait around for me after work to go drinking. The Saturday that Kretch gives Nick the hot dog job, I finally say something. He's starting his shift, I'm ending mine, and we're in the locker room. The bar's rocking away upstairs, but the silence between us is way louder. "Did I do something wrong?"

"What?" He acts like he can't hear me over the roaring silence.

I come over to him. I want to explain myself, but first things first. Actions speak louder than words. I reach in my pocket and pull out a pack of bills. I hand it to Terry. It's $250. That's what I figure I owe him—and it's probably more. "I told you I'd pay you back. And I want to keep my promise. Just-just… thank you… for helping me get on my feet." I hold out the money.

Terry doesn't take it. "You don't need to do that."

"Yeah, I do."

He backs away. "I've gotta get up on the floor."

"I know you're pissed off about the other night."

"Not pissed…"

"Well, disappointed or something. But I'm trying to save money." Terry's probably thinking: *then why are you handing me a wad of cash?* "I want to be smart. I want to get something out of this. Like you."

Terry reaches out and slides the money out of my hand, like it's something fragile. "I'm just holding on to this. Whenever you need it back, just ask."

He heads for the stairs. I wait to hear him tromping up the steps. Nothing comes. Then his head peeks around the edge of the locker room doorway. "I wasn't mad," he says, half in, half out of view. "And I wasn't disappointed in you. I was more ashamed of myself than anything. For putting you in that spot."

I start to dismiss him. "No—"

"I just wanted you to see what it's really like here. What it can be. Learn something, you know? Your dad is Bud's best friend. Bud really cares about you. Everyone's looking out for you. And you seem like… like a good kid."

He leaves then. And this time I hear him bounding up the steps. I let out a huge breath. Had I been holding it in that whole time? I can't believe how relieved I am. And happy. Terry cared. He saw something in me.

I get dressed, go upstairs, pull open the bar door—and there's Susie. I've never seen her sitting at the bar before, taking up a spot on the rail. Her stool is already aimed toward me; she's been waiting. Terry bustles past her. Her eyes shift to him ever so slightly. Then she sees me. And she straightens up on the stool and gives me this big smile. Susie's smile is never big.

It crosses my mind just then: Terry called me a good kid. *A kid.* That's what he thought of me now. Maybe that's what I am. But maybe I don't want to be that anymore.

## Hot Blooded

*I'm hot blooded, check it and see. I got a fever of a hundred and three.*
*- Foreigner*

Terry stops freezing me out. We go to a Cubs game; have a drink, just him and me; take his Triumph down to a stereo shop south of the river. He's got his eye on these high-end speakers. They're Magneplanars. Terry calls them "Maggies." They look like black doorways—they're that tall, wide, and thin. But the really cool thing is they don't have woofers and tweeters like other speakers. The music comes out of long wire ribbons that cover the entire surface of the Maggies. The sound is pristine. You can hear the singer breathing. They're pricey—and they need a special amp. Plus, you need the right room placement for them to sound perfect. Terry hasn't pulled the trigger on buying them yet. He just likes to go to the store every once in a while and listen to them.

I'm glad he isn't giving me the silent treatment anymore. Still, something's changed between us. I always seem to be in Wheaton or working when Terry does his serious partying. He still leads the gang out on Friday nights, and I'm up for going. Problem is, Terry doesn't wait around for me like he did that Faces night. And Kretch seems dead set on keeping me around until close.

It's just as well. I'm not hung over all the time. And I'm picking up more shifts, so I've got more money. Plus, I'm spending more time with Susie. We're just friends, so we don't go out partying. Hell, we hardly ever leave her apartment. We'll catch a bite to eat or go to a movie now and then. But that's about it. Everything's easy with her. We think alike, have the same temperament, and she respects me. She'd would never tell me I was a "good kid."

Susie has this weird apartment above a Mexican restaurant called the Hacienda del Sol. It's at a six-way intersection. Sedgewick and Lincoln squeeze the building into a wedge. Imagine a slice of pie where someone snuck a forkful off the tip. That's what the building's shaped like. Susie lives on the other side of that missing bite. Her whole apartment angles towards it, and there's a big window there that looks across Armitage. The entry to the restaurant is right below that. If you're standing there, you can hear the bell above the door jingling when people come and go.

Honestly, the place is a dump. Once, when Terry asked if I wanted to go out with him and Jill for drinks, I said I was going over to Susie's. He laughed. "What are you gonna do there? Watch the cockroaches fuck?" I guess Terry tried to steer Susie away from the place—which she affectionately calls "The Pie"—and into one of his units along the wall. He said he knew her landlord, and the only reason he signed month-to-month leases was so he could keep jacking up the rent on her. Susie didn't listen to Terry. Big surprise.

Susie thinks she can be a stand-up comedian. A lot of what we do is lie around and write. Well, she does, anyway. I've tried to write some poetry there, but it just brings me down. Oh, and we smoke weed. And laugh. God, we laugh harder than I have since I was a kid. A lot of that has to do with the pot, I know. A few times, we've gotten laughing so long Susie'll say "I've gotta write that down." She carries around this notepad everywhere she goes, and she's always scribbling ideas in it. Whenever we reread those stoned entries later, they're never as funny as we thought. Sometimes, they don't even make sense. Like a dream.

Susie grew up in some backwoods town in Indiana, down by Bloomington. In a lot of her jokes, she's the naïve country girl coming to the big city. She's got a few funny bits. Like the one about the boys she knew there and the ones she's meeting here. The upshot is, they're both the same sex-obsessed oafs, but she likes the country boys better because they're slower and have a sense of shame. Plus, you can always run into a cornfield when they try to attack you. Try getting away in the back of an alley. Something like that. I'm not doing it justice. Trust me, it's funnier than it sounds.

My favorite joke of hers is about the trouble you can get in saying hi to people in Chicago, and how it's nothing compared to the trouble you'll get in if you *don't* say hi in her town. Everyone'll be talking about you. You'll be the big topic at dinner. *I saw Henry Morton today, and he walked right past me without a word! Like he's Mr. Important. Can you imagine?* "Not saying hi to someone in my town," Susie tells me, "is worse than trying to molest them. People laugh that off. *Did you see little Henry Morton trying to make the moves on Susie? It was so cute. He had his pants down at his knees, and he was waddling like a duck after her. Too bad she ran into a cornfield. It would've been funny to see what he did if he caught her.*" I liked the joke much better without the link back to the sex assault bit. But Susie thinks it isn't edgy enough.

Then there's the one about the kinds of creatures you find in the country versus what you come across in the city. Susie goes into how she'd rather be any city creature than a young woman alone on the streets of Chicago. "If you could have one animal's superpowers," she asked me once when we were stoned, "which would it be?"

"What animals?"

"I just told you," she laughed. "Any critter in the city."

"I don't know." I thought of animals I'd seen downtown. Sea gulls. Pigeons. Cats. Dogs. Raccoons. Rats. None of them seemed possessed by any powers that I'd want, and I told Susie so.

"What about squirrels? Whenever you see them, they scurry away, climb up a tree, and wind around the trunk, just out of view. They basically disappear. I wish I could do that. You see some creepy guy coming at you—and bang! You're off like a shot and crawling around a pole just out of his sight, completely invisible."

"Okay…" I wasn't sure where the joke was.

"Or a rat," she went on. "Their superpower is that they're disgusting. Nobody fucks with a rat. Whenever you see them, they're climbing over some pile of garbage. If I were a rat, no one would come near me. And I'd have the added bonus of being able to rummage around in dumpsters and gorge on leftovers."

I laughed at that. It got me thinking. "I guess I'd wanna be a monkey in the zoo." I'd been to the Primate House a couple times since Terry told me I lived so close. "Everyone likes you, everyone thinks you're funny, and you get to swing around in a giant cage all day."

"And if anyone tries to come at you, you just throw poop at 'em."

I connected something, then, about the kinds of jokes Susie liked. "You're always worried about getting attacked."

"That's because there are so many wolves out there."

"Not all men are like that."

"Most of them are."

"I don't know." It was a funny idea, but I didn't think she'd want to alienate half her audience.

Susie sensed that I didn't buy it. "Okay, then what about this? Have you heard that new song on the jukebox? 'Hot Blooded?'"

We talked about the tunes on Bud's jukebox all the time. People were always begging Kretch to change it up and get better songs— never mind that most of what they didn't like was the stuff Kretch dug. I knew the song Susie was griping about, but I kind of liked it. It was one of those ones that got you bouncing along as you were working. "Yeah, I've heard it."

"It's the number one song in the country, and it perfectly describes how men think. It speaks to them."

"But isn't it just about a guy coming on to a girl?"

"Yeah. But think about how he's coming on to her. *I'm hot blooded, check it and see. Got a fever of one-hundred and three.* Would you get anywhere near somebody who had a fever of a hundred and three?"

"But it's just—"

"Of course you wouldn't! They're fucking *sick*! Go home, take some aspirin! Get some sleep!"

Nearly every rock song is stupid if you break down what they're saying. But Susie was on a roll. I couldn't get a word in edgewise.

"The guy's next line is: *Come on, baby, do you do more than dance?* Oh, so we're dancing, and you jump right to sex, never mind that you're getting everyone around you sick. If I was that 'baby'—such a perfect word—I'd yell out right then, *Hey everyone! This guy's got a temperature of a hundred and three!*"

"What a shock. Rock and roll's about male fantasies."

"It's way worse than that," Susie had been thinking about this a lot. "Then he tells her he's going to show her loving like she never knew. Because every man thinks they're God's gift to women. Then the guy says, *are you old enough? Will you be ready when I call your bluff?* Oh, so he's going after an underage girl—and he knows it. He's fine committing statutory rape."

"Well…"

"I'm not done. He asks her then, *Did you save your love for me tonight?* Great: she's a virgin."

I started coming around to Susie's way of thinking. The song was way creepier than a simple "I Wanna Hold Your Hand."

"Then he presses her to go with him on a secret rendezvous, but first she has to *get away from you-know-who*. Hmm. Let's see: you're an underage virgin dancing at a concert. Who could this asshole be wanting you to get away from?" Susie held her hand out to me like it was my job to answer the question.

"Her dad?"

"And that's the number one song in the country right now. Not any old male fantasy, but a child rape fantasy."

"Well," I joked, "he's the first to admit he's sick." She laughed. "That's got possibilities," I told her. What I didn't say—and maybe I should've—was that it was the kind of joke that could go one way or the other. It would either make people laugh or make them mad. If I were a betting man, I'd put my money on the mad side.

It must be hard to be funny. You're always offending someone. I don't think Susie cares about that, though. What bothers her is not sticking to your principles. I learned that this morning at Bud's.

Right when we open for brunch, Kretch gives me a table of six in the side room. "You lucky dog," Nick says, while I wait behind him to get their order of Bloody Mary's.

"What?"

"That's Jane Curtain in the corner. From *Saturday Night Live*."

I take them their drinks. Sure enough, it's her. I don't do what I always do to celebrities; I don't tell her who she is. Once, when Harry Caray got sat at my table, I couldn't resist saying, "You're Harry Caray." He laughed and said, "Let's keep that our secret," like no one else knew who he was. Fat chance. Everyone knows Harry. Anyway, when I go to the kitchen, Susie's there. "Did you see who's here?"

"The ignorant slut? Yeah, I saw her." She's totally unimpressed. I don't make anything of the ignorant slut comment. That's a *Saturday Night Live* bit. She's an anchor on their fake news program, and she's debating Dan Ackroyd. After Curtain makes her point, Ackroyd always says, "Jane, you ignorant slut."

"I thought you'd be excited. A fellow female comedian and all."

"She's just another one of the guys," Susie says.

I don't get a chance to ask her what she means until after work. We're at the zoo. Susie wants to see the Primate House. She's thinking maybe she can get some inspiration for her city critter joke. "What's your problem with Jane Curtain? I think she's pretty funny."

"She's not my kind of funny."

"Your kind of funny?"

"I would never let myself be the butt of that kind of joke, over and over. It wasn't that funny the first time, and it's just stupid and demeaning every time after."

It's on the tip of my tongue to say something, like *how do you think men are going to feel when you tear them down over and over*, but I don't say it. At least Susie's humor is true to who she is.

Susie's never been to my place at Bud's, so after the monkeys, I ask if she wants to go see it. "My place is closer," she says.

"You know where Bud's is, right? It's just across the park."

"I know where it is."

"You haven't seen the basement, though. It's pretty cool."

"Fine," she grumbles, like it's this big pain in the ass to go any-where other than the Pie.

"Welcome to The Cave!" I key into the door under Bud's stair-way. Two can have a nickname for their place. She looks around at the curiosities but doesn't say anything.

We walk down to my room. I turn on the light. "It's not much."

Susie takes her time checking it out, like she's all alone. Come on. Common courtesy would tell you to say something—*anything*—nice, whether you liked it or not. Hell, it wasn't *that* terrible. "What's that?" She points to my bed. *Shit.* I left my writing notebook out.

"Nothing." I scoop it up and hurry over to the nightstand.

"Is that your writing?"

"Not really. Just random notes. Like what you do."

"About what?"

When I open the drawer to the nightstand, I see the joints Neil rolled for me. "Look what I found." I wave one in front of Susie.

"So you don't want to talk about it."

"Not now."

Susie wanders over to the kitchenette. "A little light reading?"

She holds up the Manson book. "Yeah, not the happiest story."

"Hmm." She hums like the book says something about me.

Maybe I don't want Susie here after all. "Let's go outside and smoke this." There's a narrow walkway on the side of Bud's that goes to a service alley behind the townhouses. Nobody's ever back there, so that's where we go. I light the joint. We pass it back and forth. My brother's weed isn't great, but it's stronger than Susie's. We start giggling. Pretty soon, I don't even know what we're giggling about anymore. And that makes me giggle more—

"I *thought* I heard somebody." Bud's poking his head out of a door off to the side of us. Talk about a buzz kill. I practically choke. Susie drops the joint and covers it with her shoe.

"It's nice to see you around again, Susie," he says. "You keep this guy out of trouble, okay?" He ducks inside and shuts the door.

*Nice to see you around* again… What did *that* mean? Susie's wincing like a bomb's about to go off. I expect her to explain, but she just shrugs. That makes me laugh. We get to giggling again. I motion her back to the apartment. When we get inside, it hits me what Bud just saw. I plunk down on the bed. "Do you think he'll fire us?"

Susie laughs. "Bud, *fire* us? Over that? No way." She's talking too loud. I signal to her: *quiet*. She sits beside me. "Bud doesn't care about that kind of stuff. Don't worry."

"Easy for you to say." I lie back. "He's not your dad's friend."

She lies down herself. "Trust me." We're facing each other. The pot's doing a number on me. I keep drifting off, not to sleep, but somewhere dreamlike. Susie says my name. I open my eyes, and her face is close. She says my name again, and I open my eyes again. It's déjà vu, over and over. "What are you writing?"

Did she already ask that? "I don't want to talk about it."

"Come on! I tell you what I'm writing all the time."

"That's because you want to. I never ask you."

"Oh." I see the hurt gathering in her face.

"I didn't mean it that way." I put my hand on her shoulder. "I love hearing you talk. Really. I wish I was as brave as you are."

She smiles, not much different than her usual tough smile, but a little softer. "Is it about what you're going through here?"

"No!" I catch myself. Too loud. It's just that the idea surprised me.

"I forgot," Susie's voice is still soft. "Your life isn't here."

"What does that mean?" Now I'm out of my trance.

"It's just a summer thing for you. You get to leave."

"Well, you can leave too."

"No…" Susie trails off. "It's different. I'm done with school. I moved away from my parents and came up here. This is where I live now."

I hadn't thought of it that way. The prospect seemed so final. "What I was trying to write about is gone," I admit finally. "And whenever I think about it, I just get sad."

"You got your heart broken."

"I got my heart broken."

"So it was a love poem."

"That's what I thought at the time."

"Then that's what it was."

"It feels like a cruel joke now. I can't even read it."

"Can I?" I get out the notebook and open it to the page where I rewrote Tara's poem after burning the original. Susie starts reading out loud: "*You lie beside me, sleeping still—*"

"Read it to yourself."

She stares at the page for way longer than it would take to read the poem. Then she shuts the notebook and hands it back to me. "*The song of us about to be.* I just love that."

I try to make a joke of it. "I guess I didn't hear those birds right."

"No." She takes me seriously. "That's what you felt in the moment. That's what was true then. Do you still love her?"

"It doesn't matter."

"Sure it does. It's not about her feelings. It's about yours."

"Well, now I just feel stupid."

"Then write another one about that." I think about how angry a poem dealing with Tara leaving me would be. Not leaving me, really, more like deciding we weren't important enough.

Susie's hand is on my cheek. I didn't see her reach out. "Almost everyone who falls in love falls out of love." It sounds like the beginning of a sad story. "They could use something true about that too."

I think back to that morning, lying next to Tara. If I wrote that poem today, knowing how things would end, everything about it would still be true. Everything, except what the birds were singing. "The song of you about to flee," I say and open my eyes to see if Susie laughs. Her eyes are closed now. But she *is* smiling. I close my eyes…

I wake in the gray beginning or end of darkness. Susie's turned away from me. I rub her neck, run my fingers through her hair, press myself against her. She looks over her shoulder at me, eyes open, hazy stars breaking through the gray. She opens her mouth, those soft lips coming apart…

And then, in a furious surge, we're clinging to each other. Kissing. Pulling at each other's clothes. Grasping for skin—

She bolts out of bed. "We can't do this!" She's breathing hard, half naked in the dark.

"I'm sorry." What got over me? We're *friends*.

Susie hurries away. The bathroom light goes on. Then the faucet. After a minute or so, she appears in the lit doorway, wiping her face with a rag. Her blouse is still unbuttoned. "It's not that I don't want to. It's just that I think it might… ruin things."

"You're right," I agree. *Would it really?* "No, you're right."

Turns out, it's 7:30 at night. Susie wants to take a shower, so I let her. Then I take one. We're talking about places to eat near her apartment, and she's telling me about this rib joint called Twin Anchors.

A phone rings. The phone's never rung down here. I don't even know where it is. I let it ring itself dead. Now we hear pounding, like someone's stomping on the floor above us.

"Owen?" A voice is coming from the hallway. Lights are flicking on and off. I go out and look up the stairs. Bud's at the top, looming in full view, like he's about to topple down on us. "That was your dad on the phone. He wants you to call him."

"I thought it was for you," I say. "I didn't think I should answer."

"You have your own phone down there. Your own number and everything. On the wall in the Fun Room. Just to the right."

"Okay. I'll call him now."

"Sorry to disturb you," he apologizes. Like he's the guest.

Susie comes out into the hallway after Bud closes the door. "*The Fun Room,*" I say. "That's perfect."

Susie laughs. "That's Bud."

I go down the hallway, find the phone, and call Dad. I can't imagine what he'd want this late. One thing's for sure: nothing fun.

## Ravel's Bolero

"I was wondering," Dad says. "Are you coming home tonight?"

"Probably tomorrow," I tell him. "It's pretty late now."

There's a pause. "I just thought you might need some company." He sounds strange. Downhearted but not drunk. More like he's struggling *not* to drink, like he's the one who needs company.

"I think I can still catch the eight-forty tonight."

"I'll pick you up in Wheaton."

Dad's waiting for me at the station. I get in the car and we head home in silence, except for some classical music playing through the tinny Audi speakers. I turn it down. Dad turns it back up. "Listen to this. It's Ravel's 'Bolero.' Listen to how it builds."

We turn onto Prairie, and I can see our house all the way down the road. The music keeps cycling through the same rhythm and melody, over and over, more and more instruments coming in.

"Listen to that!" Dad gushes. "Hear the trumpet? I played that in high school." So many instruments are coming in that they're mushing together. And with the shitty speakers, there's a grating buzz that's driving me nuts. We cruise up the driveway and pull into the garage. Dad puts the car in park, but doesn't turn it off, just keeps listening to that hypnotic march of music. I open the door. I've got to get out. "Wait—wait—" Cymbals crashing, trumpets wailing like elephants, everything blaring all at once. And then it's over. Dad heaves a huge sigh, as if he was the one putting in all that work. He shakes his head in astonishment. Then he puts his hand on my knee. "I went to the doctor last week."

That's when he gets out of the car. Like that was all he wanted to say. I follow him into the house. "And what happened?"

Dad mumbles something on the way to the TV room. The Cubs are on. He plops down in his chair. "I've got polyps in my colon."

"Polyps?" I've never heard the word before.

"They're like tiny mushrooms in my ass."

"O-kay…"

"Trouble is, some might be cancerous."

And there it was. I knew it was building to something. "How many do you have?"

"Over a hundred." Dad hangs his head, as if it's shameful. "Most are nothing. They just snip 'em out. But a few…" He gets this far-off look in his eyes. "Anyway, they sent them for testing, and I'll learn tomorrow where I'm going."

*Where I'm going.* He doesn't mean it spiritually. But that's how I take it. Maybe that's what makes me notice—no drink. I sit on the couch next to him.

"Down four-one, men on second and third, two outs," Dad says. As if this is the situation I want to contemplate. He roars suddenly and throws up his arms, like he's trying to scare something away. But it's just the Cubs getting a base hit. "Four-two!"

"Dad?"

"Hang on." He's on the edge of his seat now. Ivan DeJesús smacks a line drive—and it's caught by the shortstop. "Damnit!" He falls back. "Six losses in a row."

"Have you talked to Mom?"

"We were three games up. Now we're two games back."

"Dad—"

"I don't want to worry her until I know what we're dealing with." Makes sense. But there's something sad about it. He's scared. I can tell. He could use someone to comfort him. Are things that far gone with Mom that he can't even reach out on something like this?

"Are you going to call her… whatever happens?"

Dad just sits there, stroking his chin. "Damn, these Cubs'll break your heart."

I don't say anything about the not drinking. I don't want to jinx things. So next morning, I just go about the day like nothing's happened—Dad hasn't stopped drinking, he isn't confronting his mortality, we aren't waiting for the phone to ring.

Dad's makes an omelet for me. "I'll mow the lawn," I tell him. I want to take his worries away. But that's only part of it; I also need to escape all this oppressive air in the house.

"Already done," he says.

"Alright. Maybe weeding then. Or washing the car. I'm here. I might as well be useful."

"You want to help me?" he asks. I'm in the breakfast nook. He's in the kitchen. He opens the liquor cabinet. "I'm going to refill the birdbath. Can you pour all these bottles into the sink?

I pour out the booze as fast as I can. I don't want him coming back in the middle of things. I get it all done in minutes, and even have time to bag up the bottles and take them to the garage.

I look out the back window to see what's taking Dad so long. He's got the birdbath turned on its side, and he's kneeling over it, scrubbing away. I guess it's been a while since he refilled it. But he's doing it now. Another small sign of hope.

"You don't need to stay cooped up in this house," Dad says.

I've been moving from room to room on the first floor, staying close to Dad but giving him space. There's nothing to do but read and wait. I'm skipping around the big anthology of poems Tara gave me, not because I want to, but because there's something wrong about reading the Manson book under the circumstances. I brought it thinking I would, but that was before I knew I'd have to open it in a house of doom. "I don't feel cooped up," I say.

Again, it's Dad who hits the issue head on. "Look, Owen. I want you around, but I don't want you to feel like you have to stay. It's morbid. You know?"

I get where he's coming from. "Yeah…"

"Nothing changes until the call." He heads into the living room. Next thing I know, he's taking down all the screens on the windows to wash them. Things have changed already.

I ask if I can borrow the car to pick up some stuff for downtown. I don't really need anything, but I do want to get out of here. Dad's right. It feels like we're on some sort of death watch.

I drive into Wheaton and find a drugstore to pick up some shaving cream and toothpaste. At the counter, they've got a *People* magazine with Cheryl Tiegs smiling on the cover. Fitz had her bikini poster in his dorm room. What the hell. I grab that too.

On the way back to the car, I realize I'm just a block away from that record store where I asked about a job. What better way to kill time? The same guy's behind the counter. He looks at me long enough that I can tell he remembers me. I give him a nod. Not a word between us, though, about job openings.

I'm not planning to get anything, just poking around. If I were to buy something, though, it would be records. The hell with eight-tracks. I start finding stuff. The Beatles, *White Album.* Manson went nuts over this. Foreigner, *Double Vision* with a sticker on it: "Includes the hit single HOT BLOODED." Gotta get this for Susie. Iggy Pop, *Lust for Life*. Terry's driving music. *Saturday Night Fever.* What the hell. Rolling Stones, *Some Girls.* Kretch just got "Miss You" on the jukebox. He was into it at first, but now the song annoys him. "Jagger didn't learn a damn thing," he said one night. "Back when he wrote 'Paint it Black,' he put on this brave face after getting dumped. Now he's begging his gal to come back. It's embarrassing." Leave it to Kretch. I get the album anyway. It's got this cool cover of an old ad for wigs with the faces cut out and celebrities showing under the holes. The Stones are in drag, and there's Marilyn Monroe, Raquel Welch, and Farah Fawcett. Sex symbols. Susie would have a field day.

Five records—and no record player. There's my goal for the summer. Save up and get a bitching stereo, like what Terry's always dreaming of. I head up to the counter. The guy starts ringing up my record. "That one's just a joke," I feel the need to say when he picks up the Foreigner album.

"It's not Beethoven. But it's halfway decent hard rock."

It hits me then: he might know classical music. "You wouldn't happen to have Ravel's 'Bolero,' would you?"

The guy lights up like a goddamned Christmas tree. "We have three!" It's like he's been waiting for someone to ask this very question. He bustles out from behind the counter, waves me toward the back of the store, and leads me to a sizeable section of classical albums. Who knew there was such a market for this stuff?

It takes the guy no time to find the three recordings. He hands the albums to me. "The Ozawa one has a great ending, but it's an underwhelming ride getting there. Bernstein just plays it straight with the New York Philharmonic. For my money, though, Boulez is the best. The recording's pristine, and I'm telling you, your speakers will be sizzling." I take the Boulez. Dad would be happy with any of them, but that comment about the sizzling speakers wins me over.

The six albums come to over 40 bucks. I have no idea when I'll ever be able to listen to them. Still, it feels good to have a notion pop into my head and be able to act on it. It makes me feel powerful, in control. Now I know why people like money so much. On my way out, another thought comes to me. "Hey, do you know of any stereo shops nearby?" Neil's speakers definitely don't sizzle.

The store he suggests is near Naperville. He said it was 10 minutes away. It's more like 20. Dad's probably wondering why a trip to the drug store is taking so long. Nothing I can do about that now. I'm here. I need everything—speakers, turntable, receiver. But no way I'm telling the salesman that. Funny: I think of this guy as a salesman, and the dude selling records as some chucklebutt stoner. It's all in the body language—and the choice of clothes. This guy looks like an engineer selling spaceship technology: creased pants, white button-down, thin restrained tie. On second thought, he's more like a door-to-door Bible salesman. Either one.

"Can I help you with anything?"

"Nah, just looking."

"For anything particular?"

"Not really."

"Receivers? Tape decks? Speakers?"

This guy isn't going to quit. "I could use new speakers," I relent.

"Well, you've come to exactly the right place, my friend!" He's so excited for me. "We carry all the top brands."

He motions me ahead of him. With the record dude, I was following. Here, I'm leading. I guess the guy wants me to feel like I'm in charge. Smart. I see the Magneplanars right away. How can you miss them? But these are different from the ones Terry wants. Each speaker isn't a single black door. There are four thin panels hinged together. And they're taller. "Are those Maggies?" I ask, throwing in the lingo so the guy knows I'm not just some Schmoe off the street.

He nods, either impressed or faking it. "You know your stuff."

"They look different."

"They're Tympani Threes," he says. "Four base, two mid-range, and two tweeter panels. The sound is…"—he pinches his fingers together—and tosses them off his lips like Chef Boyardee. "Choice."

My first thought is: no way these things'll fit in my dorm room. But, man, do they ever look cool.

"Of course, you'll need a good amplifier," the guy says. "What kind of receiver do you have?"

"Honestly, I need everything," I confess. "I've got a Realistic eight-track system my brother gave me. It's at least five years old."

The guy winces like I told him I drive a Gremlin. "Yeah, that's not going to work. Let's get you set up right."

"I don't have enough money." The guy scrunches up his eyebrows and folds his arms, like there's no solution to that thorny problem. "Not yet, anyway," I add.

He flashes a big white smile. "We can work with that."

Dad's sleeping on the couch when I get home. Like I said, our living room furniture screams, "Don't sit on me! I'm for company!" I've never seen Dad on this couch, not even back in Cleveland. He's lying on his side, but his feet are still on the ground, like he suddenly keeled over. His left arm's sticking out, and his hand's hanging there like he's begging for change. Right below that hand, there's a broom. He must've dropped it when he collapsed.

*Wait.* Is he okay? I call out, "I'm home." He stirs right away and springs upright. I feel bad waking him.

"Just sweeping these hardwood floors," he says. "Man, they get dusty. Now I know why your mother was always sweeping."

I breeze past him. I don't want him to see the bag of records. I stop on the steps, out of his sight. "Any calls?" I ask. As if there were more than one that mattered.

"Not yet." He comes my way, sweeping. I hurry upstairs.

Everything I own is either downtown or packed away. This room looks like it did the last night Neil was here. It feels like his room, too, a relic stuck in a time long since gone. Hippies and protests and Vietnam. People you know going off to war, and the outrage and fear that would stir up. Everything life and death.

As a kid, I remember going to Abe Lincoln's house. You could see the rooms where he used to sleep and eat, be with his family, think and write. Parts of it were roped off, and they didn't want you to touch a thing. It had to be preserved for the future. I remember how dated all the furniture was, how ridiculous the wallpaper looked. I couldn't believe there was ever a time when this felt new.

That's how it feels looking at my brother's room. Only he's still alive. There's a chance he could come back. I don't think he will, though. He knows that what he wants isn't here anymore, isn't anywhere, really, except where most people are afraid to go. He knows the world no longer cares what he thinks or does or who he is. I lie down in his bed. *I still care, Neil. I still care.*

The phone's ringing. I spring out of bed and rush into the hallway. It's not ringing anymore. I go downstairs. There's Dad, standing in the kitchen, holding the phone to his ear. He's not saying anything, just making the odd hum and groan as he nods grimly. He sees me and holds up his finger. *Don't come any closer.* I retreat to the hallway, out of his sight.

"Where are you?" He calls out a minute later. We meet in front of our forbidden couch. He stops a few steps in front of me, lets out a deep breath, then winces like he's straining under a heavy weight. "Benign," he says. "Every one of them, benign."

Now he's coming toward me. His legs wobble. He falls to his knees. I brace to catch him. He wraps his arms around my waist. "I dodged a bullet," he says. There's wonder in his voice.

"Yes, you did."

"A big one," he sobs out. "The biggest there is."

We have a frozen pizza. Dad's moaning away like it's the best thing he's ever eaten. "I was so sure it was cancer. So sure." He grabs another slice, folds it like a paper plane, and steers it into his mouth. "But God showed me mercy," he garbles out. "Everything now's a gift."

I wait until he swallows. "You gonna call Mom?"

He screws up his eyebrows. "I don't want to worry her."

"Wouldn't *you* want to know? I mean, you two have been married for almost twenty-five years. You don't stop caring, just because of… whatever."

He hangs his head. I don't know if he's thinking about what I said or eyeing the last piece of pizza. "Yeah. You're right. You're absolutely right." He points to the pizza. "You want that?"

I shake my head. "You could get a hold of her tonight."

"Good idea." Dad folds the last slice and glides it into his mouth. "See? Even having you home, giving me advice, that's a gift too."

Next morning, I come downstairs to a quiet house. There's a note from Dad on the kitchen counter: *OFF TO WORK!! SEE YOU TONIGHT!* So eager, so excited. I think of the dwarves in *Snow White* heigh ho-ing and finding a million diamonds. Good for him.

*See you tonight!* I was planning to catch the train downtown after breakfast. But Dad expects me to be here. And he's looking forward to it, judging from the exclamation point on the note. Okay, so he's just half as excited as going to work, but still. I don't want to abandon him if he needs me. I can always catch a late train.

I eat Cheerios. I put my dishes in the dishwasher. It's raining outside. I have to do something. I go into the garage. The Audi's still there. Dad walked to the station, no doubt singing in the rain.

The guy at the stereo shop sets me up with a Yamaha CR-2020 receiver, a CA-1010 amplifier, a YP-800 turntable, and the Tympani III's. It all comes to over $2,300. I pay 10 percent down; $230 of my tips from last week. And I promise to get him the rest by the end of July. That gives me almost a month.

"If you can't come up with the rest," the guy warns me, "I'll have to keep your deposit. It costs to ship equipment here and back."

"I get it." With the money I have downtown, and what I'll make in four weeks, two grand should be no problem.

It isn't even noon by the time I get back to the house. Dad's usually home before five, but that's when he was drinking. With his new-found work enthusiasm, it could be after six. Then making dinner, eating, and cleaning up; probably eight by that point. So: catch the train at nine, take a cab, and you're at Bud's apartment in plenty of time for a good night's sleep.

I have PB and J for lunch. I make Neil's bed. I pack up for Chicago. I try to read more poems from the anthology. It goes from oldest to most recent poets. I start in the back. I'm tired of old poets. The only poem that sticks is "Mid-Term Break" by Seamus Heaney. It's about a teenager coming home from school to a grieving household. It's only in the last lines that you learn his brother got killed in a car accident and lay in "a four-foot box, a foot for every year." Death just grazed me this time. Sooner or later, it's going to hit.

I go for a walk. I take roads I've never been down. I keep turning away from what's familiar. I know where I'll end up; I've known since I left the house. But maybe if I get one more street away from it, I'll stop wanting to go there. No such luck. Here I am in front of the house that blared out the Doors' "Love Her Madly"—the closest I'll get to a Manson hideaway. I stand at the end of the driveway, looking through the overgrowth at that high boarded-up window.

And now I'm walking to the house. I'm past the viny bushes that guard the front, and I can see the door. There's a girl my age, maybe a little older, sitting in a chair on the far side of a long porch. When she sees me, she stands, looks back into a wide-open, screenless window, then walks across the porch and comes down the walkway toward me. She's wearing tattered overalls and nothing else.

"You looking for Vince?"

"No."

"Because you're supposed to call."

"I was just walking. And I wondered if anyone lived here."

"Do you party?"

"Not much."

"That's all we're doing here," she says, like it's the most innocent thing in the world. We stare at each other, her with a sleepy smile, me trying to figure out what to do. "You wanna come in?"

"I better not."

"Too bad." She goes inside. I hesitate a second before turning to go.

Just after five, the phone rings. It's Dad. I can barely hear him over the noise in the background. After his third try, I make out what he's saying: "Something came up at work," he shouts.

"All right. Then I'm going back to Chicago."

The noise. His voice. The excuse. He's in a bar, drinking. It knocks the wind out of me, like a punch I knew was coming, but didn't expect to be so hard. "Did you call Mom?"

The phone clicks. I make a fast decision. I know the number by heart. "Hello?" It's Tara. I hang up.

I lock up the house and hurry out to catch the six o'clock train. It's going to be close. I'm not going to run—there's always the seven o'clock—but I'll go as fast as I can without breaking a sweat. If I have to sit around and wait, I will. But I'd rather not. That just means more thinking.

When the train pulls up, I'm just across the street from the station. I start running. Down the sidewalk. Through the parking lot. Around the station. Up to the boarding platform—

The train pulls out. Okay. Just sit. Just wait. Don't think. I suddenly remember: I put that *People* magazine I bought in my gym bag. I sit down, take it out, flip through it. I read the article about Cheryl Tiegs. It's more about the old dude who married her, Stan Dragoti. He's an advertising guy, and he dresses like Dad. I read about David Bowie's bodyguard. I read a piece on this psychologist named Salk. He says kids with divorced parents are more sensitive about life. Foghat has a new album. Fitz'll be thrilled.

The seven o'clock comes, I'm surprised time went so fast. I get on the train and watch buildings flicker by. It isn't so hard to stop thinking. You just throw yourself into what's in front of you.

Pulling out of the Lombard station, I start humming that hypnotic melody of Ravel's "Bolero." Just as we're coming into the Oak Park station, before we even get to the platform, the train wrenches to a stop. We sit there. And sit. And sit. The buildings outside my window don't move. I keep humming.

The conductor comes into our car. There's a problem with the engine. He doesn't know how long it's going to take to fix. He doesn't know if we'll have to wait for another train. He'll get back to us as soon as he has more news.

And there it is: a fitting end to my trip home. The perfect crescendo of shit.

I stop humming.

## I Wanna Be Sedated

*Nothin' to do, nowhere to go-oh. I wanna be sedated.*
*- Ramones*

I keep my head down the rest of the week, work my usual shifts, go out as little as possible. After Sunday brunch, Kretch asks if I can work Monday night. Then Monday, Clancy asks if I can pick up his Wednesday shift. Why not? I need the money. I call Dad to tell him I won't be coming home that week. I'm glad when he doesn't answer.

Things are weird with Susie. We never talked about what happened, except to agree at the time that it was a mistake. She's not really avoiding me; she just isn't trying anymore. Whenever we're waiting for orders together, it's always me thinking up something to say. And no matter what I talk about, she doesn't seem interested. Susie used to wait for me after work. But that's over too. It's probably for the best. I need to get better at being alone. Still, I can't help wondering. What's the point of her indifference? Did she think I was getting too close to her? That I was falling in love? I should tell her: She doesn't have to worry. I don't know what love is. I don't even love the idea of it anymore. In fact, I sort of hate it.

I never miss a chance now to eat when I'm working. Sometimes, I'll eat before *and* after my shift. There aren't any hard-and-fast rules for letting employees hang out in the bar after they get let off. Kretch just doesn't want us hogging the good seats. I've taken to sitting at the far end, where the loners turn their backs on the crowd and play pinball. Part of the reason is, I don't have the gumption to get a beer anywhere else by myself. The other part is Jill. I only do it when she's bartending because she gives me free beers. And when she isn't busy, she rests against the counter in front of me and talks. Nothing personal or important, just idle chit-chat—what she thinks of a song, who's driving her nuts at the moment. She likes to make jokes about customers. She makes me laugh.

Once, when she came over and didn't start talking right away, I couldn't just sit there and be quiet. "What are you doing tonight?" I knew the second I asked, I'd made a mistake.

Jill acted like she didn't hear me at first. Then she frowned. "Nothing fun, I'm sure." She got cut just after that, and I saw her leave with Terry and Moose.

I'm starting to go out more with Nick. He lives with his parents on La Salle, and he knows some pretty cool bars nearby. One's called Burton Place. It's supposed to be rowdy, but the two times we've gone, it's been laid back. Nick keeps apologizing for how dead it is. Truth is, I like the quiet. I like just sitting there, unwinding with a beer. Nick isn't a talker like Jill. But things come out. I told him about the stereo I'm saving to buy. I told him there was a girl at school. And I know he dropped out of Northern Illinois. I know he wants to open a breakfast place. I know he's head over heels for Jill. He didn't come right out and say that. But he always brings her into the conversation. Just last night, he told me, "I'd never stand a chance with her."

Tonight, Nick wants to show me a new place. "Ever been to Old Town Ale House?" We're waiting to put our drink orders in with Jill. Nick's talking loud enough for her to hear. It's pretty obvious.

"No. Where's that?"

"It's, like, right around the corner from Burton."

"What kind of place is it?"

Nick starts to answer—

"It's a comics hangout," Susie says behind us.

"That," Nick says, "and musicians and locals and other oddballs."

"What about O'Banions?" Jill says, sliding two pints Nick's way.

Nick laughs. "That's a punk bar."

*Wait.* Is Jill suddenly interested in our Friday night festivities?

"I've been there," Garrett calls over from the taps. "It's crazy."

"I'm up for it," Jill says. "Boys?"

"Sure," Nick agrees. Of course.

"I'll go," Garrett says.

I glance at Susie. *A comics hangout.* I know where she'd rather go. "I'm not up for a late night," I say.

Later, when we're the last two on the floor, and Garrett and Nick are waiting for Jill, I catch Susie alone by the kitchen. "Hey, you wanna go get a beer at that Old Town place?"

"I don't know."

"Come on. It's a comedian's hangout. You said so yourself."

"Okay." She acts like she's giving in, but I can tell she wants to go.

Kretch cuts me right after that. I go sit on that last stool at the end of the bar and start cashing out. Jill comes over.

"So you're not coming to O'Banion's. What, too wild for you?"

"Susie really wanted to go to Old Town."

"Well…" She slides me a book of matches. "If you get done early, this is where we'll be." Under the flap, Jill's written *661 N Clark*.

That's John Belushi's brother." Susie and I were lucky enough to get seats right by the front door. We can see everyone coming and going. Susie's pointing at a loud guy holding court under a faded painting of a bunch of faces. They look like a crowd of barroom denizens, stuck in time, doomed to watch the goings-on until they fade away. Above the painting, it says *ESTABLISHED 1958*, a year before I was born. They'd been watching this dive my whole life.

"How do you know he's Belushi's brother?" I'm skeptical. The guy's way taller than Belushi, leaner, more rock-jawed. He does have the same arching eyebrows, though. I'll give him that.

"I saw him at Second City. Him and that girl he's talking to."

"You should go talk to her, tell her you want to do what she does." I'd never have the guts to do that, but Susie would.

"God no! There's a whole tryout process at Second City. If you ask for advice, they think you're trying to weasel your way in."

"How about this?" I let out a big belly laugh.

"What's so funny?"

"You. I laugh loud, and everyone thinks you made a joke."

"Then I get a job, all because some goofy kid laughed."

"So is *that* what I am?" Not just a *kid*, like Terry said. A *goofy kid*.

"Sorry." She puts a hand on my arm. "I've been a bitch lately."

"What do you mean?" As if I didn't notice.

"I just want us to be back to normal, back to the way it was."

"It was dumb of me. I let my feelings take over. I do that a lot."

"So… nothing personal."

Did I hurt her? "I wouldn't say that."

"Truth is, I've missed you. There's no one to bounce jokes off."

"By the way," I remember, "I bought you a gift. That Foreigner album, the one with 'Hot Blooded.' You can use it as a prop."

"I didn't think you liked that joke. I was going to drop it."

"No, no. You should keep it. It's right on."

We drink our beers and watch the action in the bar through a smoky haze. I keep staring at those faces on the wall, and they keep staring back. We're just as trapped in time as they are. The only difference is I can get up and walk out any time I want.

"I've been meaning to ask you something," Susie says after a while. "But I just—I didn't know where we stood."

"Ask away."

"It's a favor, really. You can say no."

"Okay."

"I've got a five-minute bit at this jazz bar," she says. "It's a tiny place, and no one's coming for the comedy, so if I bomb, it's no big deal. But I could use a friendly face in the crowd."

"You got hired?" This was a big deal.

"Well, they're not paying me anything. It's just exposure."

"Still, you're gonna be on stage."

"Yeah…"

"How did they find you?"

"I found *them*. One day, I just started going bar to bar, asking everyone if they could spare five minutes for a comedian. And this place, Los Toros, said they'd give me a shot."

I can tell: Susie's proud of herself. She should be. "Man, that is so fucking cool, Susie. That took some serious balls."

"Well, ovaries. But yeah."

I hoist my mug. "Here's to your serious ovaries."

"Here, here." We finish off our beers. "And now those ovaries are scared shitless."

"You'll be great."

"And if I'm not, it's just five lousy minutes, and nobody cares."

"So it's good no matter what." I motion the bartender over. "Can we get two kamikazes here?"

I'm not a big shot drinker, but Susie deserves to see this as a success. After we down the shots, she orders more. I can't say no. And they go down so easy too. I'm getting drunk. When Susie calls over this guy from her improv class, I tell her I have to go. She says she'll go with me. But she keeps talking to the guy, waving her hands like she's holding wands, all boisterous and animated. He's doing it right back at her, both of them showing off, the way people do, I guess, who want to be comedians. They talk and talk, telling each other how good they were in class, laughing about some poor dope who had a meltdown on stage, bitching about the teacher. I can't take it anymore. I tap Susie on the shoulder. "I'm gonna go."

I get out on the street. North Avenue isn't the safest place at two a.m., but the streetlights work, and Susie doesn't have too far to go. Susie with that guy… She was a completely different person. Was that who she really was—or wanted to be? Is that why you chase a dream—to become someone you wish you were, someone you weren't already? What was *my* dream?

Two beers and two shots. I'm not *that* drunk. Anyway, 10 minutes and I'll be home in bed. I get to Clark Street, across from Lincoln Park. Clark Street… I feel in my pocket for the matchbook. *661 N Clark.* How far down would I have to go to get to O'Banions? I start walking. It takes three blocks to find an address. I'm in the 1200 block—six more blocks. It feels like that first night when I walked to the train station. Only I'm not scared anymore. Not that there aren't good reasons to be. Clark's a sketchy road—boarded-up storefronts, empty garbage-strewn lots, flop-house hotels, someone screaming in the shadows of a fenced-off park. Maybe it's the booze. Maybe it's that I'm used to the city now. Maybe it's this funk I'm in. Whatever. I'm not scared. I'm not looking over my shoulder. I don't really care what's around me.

O'Banions is as rough as any dump I passed along the way. Worse even, with its black chain link-covered windows and all the graffiti. I would've walked right past it if it weren't for the guys laughing on the corner. They look like bikers. Not real ones, though; more over the top, with black leather, chains, and handcuffs, like they're dressed for Halloween. The entry to the bar is just a black metal door, no way to see what you're getting into. But there's thumping behind it. When I start to go inside, the fake bikers get quiet. They're glaring at me. I'm not in work clothes, so I don't look totally out of place. But I *am* wearing the white shorts Terry bought me. I definitely look more disco than punk. I nod and go inside.

It's like walking into a wall of rage. The music's loud and discordant. The singer's voice is roaring, garbled, strident. Bodies are packed together, bouncing and shoving, swinging and flailing. I shouldn't have come. Now that I'm here, though, I can't turn tail and leave. The bar's off to the side. I edge my way over there against the lurching riot, hands out, pushing bodies clear. Everyone seems to be dancing alone, bobbing out of rhythm; women with eyes circled in black, spiky hair, ripped-up t-shirts; men not wearing any shirts at all, bodies gleaming in the pale blue light.

And one of them is Garrett. I turn, and Nick and Jill are right there, standing at the bar like they're keeping safe at the edge of a deep pool. "You came," Jill shouts over the noise.

"I did."

"I bet Jill you wouldn't," Nick leans in.

Garrett crashes into the bar, like he's coming up for air after a long dive. "Owen!" he roars, as if we're best friends. This is the guy who still chirps "make that" whenever I screw up an order. He's better now, mostly because I don't screw up as much anymore. But he never seems happy at Bud's, like he enjoys being there. Here, though, the guy's in his glory. He's loud and gushing and grinning, all energetic, like Susie was when she was talking to her improv friend.

"Shots!" he declares, thrusting a finger in the air. That's the last thing I need. But Nick and Jill seem up for it, so who am I to argue? Garrett gets us each two kamikazes—the Bud's workers' shot of choice. "We gotta get busy!" He downs one then the other before diving back into the tangle of bodies.

I do one shot and leave the other. Jill's just sipping hers. "You're not dancing?" I lean in close so she can hear me.

"Nobody's asked me."

I laugh. "You don't need to worry about that here."

"You don't either." She holds her near-full shot glass up to me. "Finish this." I down it. Then I look out into the convulsing mass. Does Jill want me to ask her to dance?

"Here." Nick holds up my second shot. "You need to catch up."

What the hell. And why not dance? "Come on!" I wave Jill into the thrashing pool, off the safety of the bar rail. She doesn't budge. But now I'm out here. And like the song says, there's *nothing to do, nowhere to go.* I start bouncing along to the beat. People are pogoing into me and knocking me all around. Garrett and I collide. He shoves me into the throng. Now there isn't anything to do but let go. I close my eyes. I throw my head back. I give myself over to the senselessness, the swirling, stomping, staggering seizure of spontaneity. I don't care what anyone thinks. I don't care about myself. It's a trance. It's an escape. It's me finally just being me.

And now the music's over, and I'm swaying and I'm dizzy and I might get sick. Garrett steers me back to the bar. "Dude, where'd you learn to dance like that?"

"Like what?"

"Are you okay?" Jill's asking.

"I'm fine." I shake my head like I'm waking up. "Just fine."

The music starts up and seizes me again—the grating, the stuttering, the whirring—a loose motor in my chest. I lurch out onto the floor.

"Oh, no." Jill grabs me and sets me against the bar. I don't resist. My body isn't mine anymore. "You're not going anywhere."

"I'm just drunk."

"Can you walk?"

"Probably."

Garrett and Nick aren't around. Jill takes my hand and pulls me through the crowd. We're out the door, away from the noise, and on the street before I can grasp what's happening.

"Are we going?"

"We're going."

"Where?"

I hear the biker punks laughing behind us. I see the road I need to take stretching into the darkness. I feel the giant droning presence of the city, asleep and dreaming. Jill takes my face in her hands... and kisses me.

"We're going home."

**Use Me**
*If it feels this good gettin' used, just keep on usin' me until you use me up.*
*- Bill Withers*

Through alleys… between buildings… up an elevator… down a hall-way… into a dark room of windows. The glow of unseen lights… the lake, a sheet of shimmering black gold, shuffling toward us.

And now the urgency—the tearing at clothes—the tangling of limbs—the tumbling nakedness—the rapture of skin.

Jill's eyes burn low in the dark city light. Her body catches the blue glow, curves it into form, undulating, irresistible. My hands glide along the contours. I mold and spread them in the light. To see. To see myself doing it. To remember.

"Slow," Jill says. I stop. I try to settle my breathing. I'm shivering. "Slower." I start again. "Easy… easy… so slow," she whispers.

I want to do what she wants. I want to give myself over to her, to see her enjoying this. I want to know I did that.

We wake in bright morning light on the living room floor. Sun slants into Jill's window from just above the lake's horizon.

"What time is it?" Jill rolls away from me. The sheet we put over ourselves slips off her hip. I see her naked back, stark in the red-orange morning. The wonder of what we did comes back to me. She's looking across the room, to the clock on her kitchen wall.

"Just after six," I help her out.

Jill lies back down, breasts settling gently to the sides. She rests her arm on her forehead and gazes at the ceiling. She's quiet, solemn. Maybe she's regretting what we did.

"I can go."

"No." Jill looks at me and smiles softly, reaches out, brushes my cheek. "I'll make us breakfast."

She gets up, strides unabashed across the room, disappears, then comes back in a short pink robe, cradling a blue bundle. "Here." She tosses it to me. A man's robe. I don't say anything about it.

Jill's stereo is beside a sliding glass door that goes out to a balcony. She turns on the receiver and cues up the record that's already on the turntable. It's warm and funky soul, the singer's voice smooth and deep. Jill turns the music low. "I love this album," she says. I find the cover slotted next to the turntable. Bill Withers. It sounds old, the kind of music Neil would like. He hits me then: Neil and Jill are the same age.

Jill has one of those automatic coffeemakers. She brews a pot in minutes. Then she starts making a bacon and cheese omelet.

"Need any help?"

"I've got it." She turns her head, inviting me to kiss her. "Just go relax. Check out the balcony. We'll eat there."

When I leave the kitchen, I notice how big Jill's apartment is, how modern the furniture looks, how pricey the décor is. Table lamps, floor lamps, hanging lamps, all coordinated. Bookshelves filled. Vases with big, drooping plants. Jill's settled in. This is her life. She has exactly what she wants. I flip through her albums. She has a lot of the same records as Neil's mystery girlfriend. I don't want to go out on the balcony alone and run into a neighbor. Honestly, I just want to leave. I'm hungover. I have to work in a couple hours. And I'm sure Jill would rather not have me here. Hell, she's probably wondering how she got herself into this. She comes out carrying a tray with two plates for the omelet, toast, and banana slices; little glasses of orange juice; salt, pepper, butter, jam.

Turns out, the balcony's totally private, walls on either side all the way up to the floor above, plenty of room for a table, two chairs, and clusters of red, yellow, and purple flowers in every corner. We start eating. It's so good, I keep thanking her until she seems embarrassed about it. When I'm done eating, I pick up my coffee cup and look out over the lake. Boats are already heading out for the horizon. They look so small, all of them, far and near. "How high up are we?"

"This is the fourteenth floor."

"Prime real estate."

She shrugs. "You get what you pay for. Like anywhere else, though, it's got plusses and minuses."

"Well, not *any*where. My place…" I shake my head.

"Your place is great. You're five minutes from Bud's. It's free. And you don't have to worry about taking care of things."

"In other words, I'm poor."

She laughs. "You're poor. Give me a break." Is that some sort of a put-down? I push away from the table.

"You know, I'm not just some spoiled kid from the burbs. Not anymore. But that's still what people think."

"No, they don't." Jill leans forward to make eye contact. "*I* don't. What I meant was… well, you haven't really *seen* poor."

I get it now. "Sorry. I'm just sensitive, I guess."

"That's a good thing," Jill says.

I go inside and get more coffee. When I come back out, Jill's standing in the middle of her balcony with her back to me. "Quiet," she says, pointing to the corner. There, on the end of the rail sits an owl. I come up behind Jill slowly. She's having a stare-down with the thing. Both of them glare at each other, eyes hard, unflinching.

"That's their superpower," I whisper. "They gaze right into your soul. They know your fate."

"You think?"

"Just look at those eyes."

Jill straightens up, slips her robe off her shoulders, and shrugs. The robe falls to the deck. She leans back into me. I put my arms around her, cradle her stomach, rest my chin on her shoulder. Jill just goes on staring. I kiss her neck. Finally, she turns her head and gives me a small tender kiss. I don't know why—it was nothing compared to what we did the night before. But it takes my breath away. When we stop and look to see how the owl's taking this, it's gone.

We shower together, then I dress back into what I wore the night before. As I'm putting on my shirt, I notice two buttons missing. They're probably somewhere on the carpet where we took off our clothes in the dark. It's just the top buttons. If I hurry down to my locker at Bud's and get my white shirt on, it'll be fine. Jill isn't so sure. "Hang on." She rummages through one of her dresser drawers. "Here." She throws me a light blue shirt. It's an Izod polo, the kind Terry said branded me as Joe College. Why does Jill have it?

"Really, it's okay." I'd rather walk into Bud's with a torn shirt.

"Just wear it. You don't want to be getting a lot of questions."

It hits me—Nick's on the Saturday lunch shift, Garrett sometimes too. I disappear with Jill then show up next morning wearing the same stuff. What are they gonna think? I put on the shirt. "They're still gonna ask me where we went," I say, watching Jill dress.

"I'm sure the rumors are already going around."

"Rumors?"

"You can't keep a secret at Bud's. Shit'll start flying. By the end of the day, everyone'll know you and I left O'Banions together, and they'll be drawing conclusions."

"So why do I give a shit what shirt I wear?"

"Well, first of all, your shirt smells. Secondly, smoke's always floating around Bud's. But there's a difference between smoke and fire." She leaves me then, standing in her room, pondering what that difference might be. When I come back out, Jill's in the kitchen making a new pot of coffee. I don't have any reason to go home, but I don't want to be a nuisance.

"I should be going."

"Why? You've got an hour before work."

"I'm sure you had things you were going to do."

"No."

"Okay. I just—I don't want to overstay my welcome."

Jill turns, and she's holding our two cups of coffee. But it's like she's forgotten what to do with them. She's just standing there looking at me. "I thought this went well," she says finally. "Didn't you?"

"Well, yeah…"

"Really well. A lot better than I expected." She hands me my cup.

"You *expected*?"

"At a certain point, you always expect."

"And you didn't think it would go that well?"

"Not after we got here."

So I sit back down with Jill at her little dining table. And we drink our coffee, mine black, hers with cream, and we don't say anything, and now and then we look at each other, and we smile.

"You know what?" she says, after I've gotten comfortable with the silence. "I should get you a different shirt."

"Okay."

"I don't know if that's Terry's or not. Either way, he might remember it from here."

This could be Terry's shirt? I gotta admit: it's more surprising to me that he'd own an Izod than he'd be screwing Jill.

"You knew we went out for a while, right? Everybody knows that."

"Nobody told me." So Jill and Terry had gone out. More than just a fling, by the sounds of it. Okay, so what? Unless he still cared…

"I guess I'm telling you now then."

"What happens if he finds out? You said everybody'll be talking."

"This is why smoke is better than fire."

"So he's not going to be pissed at me."

"I don't think he cares anymore. I'm telling you so you'll be ready. Just in case." Jill heads back to her bedroom.

Ready for what?

## Money

*Grab that cash with both hands and make a stash.*
*- Pink Floyd*

When I get into work, Nick asks where I went last night. He doesn't seem to know I left with Jill. I tell him I was getting too drunk, so I went home. It's almost the truth. All Garrett says is, "Man, you're a whirling dervish on the dance floor." Susie tells me how she met Belushi's brother after I left. She doesn't know I went to O'Banions, and I don't tell her.

It's a normal Saturday lunch shift—hardly any sit-down business, a bunch of one-drink tourists in the afternoon, then the crush of regulars coming in for 10-cent hot dogs. The only one killing it is Nick. The hot dog guy isn't pinned down to a section. He gets to go anywhere from four to seven. So the faster he hustles, the more money he makes. If it were me, I'd be busting ass. Whatever you take in is yours. Nick says he gets $10 sometimes for a single dog. For whatever reason, though, the money doesn't seem to motivate him. He was into the gig at first, but now he acts put out by it. Tonight, when seven o'clock rolls around and Nick goes into the kitchen to dump out the dogs he hasn't sold, there are at least a couple dozen left. Terry notices. "Tough night?"

"I don't know," Nick says. "Maybe I'm just no good at this."

Hot dog night is Terry's brainchild. I'd never say something like that to him. Terry stares at the dogs in the trash can. Nick looks at me with a sort of breathless dread. "You'll get the hang of it," Terry says, more insisting than encouraging.

Kretch lets Nick and me go 10 minutes after that. We head down to the locker room. As I stand there, wolfing down a dog I salvaged before Nick dumped the rest, Nick sits in front of his locker, gazing at the floor. "You okay?"

"I don't want to do it anymore," he says. "It's too much pressure."

"The hot dogs?"

"It's more than I bargained for. Making the dogs, running all over the place, people yelling at you, getting pulled in every direction."

"You're *making* the hot dogs?"

"The kitchen guys don't want to have anything to do with it. I've gotta unpack 'em, boil 'em up, put 'em in the box, steam the buns. And that's not even the worst of it."

I didn't know about boiling the dogs, but I'd seen Nick doing all the other stuff. Okay, so maybe it's a little stressful, but no worse than a busy Friday night. "Well, how much money did you make?"

"I don't know. A couple hundred? It's not worth it." Not *worth* it? Two hundred dollars for three hours work? I'd take that in a heartbeat. "I'm going to tell Kretch I don't want to do it."

It's on the tip of my tongue to tell Nick I'll do it, but it seems sort of heartless after all his complaining, like I don't believe him when he says it's so tough.

When I get upstairs, Terry and Kretch are talking by the front door. I give them a nod as I pass. "Hey, Owen," Kretch calls out. "How would you feel about taking a turn as the hot dog man?"

"Sure." I leave Bud's with a little spring in my step. Nick gets what he wants. I get what I want. Nobody gets hurt.


I stay downtown for another week. Jill doesn't say a word to me, so I don't say anything to her, other than ordering drinks. There aren't even any smiles or glances. She's all business, like what we did together never happened. Worse than that, really. Like we don't even know each other.

Susie keeps wanting to rehearse her routine for Los Toros. She's getting really good at the "Hot Blooded" bit, perfecting her timing, getting the right mix of bewilderment, sarcasm, and outrage. She's still not quite there with the bit about city creatures, though.

"I figured out what I want to be," I blurt out. "An owl."

"An owl? Where'd you see an owl?"

*Oops.* "Just out my door," I lie. "Sitting on Bud's steps."

"So what's its superpower?"

"I felt like he was staring into the depths of my soul. I tried to hold his gaze, but it went on forever. It was unnerving. His eyes were so harsh and severe."

"How did it end?"

"I started getting weirded out." Another lie. "Like he could see something in me, something I was hiding. I looked away for just a second. Then, when I looked back, he was gone."

"Ooh, that's good!" Susie's all excited. "The power to see people for who they really are. I'm gonna use that."

"In your routine?"

"Why not?"

"I don't know." I think of Jill. "It's more creepy than funny."

"It needs work. But I can make it funny."

Who am I to argue? It's not like Jill's going to go see Susie.

By the time Saturday rolls around, I'm the hot dog man. Whether Nick begged off doing it or Kretch axed him, I don't know. Either way, he seems fine. If he wasn't, he wouldn't be so chipper about showing me the ropes. Honestly, it's not as hard as he made it out to be. The only thing Nick says that worries me is about Kretch and Terry. "Just remember," he says, "Kretch is your boss, not Terry. You don't have to do what he says."

I make $238 my first shift hawking hot dogs. Then I work every day for the week after that and make another $254 the second Saturday. By this time, I've got more cash than I can fit in my nightstand—$2,482 in twenties, tens, fives, and a lot of singles. I separate the bills by denomination. Then I wrap a rubber band I found around the stack. I put the stack in a sock, and stuff the sock into my gym bag.

I call the stereo shop and tell the salesguy I have what I owe him. He says he can deliver my stuff the next day. For the first time in weeks, I go back to Wheaton. It's just before sunset when I get to the house. Dad isn't here. The sink's filled with unrinsed dishes. I kill half a dozen ants crawling around the counter. There's an empty J&B bottle on the breakfast table and a Canadian Club fifth on the floor next to the couch in the TV room. When I pick that one up, there's still a hefty slosh left. It's a sad consolation.

The lawn needs mowing, and there's still a good hour of daylight left, so I get that done. Then I come back in to tackle the house cleaning. The dishwasher's full. Has he even run it since the last time I was here? When I start clearing out the sink, more ants scatter. You have a brush with death, and what do you do? You live your life more recklessly. What sort of gratitude is that?

Neil's room is exactly the way I left it—not expecting to return. I was thinking I'd set up the new stereo here, but looking at it now, there's no way the speakers are going to fit. The salesguy said these Tympani III's need to be at least three feet away from a back wall. They'd be right at the foot of the bed if I did that.

The speakers would fit perfectly in the TV room; it's nice and long. But I'd have to move the TV, plus Dad's lounge chair. No way I'm doing that. The living room'll work. I can put the speakers on either side of the fireplace and aim the sound across the length of the room to the kitchen. The only issues are where to put the receiver, amplifier, and turntable and how to hide the cords.

I'm tired. I take the cushions off the couch, find a blanket Mom knit, position throw pillows between my knees and under my head, and nestle in. May as well sleep the night here. I'm not messing up Neil's room. The phone rings. Great. I go and answer it. It's Mom.

"There you are! I've been calling for days. Where's everybody been?"

"I've been working in Chicago."

"So you decided to stay."

"Yeah." I can't remember the last time we talked. Did I tell her I was thinking of going to New Jersey to be with Tara?

"And you're happy with the decision?"

"It's been good. I'm working in a bar, making a ton of money."

"Don't tell me. Bud's."

"That's right." Figures she'd know. Mom and Dad met in college, and Bud was his roommate.

"And you're being careful?"

"Of course, I am."

"But you're having fun, too, right? I mean, you're doing what you want, like we said." Oh yeah. This was supposed to be the summer of doing what you want. That's a laugh. "So, no," she reads my pause.

"It's fine, Mom. Really. I've made a few friends. I'm seeing the city. And I'm saving a lot of money."

"How's your father?"

What do I say? "Oh, you know. Still drinking a lot."

"But he's coming home at night, right? You guys are having dinner together, hanging out?"

"Oh yeah. I mean, I work downtown four or five days a week."

"And where do you stay when you're in the city?"

"Bud's letting me use an apartment in his basement."

"Bud's infamous basement." Mom laughs softly. "Your father's favorite excuse for where he was when he doesn't come home."

"How are *you* doing?" I'm tired of being the one getting grilled.

"Good," Mom declares with a lilt of surprise, like she just came to that conclusion. "I'm getting perspective, starting to understand myself, coming to terms with what needs to happen."

"That's good." *Please don't tell me what that is.*

"Owen, I think you need to be prepared for things to change."

Oh, God. I am *not* ready for this. "I don't want to talk about that now, okay? When you guys decide what to do, I'll deal with it then."

"Fair enough. Tell Dad I called, okay? I still worry about him."

If she only knew.

The stereo shop doesn't deliver my equipment until after three. I paid to get it installed, so the guy brings everything in and unboxes it. I tell him where I was thinking of putting the Maggies. He gives me a handful of reasons why that's a bad idea—they'd be too close together, the sound wouldn't fill the length of the room, he'd have to run cords across the mantel, it could be a fire hazard.

Now I'm starting to worry that I bought too big a system, not just for here but my dorm room. "Where would *you* put things?" I ask. He goes out to the center of the room, points to opposite corners and starts twirling around like a roulette scarecrow. Part of me thinks it's an act. He's just the delivery guy. Then again, all he does all day is set up stereo systems, so he can't be completely clueless.

"Right here." He stops in front of the couch I slept on. "One speaker on that side, the other on that side. Three feet from the wall, angled in just a touch."

He's got the Maggies aimed at the width of the room, playing out toward the sliding glass door to our backyard. "But there's nowhere to sit over there."

"I'm thinking you move the couch in front of that door."

There's a chair off to the side and a table made from an old lobster trap. Mom loves that table. "What do I do with those?"

"Put them in between the two speakers and set all the equipment on that table. Then it's easy to hide the cords."

Dad's going to shit a brick when he sees the room all rearranged. But he's never here anymore. And who knows if Mom'll *ever* come home? We set things up like the guy suggested. It doesn't look too bad. The only weird thing is the couch in front of the sliding glass door. But we move it away far enough that there's a little lane you can walk behind to get outside.

The guy calibrates the settings for the speakers, shows me how to turn on the system, and explains every knob on the receiver and amplifier. "I forgot one thing." He goes out to his truck and comes back carrying an album. "We always like to give new customers this." He pulls out Pink Floyd's *Dark Side of the Moon*. "It's a mind-blowing record for testing the quality of a system."

He unwraps the record, puts it on the turntable, then shows me how to drip the cleaning fluid on the velvety brush and wipe it along the vinyl. Finally, he sets the needle on the record. I've heard *Dark Side* before, but on Neil's crappy eight-track player. I never listened to the heartbeat that starts it. The Maggies drive that pumping straight into my chest as if it was my own heart I was hearing. Then the clock ticks, the cash register rings, the madman mutters…

*"Holy shit!"*

The delivery guy holds his hands up in a big victory sign. "The placement is primo," he says, and I can tell he isn't bullshitting me.

There's a helicopter chuffing, some insane chuckling, then a woman starts screaming. The delivery guy takes out some papers, shows me where to sign, and leaves. I settle back on the couch we moved. The music's whirring in a circle, like a motorcycle tethered to my mind, winding around. Now a wobbling watery synthesizer… a woman droning over an airport loudspeaker… the clattering of shoes running on a bare floor… a twirling buzzsaw… then that wobbly synth again, burrowing and burrowing and burrowing. Now back to the clatter of running… and ragged breathing… and an old clock ticking. And more clocks and more ticking. Then: the eruption of alarms, the tolling of chimes! Now: deep guitar twangs, one, a long wait, then another—stark, haunting, portentous.

A few times, I catch myself looking around the room, thinking the noises are coming from somewhere other than the Maggies.

That's how I feel, too, about the wailing woman and the mad mumbling under the surface of the sound, like it isn't part of the music but something inside me, something exhilarating, terrifying.

I listen to the entire record, awestruck, dumbfounded. After it's done, I put on the Stones album. It's one thing for *Dark Side* to sound so mind-blowing, but what about stripped-down rock and roll? "Miss You" comes on—tight, lean, urgent. Damn… this system is so fricking choice.

There's no reason to stick around, but I have to let Dad know why there's this big-ass stereo in his house. I write him a note, explaining that I bought it with my money, but I still have plenty left over. That's not quite true, but it will be by the end of the summer. I tell him the delivery guy said the living room was the best place to put it, and I'll be happy to move it if he doesn't want it there. Then I tell him that I've got Ravel's "Bolero" cued up, and I write down the instructions as plainly as I can for how to play the system.

I have a ham sandwich while I listen to the rest of *Some Girls*. Then I put "Bolero" on the record player like I said I would. I'm just wiping the clean-up brush across the album when Dad comes bursting through the back door. He's got his head down. He doesn't see me standing there in the living room. "Dad."

He jerks so hard he nearly falls over. "Owen! Shit!" Not the warmest greeting. "Hang on. I gotta pee."

He rushes past me—and comes up beside one of the Maggies. "What in the holy name of Jesus?!"

Thank God he had to pee—a forced cooling off. "All right." He comes back, zipping up. "Now what the hell is all this shit?"

"It's a stereo system I bought. It's, um…" I look down at the letter I was writing. "I still have a lot of money saved up."

"And what's it doing in my living room?"

"The delivery guy said it would sound best here. I can move it upstairs if you want me to."

Dad studies the equipment. "Looks pricey."

"A couple thousand, but I'll have this for the rest of my life. And you don't have to worry about money. I'll still save over four thousand dollars for school."

Dad looks around the room. "Your mother would have a heart attack if she saw what you're doing with this furniture."

*Mom might not ever step foot in here again*, I think to myself. "Like I said, I can always move it upstairs." Dad just gazes down at the turntable, flummoxed. "But you've got to hear it first, Dad. Have a seat on the couch. I have a surprise."

"Let me get a drink."

"So… you started up again." I shouldn't have said anything. This is all about getting Dad to fall in love with my stereo.

"I don't need any shit right now." Dad goes to the kitchen. "I'm going to die one of these days. I can't be worrying about it anymore. Now is now, and that's all there is. Might as well make it fun."

It's hard to argue with that. "I'll have a drink with you."

Dad gives me a searching glare then nods his approval. The drink he brings me is half as full as his, but it's a strong pour. I get him to sit on the couch, then drop the needle on "Bolero." When the snare drums start, Dad looks off to the front door, like someone's rapping on it. The flute comes in. "Oh…" He smiles. Then the bassoon surprises him. "Whoa!" Every new instrument that loops into the melody inflates Dad with more amazement. "Holy shit! Ho-ly *shit*!"

He lifts his glass and gazes into it. It's empty. He starts to get up. "N-n-no. You sit and listen. I'll get us a refill."

I pour us about the same amount this time, a little less than what Dad had, a little more than I got. Dad takes his glass, eying mine. "Are you working tomorrow?"

Dad worried about me. That's rich. "I thought now was now."

"Not for you. Your now isn't coming for a long time."

"That doesn't seem fair."

"Life's not fair," Dad informs me.

We listen to the rest of "Bolero." I know I have to tell him about Mom calling. But I don't want to bring him down from the high he's feeling. I'm still selling him on keeping the stereo where it is…

I wake up to Dad snoring. We're both slouching back, the house dark, save for the kitchen light. I nudge Dad awake. He rouses, reaches for his glass, and jiggles it with disappointment.

"What time is it?" he asks.

"You've got the watch."

"Twelve-thirty. Shit." He pries himself off the couch and takes our glasses into the kitchen. I watch him pour another finger of whiskey in his glass and throw it down. Then he shuts off the kitchen light. The glow of the stereo is enough to guide him through the living room.

"You coming?"

"I'm going to sleep here. I don't want to mess up Neil's room."

He nods. For half a second, I consider telling him about Mom's call. But as late as it is, I know he wouldn't take the news well.

Next morning, we walk together to catch the nine o'clock. And we sit next to each other. He reads a newspaper. I look out the window. We don't talk. At the Elmhurst stop, a sharp looking guy with a three-piece suit and one of those fancy hankies in his breast pocket gets on and takes a seat across the aisle from us. He looks over at Dad and gives me a quick glance. "Hey Mike."

Dad looks up from his paper. "Oh, hey Jeff."

"That's gotta be your boy. He's the spitting image of you."

"Not nearly as handsome," Dad jokes. "Jeff, this is Owen. Owen, this is Mister Roth."

"Jeff," the guy reaches his hand across Dad. I shake it.

"Owen's back from college at Michigan," Dad brags. "He's getting a little taste of working downtown."

Jeff grins at me. "Father and son, going to work together. Nice!"

I force a smile, wait for the moment to pass, then look back out the window. I've spent my whole life wanting to be like Dad. Now I know that I could be. Problem is, I don't want to be anymore.

As we're pulling into the station, I turn away from the window. "So, did you want me to move that stereo or not?"

"It's fine for now. But you have to teach me how to use it."

"I wrote down the instructions."

"Now, if Mom comes home, all bets are off."

"Yeah. About that. She called yesterday. She's been trying to get in touch with you."

"I know."

I figured he did. "She told me to be prepared for a change."

Dad doesn't say anything for a while. But I can tell he's thinking about it. He's tapping his finger against his lips. Then, just after I turn to look out the window, I hear him say, "She's probably right." His voice is so soft, I'm not sure if he's talking to me or himself.

## Helter Skelter

*I'm coming down fast but I'm miles above you.*
*- The Beatles*

Only six weeks left of summer. I told Dad I'd have over $4,000 for school. Right now, I have $294. I need to save about $600 a week between tips and my shitty paycheck. But then there's expenses—eating and the occasional night out. Say, $200 a week. How am I going to make $800 a week? That's over $200 a shift. I can make that much on hot dog Saturday and maybe Sunday brunch, but no way on Thursday and Friday. I start picking up all the shifts I can. Problem is, all the summer hires are doing the same thing.

I have one day off after coming back from getting my stereo, then I set it up so I work the next 12 days. Monday through Thursday sucks; I barely make $60 a day. I head into the last weekend of July needing to make $550 on my three big shifts. It's doable, but am I going to have to work every day now to keep up this pace?

To make matters worse, tonight's going to shit. Usually, you can rely on regulars to see you through on Friday night. But Kretch gives me section three by the bathrooms, and no one's coming back here. I don't mind normally. Jill works Fridays, and when it's slow, we hang out in that back corner. But ever since O'Banion's, she's been standoffish—not mean or anything, just treating me like everyone else. I don't know what I was expecting.

It's getting late, and I'm starting to wonder if Kretch is going to cut me. Most other nights, I'd be okay with it. But I haven't made enough tonight. I go up to the door and tell him I'll stay as late as he needs me. "You sure? You've been in here more than me lately."

"I need the money."

Terry hears me. "He can have my section."

Kretch scans the length of the bar. "Sure you can handle all this?"

I'm just about to answer, and Fitz walks in. I'll be damned… *Fitz!* I haven't seen him since he dropped me off from school. He's with a couple guys I don't know. Moose cards them all, and they come strutting into the bar, right past Terry and Kretch and me.

"Hey Fitz." I play it casual. He does an awkward double take. I can already tell he's drunk.

"Maloney! What the hell're you doin' here?"

"I work here."

"You work at Bud's? No fucking way!"

Kretch is standing there, arms folded, that flat, pained grin he always has when he's trying to be patient with annoying customers. "Come on." I wave them to the back. "Let's get you a drink." Anybody else and I would've asked Kretch if I should serve them. They're pretty drunk. Fitz says they've been barhopping up Rush Street. If they'd ordered anything stronger than a beer, I might've shut them down, but Fitz tells me they're having one last Guinness before they catch the train. So no big deal.

I set them up near where Jill and I hang out, and she pours them their pints. When Fitz goes to pay Jill, I say, "This one's on me," and put a twenty on the bar.

Jill nods and takes the twenty off the bar, all very business-like. After she walks away, Fitz breaks out laughing. "Man, Om! You are large and in charge. You got city babes bowing down to you."

He's so loud, I'm sure Jill heard. "Nobody's bowing to me."

"So you took my advice. Got your ass downtown." Fitz looks over at his buddies. "This guy was going to sit around all summer in Wheaton, moping over some chick hundreds of miles away, but I told him, 'Forget that bitch and go cut loose in Chicago.'"

Jill's eyeing me, and now Susie's coming over to the drink station. I'm starting to wish Fitz hadn't come in. Susie orders a couple drinks right next to Fitz. It feels weird not to say anything. "Guys, this is Susie. Susie, this is Fitz and…"

"Kip and Hal," Fitz fills in the blanks. "We went to high school together in Oak Park. The Buzz Boys!"

"You don't say." Susie barely feigns interest.

"And who's that fine babe?" Fitz slurs out, pointing to Jill. She's standing over by the taps, within easy earshot.

I lean my face down between Fitz and Kip or Hal, I'm not sure which of the Buzz Boys it is. "You need to watch what you say. They don't put up with any shit here. See that big guy at the door? He'd like nothing better than to pound your ass."

The three of them go quiet. Susie catches my eye and smiles. "Fucking-A, Om." Fitz's voice is low enough that no one else can hear. "Nobody else gave us shit tonight."

"Well, nobody else knows you." I walk away, up to the front of the bar. A couple is just sitting down at the table by the jukebox. They're mine now. Thank God I have more to do than stand there and get embarrassed by Fitz. When I walk past Jill, I swipe a finger across my neck. She nods. That's the last drink for the Buzz Boys. Not five minutes later, Fitz leads his pals out of Bud's. I'm relieved but kicking myself a little too. I didn't need to be such a prick. I'm all set to apologize as Fitz comes my way, but he beats me to it. "Hey, man. Sorry. You know what an asshole I am when I drink."

"I just didn't want you getting in trouble."

"Looking out for me, right?"

"What are friends for?"

"Hey, I got some tickets for a Sox game next week," he says. "You wanna go? We could ask Stu too."

"That'd be great. What about Eddie? Is he around?"

"Eddie's got some shit going on."

I give Fitz the number to Bud's basement phone, and he leaves with his buddies.

"So those are your college friends." Susie comes up beside me.

"Just the loudmouth."

"You seem so much older than him."

Terry's sitting near us at the bar. "That's what you were like when you first got here," he says. I don't think I've ever been like Fitz. But who knows? We never see ourselves the way others do. It's just good to know that Terry thinks I've changed.

When we close that night, he's still hanging out. Susie's gone, but Jill's there, cleaning up the bar. "Hey, wanna go grab a drink?" Terry asks me when I come up from the locker room.

"Maybe just one." As bad a Friday as it was, I can't afford to be burning through money after hours. Terry gets up to go.

"Aren't you going to wait?" Jill asks behind us.

"I'll wait for you," Moose says. "We'll catch up with you guys."

O'Leary's is a hole-in-the-wall down the alley beside The Lodge. Bud's people like to go there after work because it's right across the street, and you can wait there for others to get off without Kretch looking cross-eyed at you for taking up bar space. It's just a long brick cavern. There's really nowhere else to sit but at the bar. Terry gets a Guinness and asks what I'm having. I get one too. When I go to pay my share, he waves me off. "I got this." I've learned by now: there's no arguing with Terry when he wants to pay. "Man, you've been working your ass off," he says, as we wait for the beers.

"I've got to make money in a hurry. I went a little crazy and bought this new stereo. My dad was not pleased. Now he's squeezing me to make four grand by the end of the summer."

Terry shakes his head and whistles. Even he thinks that's a tall order. "What kind of system did you get?"

I wasn't going to tell him about the Maggies. I know what he'll think: must be nice not to have any other worries in life but to get a bitching stereo. Still, I know Terry'll be impressed. "I got a Yamaha turntable, receiver, and amplifier. And Tympani Threes."

"Are you kidding me?"

"It wasn't the smartest thing. It pretty much broke me."

Terry shakes his head. "Look at the balls on Owen Maloney!"

"I don't know." I shrug it off, even though it makes me feel pretty good. "I've put myself in a big hole."

"Hey, I've been there." The beers come. We start drinking. "I might be able to help you with your money troubles."

"I don't want to borrow anything."

"Nothing like that. It's just a favor. And we'd both make money."

"What is it?"

"I promised these guys I'd find them a little blow. I know: it's not legal, but neither is weed, right?" *Cocaine. Whoa.* "Anyway, they're coming in tomorrow, and I'm supposed to be shadowing Kretch. So I just need someone to hand it off to them."

"Shit, Terry. I don't know…"

"Honestly, it's no big deal. You just hand it to them while you're working. The packets aren't any bigger than a tea bag."

"They're going to come up to me while I'm working?"

"This is the beauty of it. I got it all worked out, simple as can be. Tomorrow night, you're selling your hot dogs, right?"

"That's right."

"So, at some point, three different guys are going to ask if they can get olives on their dogs. Crazy, right? You say no, then they'll ask for double mustard. That's how you know they're legit."

"So, that's when I give them the packet?"

"They'll give you a twenty and ask for five in change. You'll have three folded-up fives with the packet inside. Just pull one out of your pocket and hand it to the guy. Easy."

What Terry's asking isn't right. I know that. But I do things every day that aren't right. It's really a question of risk versus reward.

"Tell you what." Terry reaches into his pocket and pulls out a wad of cash. "I'll give you fifty bucks a packet. Here's the money.

On faith." A hundred and fifty dollars to hand out three lousy packs of cocaine. Like Terry says, it's not much worse than a few joints.

"So when do I get these packets?"

"Moose'll get 'em to you. You barely have to do a thing."

"Okay, I'll do it." It seems easy enough. Especially for the money.

Terry counts out eight twenties. "There's a little extra." He hands the bills to me. "Like I say, on faith."

I'm just pocketing the money when Moose and Jill walk in. Terry springs up and pulls out a stool for Jill. She and I look at each other. I smile. She gives me a quick grin, then turns away and gazes up at the bottles behind the bar. What would she think if she knew what I was going to do?

"Gentlemen." Moose's huge hand lands on my shoulder. He's looming between Terry and me. Moose hardly ever drinks, but tonight he orders a shot of Dewar's. "And get a round for these three," he tells the bartender.

"I'll have a glass of Chablis," Jill says.

The drinks come. Moose raises his shot in a silent toast. I raise mine. He clinks it, then Terry's. Jill doesn't hold out her wine glass. After we down the shots, Terry motions Moose to the back of the bar. Now it's just Jill and I sitting next to each other. She sips at her wine and stares into the wall of bottles. I don't have a drink anymore, but I'm thinking of ordering one. It's awkward just sitting there.

"How've you been?"

"Good," Jill says. "And you?"

"I'm okay."

"That's good."

"Did I do something to piss you off?" I can't help asking.

"No."

"Okay. I just thought—"

"I've had a lot on my mind lately."

"I wasn't expecting anything more, you know."

Jill smiles, but she seems sad. "You're sweet, Owen. Stay sweet."

Terry and Moose come back. "You ready?" Terry asks Jill.

She makes a show of assessing her glass. It's almost full. "Guess I have to be." She gets up, sneaks me a glance, and leaves with Terry. Why did it never dawn on me that they were together?

Moose sits down and orders a couple more shots. When the bartender walks away, he slides the folded bills across the bar to me. Three fives, folded into quarters, thicker than they ought to be. I put them in my pocket. The shots come. Moose raises his in front of me, like he's about to force me to drink it. I raise mine.

"Here's to not fucking up," he says. We down the shots. "Terry's put a lot of trust in you." He wraps his knuckles on the bar and stands up. "You can afford to take care of this." Then he walks out.

Two Guinness, five shots, and Jill's wine. Plus the tip. This is going to set me back at least 50 bucks, nearly half my take for the night. Or the pay for handing out one of these fives in my pocket.

Olives. Double mustard. A twenty. Then one of the fives in the left pocket of my server apron. Easy.

I see the first guy coming a mile away. I'm swinging through the dead section at the back of the bar, and he locks eyes on me. "I want a hot dog," he whispers, all nervous, like some rookie spy. I don't know yet if he's one of the three, but I have a good idea. Sure enough, when I'm taking the tongs to his dog, he asks, "You got any olives?"

"No, I'm sorry. We don't."

"Then I'll take double mustard."

"Okay." When I hand his hot dog to him, he's already holding out the twenty. "Gimme five back, and you can keep the change."

I reach into the left pocket of my apron, pull out one of the fives, and hand it to the guy. He puts it in his pocket, takes a bite of his hot dog, then hurries out of the bar, dumping the rest of the dog in the trash can by the jukebox. And just like that, it's done.

The second guy surprises me. I'm in the side room, and there are two couples at a four-top, dressed like they're on a double date. I ask if anyone wants hot dogs, and they all say yes. It's only as I'm dressing up the last one that the guy asks, cool as can be, "You got olives?" We go through the routine, I hand him the folded five, and they go right on laughing and drinking, in no hurry to leave, like *nothing to see here*. That's the way to do it.

The last person to ask for olives is Hadley. I should have figured. He was after Terry about hot dog night the day we met. I tell him we don't have olives. He says he'll have double mustard. I make the dog and hand it to him. But then he gives me a ten. It's not a twenty, like Terry said it would be. I don't want to screw this up. I hand him back a regular five. He pulls it slowly out of my hand, staring me down. I hurry away. Did I make a mistake? What are the odds that someone would ask for olives and double mustard—but *not* want a packet? The rest of the night, I'm praying that someone will ask for olives and relieve me of the last folded five. Nobody does, but Hadley eyes me every time I go by. Should I just give him the five? What would Terry say? It's not my fault Hadley messed up.

Kretch cuts me right after I sell all my hot dogs. I go downstairs, get out of my work clothes, come back up, and sit at the far end of the bar, where Jill's bartending. Terry's still working, still shadowing Kretch. I need to catch him alone before I leave, explain what happened and find out what to do. Jill senses I'm worried. When she brings me my beer, she asks, "Everything all right?"

"Everything's fine." I wish I could get her advice, but I have no idea if she knows what Terry's up to. My guess is she does. But this is the kind of thing you can't guess about.

How long am I going to have to wait here? I keep an eye on Terry, trying to get his attention, but not too obviously. Not like Hadley's doing, glaring me down. I head to the bathroom. I need to be alone. I'm in there peeing when the door opens behind me. The guy stands at the urinal right next to me. I look down at the blue sanitizer puck. "You did the right thing." It's Hadley. I glance at him. He's holding a $50 bill in his hand. "Good job. Keep that other five for next time."

I take the bill and nod. Then, just as fast as he came in, he's gone. It's only when I'm washing my hands that it comes to me: he didn't have his usual high-flown accent. He sounded more like a typical Chicagoan. And what was that about *next time?* Wasn't this supposed to be a favor? I had a feeling this was going to be more than a one-time deal. Just how planned out and elaborate the whole olive/double mustard thing was. And Moose with the fives all folded and ready to go. Then his warning not to fuck it up. I wonder if this was why Nick said the job was too much pressure. Maybe one day, I'll ask him. Then again, maybe I won't.

I made $210 more than I would've tonight, thanks to those packets. And it puts me just $24 short of my $800-per-week goal. Without that money, I would've fallen over $200 behind in the very first week. No way I'd make four grand. So what's wrong with seeing where this goes? With Hadley getting in the picture, it seems like tonight was a test run. Maybe next week, they give me 10 packs to distribute. Three, 10, 20—what does it matter? It's not like it takes a lot more work.

I pick up two extra shifts for the coming week, Monday and Wednesday lunch. Lousy shifts. You're lucky if you make $50 those days. But with summer winding down, you take what you can get. So it's going to be another week of needing $200 shifts Friday through Sunday brunch. A longshot—unless Terry comes through. But I'm nearly done with my Thursday lunch shift, and Terry hasn't said boo to me. And, just my luck, I'm first to get cut. I was going to go out to eat, but the day was so shitty, and I'm so deep in the hole, I can't afford it. There's peanut butter and jelly at the apartment. I'll just do that and call it an early evening. I'm out the door and almost to Dearborn when Terry calls out behind me. He's running to catch up. "Hey, you wanna go grab a drink at O'Leary's?"

I make a show of thinking about it. I don't want to be too eager. I need to plant the seed that I'm not so sure about this. It'll make it easier to back out whenever I want to. "Yeah. We should talk."

Terry has an envelope all set for me—five more loaded fives and $300 to pass them all out, plus the one I kept. I tell him this is more than a favor, and I'm not sure how I feel about doing it. He says he gets it. He only needs my help a couple more times. I fret about the big risk I'm taking. He laughs. "Are you asking me for a raise?" We agree that I get an extra $50 for every five I do each night. So 10 is $100, 15 is $150, and so on. I also get him to promise we'll just do it those two more times.

Friday night's decent—I make $185 and go straight home. The next morning, it's raining. I have a bowl of Raisin Bran, make a pot of coffee, pour a cup, and take it out into the Fun Room. There's a big cushy chair right by the entry. Sitting there, I can look up through the door's curtained windowpanes and see people flash by under umbrellas. Drinking my coffee, I think how nice it is not to feel like I should be doing something. The rain's given me that permission. When I go back to get more coffee, I see the Manson book on my nightstand. I get it, then I refill my cup and head back to the chair. Today's the day I finish this damn book.

I think about what I'm doing, slipping people these packs, then I read about all the gruesome shit Manson and his family did. A lot of them were as old as I am now. How do you get talked into doing something like that? Can you go from knowing right and wrong to butchering people, just by degrees? Can drugs and mind games make you take such an unpardonable leap? I've given two people the smallest means to get high, and already I feel guilty. Tomorrow night, I'll do six more. Maybe by the end of this, I'll have given 20 people a thimbleful of coke. It's wrong, yes. But it's not like Terry's telling me to hurt anyone.

Strangely, it isn't the victims of the Tate murders who move me the most. It's William Garretson. Nineteen years old, just like me. On the night when five people were brutally slaughtered in Polanski's home, Garretson, the caretaker, was mere feet away from the scene, happily listening to music in the guest house. By some miracle, Manson's ghouls didn't attack him, even though they knew he was there. And he never had a clue about the horror playing out around him. You could say he was lucky. Then again, his first awareness of the murders came when police burst into the guest house, led him over to see the butchered bodies, and arrested him as the key suspect in the killings. The poor guy. Innocent as can be… and he has to live with that for the rest of his life.

I'm not that innocent—but I'm a lot closer to Garretson than the deranged teenagers in the Manson cult. Okay, I can see how doing bad is a slippery slope. But going from being in high school to bludgeoning people seems like an awfully long and gradual slide. Who knows? Maybe it's like the Beatles say in "Helter Skelter," the song about a spiraling slide that spurred Manson's crazy vision and prompted his family's killing spree: We think we're miles above serious trouble, but we're coming down fast, every one of us.

Saturday night can't go any better. Two of the six people are the same ones I handed packets to the week before. The other four, three guys and this out-of-place woman with a beehive hairdo, are very cool about the whole thing. Within an hour, my work's done.

It's a weight off my shoulders. And not having that weight gives me a kick of energy. I sell out my dogs with 45 minutes to go, make more, and sell those too. I'm easily over $500 for the night, probably close to $600. To top that off, Kretch slides me a couple tables in the side room after I'm done cleaning up from hot dog detail.

Susie's working the room with me. "You get two tables, and I get a bunch of meandering loners. It's not fair. You're killing it, and I'm dying over here."

She's not serious, I know. But I do feel bad. "I don't know what to tell you," I joke. "Some people have it, and some don't. How about if I take you to dinner to make up for your shortcomings?"

"Are you taking pity on me?"

Kretch comes bustling into the side room. "Maloney. There's a lady here for you, sitting in the window."

"Ooh! A *lady*!" Susie kids me.

I follow Kretch back into the main bar, come around the corner by the front door—and there's Tara, perched on a front stool, gazing through the smoky haze.

## Spoonful

*Everybody fightin' about a spoonful.*
*- Howlin' Wolf*

"**D**on't beat yourself up," Susie says. "I would've done the same thing." We're at Twin Anchors, this tavern by Susie's place, finishing a plate of ribs. Some blues tune's playing on the speakers. "Spoonful." I thought it was a Cream song, but it's a black guy singing, and he's got this gravelly voice that shakes right through you.

"I don't know…"

"She's the one who broke it off, right?" God bless Susie. "What did she expect? That you'd come running out and throw yourself at her feet? No, I would've done the same thing."

"Who *is* this?" I don't know why I'm asking Susie. She isn't going to know. But the singer's growl, so haunting and ferocious… I can't think with it threatening in the background.

"Howlin' Wolf," she says.

I laugh. It's an apt description. "Or growling dog."

"No, that's the artist. Howlin' Wolf. He's a big Chicago blues guy. I saw him two years ago with—"

"With who?"

Susie ignores me. "He was good. He's this giant of a man, but he got down on the stage and crawled across it. The crowd went nuts."

*Everybody fightin' about a spoonful.* I always thought Cream was talking about coke, but this Howlin' Wolf guy sounds like he's talking about any craving—drugs, money, love, sex, whatever.

I finally face my failure. "I saw her—and just turned around. I don't even know if she saw me. It was a reflex. My feelings were all mixed up. I was scared, angry, hurt. Now I feel like a coward." I pick at the label on my beer. "I should've told Kretch I didn't want to see her when he came back the second time. It would've been over. Instead, I have him tell her I stepped out. So she asks if I'll be back. And what does Kretch say? *Maybe.* Now I have to think about it more."

"You don't have to think about it."

"Maybe I should go back to Bud's and wait."

"Hell, no! What good's gonna come of that? Why don't we go to that punk bar? O'Banion's. Have some drinks, kick back."

"I don't want to spend the money."

"Or…" she pauses until I look up at her. "We can go back to my place and hang out. You could help me with my routine."

"Susie Starling… are you coming on to me?"

She laughs. "Sometimes I think about that night." Now she's picking at her beer label. "It seems so long ago, doesn't it?"

"It does."

"We would've had a lot of time." Susie's quiet, like she's talking to herself. "Now you're leaving soon. I'm glad I don't have to go through what you did with Tara."

"Well, you've always known I'd be leaving."

"Yeah…" she agrees, but she doesn't seem all that convinced.

After I pay the check, I tell Susie I'm going to make it an early night. And I mean it. I get all the way to my apartment. Then, just like when I turned away from Tara, something snaps, and I keep going—down Dearborn and right into Bud's. Terry's at the door with Moose. Not Kretch. It always feels different when Kretch isn't there, no matter who's filling in for him—less supervised, more dangerous. "Well, look who's back," Terry says. Moose gives a little chuckle, like I'm some private joke. This guy… sometimes…

I head to the back of the bar. Jill isn't working anymore. I'll have to buy my own beer. Another bad thing about Kretch not being here is I don't know if Tara came back already or not. How long am I going to wait?

Bud's people are gathering up front. Kretch would never let so many hang out in that prime real estate. A few bartenders. Nick and Garrett. Clancy. Travolta-man from Faces. Astrid. This is more than a quick meet-up. Shots are flashing in the air, and the noise they're making has overtaken the bar. I hide behind the thicket of beer taps. The last thing I want is to get roped into this crew. But that Astrid; she's an eye catcher tonight. Her dress looks like a skimpy, deflated disco ball, sequins clinging to all her curves. Her face is lit up, and she's shouting and laughing. That night I went out with her, she was quiet. I'd say demure, except that she put her hand between my legs. Tonight, she's a firecracker, sparkling and loud.

Jill comes up from downstairs. The taps don't hide me from her. She looks at me and holds her gaze, like she's considering coming over. Instead, she joins the crowd by the window. I order another beer and ask the waiter what time it is. Ten-forty. I'll wait for Tara until 11, then call it a night.

Astrid's suddenly louder. She's wagging a finger at someone. Jill's there. Is that who she's yelling at? I get my beer and head that way. The hell with it. Just as I get near the front door, Susie breezes in. Is she checking up on me? Didn't she believe me when I said I was making it an early night? I guess she knows me better than I know myself. When I come toward her, she holds her hands out. "You said you were going home."

"You came all this way to see if I was lying?"

"I thought you might need some support."

"She didn't show—"

"Either way."

"I forgot to tell you, Maloney," Moose cuts in. "Some chick asked for you." Damn Moose anyway. If he'd said something when I walked in, I'd be in bed right now. "She left this." He hands me a drink coaster. It's folded in half. "I gotta say," he smirks, "A pretty fine piece of ass."

That smirk. That damn smirk. "Fuck you, Moose."

He rocks back a little. I couldn't have done that damage if I sucker-punched him. "Fuck *me?*" He's more surprised than angry.

"Use your brain and think about what you said," Susie breaks in.

Moose glares at her, jaw pulsing. Then he cracks a wide smile. "Okay. Fuck me." He turns away and rejoins Terry at the door.

I look inside the folded coaster. *I was hoping to see you. Tara.* Below that, there's a phone number. I put the coaster in my wallet.

Glass shatters. I turn in time to see shards raining down on people in the front window. Astrid's trying to fight her way past Nick and Garrett. "You bitch!" she shrieks with her Swedish accent. "You have it! I know it! That's what you get for the fucking!" Astrid slips by Nick and starts clawing at Jill. Jill keeps her cool, leaning back, just out of swiping range. Moose hurries past Susie and me. I follow him. I have no idea what I'm going to do. Moose bear-hugs Astrid from behind and picks her right up off the floor. When he swings her away from Jill, she's in front of me, kicking furiously. One of those kicks gets me right in the family jewels.

Astrid's still screaming, but not at Jill anymore. "I'll fuck you again, Terry! I'll keep fucking!" Terry's standing out of the fray, arms folded. "Please, Terry! Just a little. Please!"

Moose clamps his huge hand over her mouth and slings her onto his hip. Then he hustles her to the back door.

"Hey!" Susie barks at him and follows. Garrett chases after her.

Someone jostles me. It's Jill. "You okay?"

"I just got one right where it counts."

Everyone's backing away from the broken glass. Jill leads me over where we usually talk. Moose is trying to stuff Astrid through the alley door. Susie's yelling for him to stop. I want to see what's going on. Jill pulls me back. "Stop jumping into trouble." I should get Susie out of there. But I let Jill steer me to the back stools. "Why are you here anyway? It's way past your new bedtime."

I can't decide whether she's teasing or not. "Why go out and waste money when nothing ever happens?"

"Something's always happening."

"I'll take a wild-ass guess that it's drinking and snorting coke."

Terry's coming back toward us. He stops and puts his hands on his hips. For a second, I think it's Jill and me he's worried about, but he's looking past us to the back door. It's cracked open, and all you can see is Garrett wedged against the frame. But you can hear screaming. And now the clatter of trash cans.

"You should come out tonight," Jill says behind me.

Garrett suddenly rocks back like he took a punch. Moose comes barreling through the door, shaking his head in grim disbelief. Susie's right behind him, and she's yelling. "You asshole! You *asshole*! You didn't need to do that!"

Moose strides past Terry. I hear him say, "Get her out of my face."

Terry steps forward and intercepts Susie. "Now, now, Susie. Come on." He tries to soothe her like she's a child. "We've got customers. Come on, now."

Susie points over Terry's shoulder. "You know what that asshole did? Go see for yourself. Just go see!"

I get up. Jill puts a hand on my arm and settles me back down. "Terry's got it under control." He walks Susie to the door, leaning in close and whispering. Moose stands off to the side, arms folded, scowling. They pass without incident.

"Who's taking care of Astrid?" I wonder.

"Wasn't Garrett there?"

Do I really want to see what happened? Knowing Moose, he probably smacked her. And as mad as Susie was, it probably drew blood. What was I going to do about that?

"So…" Jill moves on. "Do you want to go out or not?"

"Do you? You've done a lot of what you don't want to do lately."

"Oh, you think so?"

"That time at O'Leary's, when Terry wanted to go, you made sure I saw that you wanted to finish your wine. But you still went."

Jill shrugs it off. "You can't always get what you want."

"Not the Jill I know. The Jill I know gets what she wants. But maybe you don't *know* what you want."

Jill slaps me. It isn't hard, but enough to get my attention. "You don't know a thing about me," she says, any true anger already gone.

I take a risk that she's not really mad. "I know *some* things."

Jill smiles. "Fair enough." She motions to the bartender working that end. "Two kamikazes."

"So *that's* what you want."

"Fuck you, Owen."

"You really *don't* know what you want, do you?"

Jill's eyes lock on mine. I was just joking, but it came out wrong, too personal. Thankfully, she laughs. It's a sad little laugh, but a laugh, nonetheless. "Like you know what *you* want," she challenges me, jaw jutting out, eyes piercing.

"I do right now." I put my hand on her knee. Why not?

Her cocksure look dissolves. The shots come. We do them without a toast. "Sorry. I don't know what came over me. It's just that—"

Her finger's against my mouth, hushing me before I see it coming. We leave through the alley. I'm glad to see no one's there. And other than a toppled trash can, there's no clue of what made Susie so mad. *Susie.* I should've walked her home. It was my fault she was here in the first place, wanting to make sure I was okay. Now she's on Moose's shit list and maybe Terry's too. Bad shit lists to be on.

"You changing your mind?" Jill asks out of the blue.

"No."

"You're so quiet all of a sudden."

I don't want to say I was thinking of Susie. But I'm also wondering why Astrid would yell at Jill like that, and I don't want to bring that up either. "What do you think Moose did to her?"

"Astrid crossed a line." I'm pretty sure I know the line, but I'm dying to ask anyway, just to see how she describes it, to find out what she knows. I decide not to. Talking is killing the mood.

I grab her hand and stop. She turns to me, puzzled. I put my other hand on the nape of her neck, under her hair, and pull her toward me. I kiss her. We don't stop for a long time. Even when we do, it's she who pulls away. She stands there, breathing like she just came up for air, then she takes my face in her hands and starts kissing me again, harder and more tender at the same time. I think of that kiss on the balcony.

We go to my apartment. And we don't get any further than the rug in the Fun Room. The windowpanes cut the streetlight into four yellow blocks. Enough to see. We do all the things we did the first night. I go slow, like Jill wants. She moves her body in the light, like I want. And she stares straight into my eyes. But something's missing. It goes on and on, but there's no spark like there was before.

Jill cuddles up beside me. "You okay?"

"Sorry. I just wasn't feeling anything."

Jill laughs to herself, stroking my head. "Figures."

"What?"

"I finally feel something for someone—and they don't."

Now I feel bad. "There was a lot of shit going on tonight. Too much preying on my mind."

Jill starts dressing in the shadows. "I'll leave you alone."

"No..." I remember how hospitable she was the morning after the first time. "Stay. I'm done thinking."

I'm still on the rug, sitting up now. She comes over, kneels down, and kisses me on the forehead. "I'm just starting."

**Warning Sign**
*Warning sign, warning sign. I see it but I pay it no mind.*
*- Talking Heads*

**"S**o it was a slap. He didn't punch her." It's the next morning, Sunday brunch. Susie and I are waiting for our orders in the kitchen. I'm trying to get to the bottom of what happened.

"What difference does that make with a guy as big as Moose?" Susie says. "He made her bleed."

"I guess you're right." Astrid was out of control for calling out Terry. She was begging for trouble. It seemed pretty clear she was harassing Jill for coke. Then again, maybe I came to that conclusion because of the hot dog gig, and nobody knew what she was railing about. But no matter what, she didn't deserve to get hit.

I don't share any of that with Susie. We're too busy with the rush. But when we're waiting at the drink station, I ask her, "So after you and Garrett got her out of the alley, did you walk her home?"

"Yeah, she isn't that far away. Just down near you."

"I wonder what she told the Professor." He's the guy who sits in the window reading books, the one who hired Astrid as an au pair.

"I wondered that too. Garrett sat with her on the steps of the Professor's townhouse for about an hour until she sobered up. He said she was getting a pretty big shiner. No way she could hide it."

The Bloody Mary's come, and we get back to work. But I keep thinking about Astrid. Next time Susie and I are in the kitchen, I say, "I guess Astrid won't be coming into Bud's anytime soon."

"She's got bigger problems than that. Garrett thinks she was on something a lot stronger than booze last night."

"Uh-oh." I make a show of being alarmed.

"I wonder what Kretch'll do."

"You think he'll find out?"

"Something like this—trust me—Kretch already knows."

I'm getting worried. If Kretch hears it from Terry or Moose, they'll smooth it over. Anyone else will have a different version. If Garrett thought Astrid was high on something, others probably did too. All I heard was yelling across the bar—Astrid accusing Jill of having something and screwing Terry for it. That was enough for me. Then again, I'm more in the know than others. At least I think. No matter what, we were taking a big risk passing out coke in the bar. Time to tell Terry: I'm done.

I thought I'd have a couple days to figure out how to tell him. But toward the end of brunch, he comes in. Kretch leaves the front door and takes him downstairs. That right there tells me Kretch thinks whatever went on last night was more than your typical weekend craziness. Kretch never has someone else work the door on Sunday brunches. The brunch is his brainchild, and he treats every customer like he's welcoming them into his house.

They don't stay in the office very long, five minutes max. That's a good sign. And Terry doesn't leave. He takes a seat at the bar right next to the back drink station. When I go to make an order, he leans over and says to me, "Let's go to the beach today." Not like *what do you think about that*, but like *this is what we're doing*.

I'm not dressed for the beach. I look like one of those office wonks on lunch break. Terry looks like he's ready for yacht clubbing, but at least he's got on a short-sleeve shirt and short pants. It's unbearably hot. All the way from Bud's, past Rush Street and the run of quiet bars on the lake side of Rush, Terry doesn't say a word. It isn't until we cross Lakeshore Drive and find a bench to sit on looking at the sunbathers that Terry speaks. "Last night was seriously fubar."

The wind's howling and the water's crashing. The traffic roars behind us. I can't hear very well. "Fubar?"

"Fucked up beyond all recognition."

"Ah… Yes. It was."

"I don't want you worrying, though. We've got it under control."

"What did you tell Kretch?"

"I told him the truth. No use hiding things from Kretch."

"Not the whole truth, though."

"Pretty much. Astrid came in high last night, made a scene, and we had to deal with it."

"What did you say about how—how Moose dealt with it?"

"He already knew that. Bud and the Professor are friends. So Bud got an earful this morning, and Kretch got one five minutes later."

"Bud's involved now? How is this under control?"

Terry takes a deep breath. "Shit happens in a bar, Owen. Everyone knows that. Nobody's okay with what Moose did. But that's what Moose gets paid to do. For every Astrid we feel bad about getting hurt, there are ten assholes we're happy Moose handled."

"So that's what Bud's going to tell the Professor?"

"He's had to do this sort of thing before. It'll be short and sweet: *Your au pair can't come into my bar high, break glasses, fight people, and not expect that there won't be consequences. And when people resist, sometimes you have to do things you don't want to do. You understand, old friend, don't you?* That's how he'll handle it."

That doesn't sound short and sweet to me. In fact, it gets me more worried. "Okay, but what if Astrid told the Professor more—like where she got the drugs?"

I expect Terry to get mad at me. It's a pretty direct accusation. He just shrugs. "I don't think that's going to happen."

"I'm sure the Professor—or his wife—are asking questions."

"I guess they already did. But she won't talk. She just wants to go back to Sweden. So, no big deal. Just another Bud's legend: the night a meek au pair busted up the bar." He grins at me. "Now. About this Saturday."

"This Saturday? Shit, Terry. We can't be doing this now—"

Terry holds up his hand. "I know, I know. We gotta shut it down. It's just that I already got this Saturday's packs. And I can't say no."

"Even if you get in deep shit?"

"If we don't hand out these packs, we'll be in deeper shit."

*We.* Terry lets that sink in. "The good news is, it's three people, and you've already dealt with them. They each want five. Seven-hundred and fifty bucks plus three fifty-dollar bonuses. That's nine hundred bucks. I made it an even thousand." He reaches into the front pocket of his shorts and pulls out an envelope. "Here's the money. Moose'll get you the folded bills tomorrow. They'll be singles this time, since we have to give each person five packets."

I let the envelope stay in Terry's hand. "This is bad."

He drops the envelope in my lap. "No worse than before Astrid lost her shit. Now take it."

I put the envelope in my pocket. Was I going to do it all along? Probably. It's a lot of money. "I just worry about Astrid talking."

"If she said anything, Bud would be handling it very differently."

We sit and watch the sunbathers, lying prone on the beach in all manner of positions, like they'd all passed out on their towels. A mass catastrophe; nothing violent, like the Manson killings, but the same twisted arrangement of bodies. I feel like that Garretson kid.

"You know what I worry about?" Terry says after a while. "I worry about Susie. That was not cool the way she called out Moose last night. She's got a righteous streak in her. Careful what you say when the two of you get talking like you do."

I think about how Susie would react if she knew I was selling coke to customers. "You don't have to worry about that."

A boombox starts blaring nearby—the Talking Heads. It's droning, foreboding, hypnotic.

Terry slaps his hands on his thighs and gets up. "I gotta be some-where." Without so much as a goodbye, he turns and walks away.

I sit there in the heat for a minute. Then another. And more. Listening to the music drone on—the siren song of all those night-stalking subterraneans, fooled into coming up on the beach in the blazing sun. The longer I stay there, the more I wonder: have I become one of them? Even then, I don't get right up.

When I finally go back to my apartment, I call Dad. He answers on the second ring. "Hey!" He's all jaunty. "What do you need?

"Nothing. I was just wondering if you wanted to meet for lunch tomorrow."

"Oh…" And that *oh* hangs out there until I think we got cut off. Then: "This week won't work. How about next week?"

"That's okay. It was just a thought."

"So, you're alright then."

"Yes, Dad. I'm all right." I hang up before he can say anything else.

Next day, Moose is on me as soon as I come in. Nobody else is around. He points right between my eyes like his finger's a gun. "Tonight. After work. O'Leary's."

It's nearly three by the time we get over there. The place is practically empty. We take the stools closest to the entry. Even though it's still hot and muggy, Moose is wearing one of those shiny green Bud's jackets we sell. That gets my attention right away. But what makes it worse is that Moose is sweating like a pig, drops rolling down his forehead and dripping right off his nose. He orders two shots again, like he did the first time we met here. Then, when the bartender turns away, he pulls the envelope out of his coat and slides it over to me. I stuff it under my shirt. We haven't said a word to each other. The shots come. Moose downs his as soon as it's in front of him. Then he raises his empty glass and clinks mine just as I'm bringing it to my mouth. Some of it spills.

"You need to stop hanging around with that bitch Susie," he says, getting up. He brings his face close to mine and lowers his voice. "She's trouble."

## Take Me Out to the Ballgame

*I don't care if I never come back.*
*- Harry Caray*

After cancelling on Susie three times, Los Toros finally confirms she'll have five minutes before the jazz trio on Friday, four days away. Susie asks if I'll come over on Tuesday and help her rehearse. I have no reason to say no, but I'm not looking forward to it. Terry wants me to be careful around her. Moose wants me to stay away from her. And I don't want to do either of those. Problem is, I don't know *what* I want to do. I want to warn her without getting into the why of things. I want her to know that making another scene is dangerous. How I'm going to do that without raising suspicion is beyond me. But I can't *not* go to Susie's, and I can't *not* say anything.

Susie's got the "Hot Blooded" bit down cold, and it's funny. She's gonna do the city critters one, too, but it's a little shaky. The set-up is too long. She says that coming from the country, she expected there wouldn't be any animals in the city. But she's actually seen more wildlife downtown in two years than she had her whole life in Indiana. That's when she wonders which city animal has it best.

"I mean, which animal would *you* rather be?" Susie asks me. She's at the point of her pie-shaped apartment, like she's up on stage and I'm sitting in the audience. "Me," she goes on after a practiced pause, "I'd need to be something the wolves couldn't get to. It's a lot different for women. Men, they just want to be predators. Women, we gotta be something men can't attack."

Susie wants to start talking about squirrels and their ability to spin around trees, just out of sight. And she knows she's going to end with poop-flinging monkeys. But she's torn about the middle critter between your basic rat and that owl I saw with Jill. It hits me then: she'd be telling that story to a roomful of people.

"Anyone else coming from work?"

"Nick knows, but that's it."

Okay. But if Nick knows… "If you ask me, the rat's better. Everyone's seen a rat downtown. Hardly anyone's seen an owl."

"I don't know. A rat's obvious. Seeing an owl, that rings true."

"But it isn't your truth."

"Is that why you don't want me to use it?"

"I just don't think it's that funny. Plus, you have five minutes; the owl story takes a lot of set-up. If you start with the rat—something everyone's seen—go to the squirrel—a more specific instance, but still accessible—then end with the monkey, that's gold."

"Yeah, you're right," Susie says. "You're probably right."

Susie's still mulling it over as she walks me to her door. That's when I remember; I hadn't warned her to keep quiet around Moose. That turned out to be a good thing, because when I finally speak up, it comes out as natural as can be. "Hey, is Moose still mad at you?"

"What the hell do I care?"

"I don't know. He's a scary dude."

"He's a moron. He just does what Terry says, like all his other coke groupies."

That stops me cold. "What do you mean by that?"

"What else did you think Astrid was begging him for?"

"Jesus, Susie. I wouldn't be saying that to anyone. How do you know it's even true?"

"It doesn't take a genius. Just watch the goings-on when the gang gets together—all the trips to the bathroom, the sniffling and rubbing of noses. Hell…" Susie shakes her head. "I even did lines with Jill a few times before I wised up."

"Okay, so someone has coke—Terry, Moose, that weird disco guy." I'm agreeing with her but injecting as much doubt as I can.

Maybe if she thinks twice about whether it's Terry who has the coke, she won't wonder about how he's selling it. "Nobody wants Astrid mouthing off about it. No wonder they got her out of there so fast."

"And now she's gone back to Sweden."

"It's probably for the best."

"Best wouldn't include getting your face busted up."

"True." Then a thought comes to me. "You don't want to get on the wrong side of Moose." It comes off like I was talking about Astrid, but it could've been a wider warning.

Thankfully, that's how Susie takes it. "I know, I know. I just can't help myself. I see that shit, and it flips a switch. My dad—"

"Your dad?"

"I oughta know better than to open my mouth."

I should press Susie on what she means about her dad, but she opens the door for me then. She thanks me for helping her and asks if I can come over tomorrow to help. I tell her maybe, but I already know I'm going to find a way to get out of it. I got Susie to say what I wanted to hear. And I didn't have to bring it up. She got there all on her own. No use coming back again and risking more talk.

I have a good night for a Tuesday—$85 in tips. With the grand Terry gave me, anything I make now is gravy. So next morning, I treat myself to breakfast at the diner where I called Dad my first night downtown. I've been here enough now that the owner knows my name. What a difference a few weeks makes. It puts me in mind to call Dad. I use the diner's payphone. Denise answers. When I ask for Mike Maloney, she realizes it's me. "Owen!" she cries out like I've been lost. It makes me wonder what it would've been like working at the agency. It almost makes me wish I did.

"Is my dad there?"

She gives this little gasp then declares, "Yes, he is," like his presence is a surprise, even to her.

Then he's on the phone. "Owen?!" Everyone seems so surprised.

"I wanted to figure out a good time for lunch next week."

"Oh." Then silence. "Shh-ure. How's Monday?"

"Yeah, that's good. I'll come to your office."

"No, let's meet at Bud's."

"Let's go somewhere else. What's halfway?"

"Is there something going on, Owen?"

"Can't I want to get together without something being wrong?"

"Sure, you can. You been to the Billy Goat before?"

"I've heard of it, but no."

We figure out a time. I'm about to say goodbye, then he hits me with this: "By the way, you gotta do something with that stereo."

"Okay…" Shit. The last thing I want to do is get on another train to Wheaton. "Can it wait a week?"

"No sweat. It's just got to be out of the living room by Labor Day. Because, well…" He pauses. "Your mother's coming home."

Talk about dramatic effect. It almost sounds rehearsed. But I can tell by the catch and huff of his breath that he's genuinely happy about it, or at least relieved. "Well, that's good—"

"And you know Mom. She'll want that living room in order."

"I'll come over next week and move it up into Neil's room."

"Don't get me wrong. I love having it. I even bought a jazz record. You heard of Weather Report, *Heavy Weather*?"

"No."

"We'll give it a listen when you're back next week."

"Fair enough."

"Very good, then!" There's a strange lilt in his voice. I haven't heard it in a while. It's the sound of Dad happy. "See you soon."

He hangs up before I can say goodbye. My omelet comes seconds later. Dad's back, the man I knew before I went off to college, the one who was on top of things, who had all the answers, who knew what he wanted and how to get it.

The thought of that prompts me to pray, like we used to years ago, when all of us were around the kitchen table together—Mom, Dad, Neil, and I. It starts as a prayer of gratitude; for Dad getting his life in order; for Mom coming home; for Neil finding himself. But when I get to me, it becomes a prayer of desperation, a cry for help. *Get me through this. Help me do what's right. Make it end.*

Wednesday night we're slow, and I get cut first. Just $72 in tips. I'd be sweating bullets if it weren't for the hot dog money. Part of me is glad I don't have to worry about how much I make anymore. Part of me wishes I could go back to when that was my only worry.

Thursday's an off day. I'm going with Fitz to the Sox game. It's at night. I've got the whole day to myself. Nick's off, too, so we get together for lunch at a deli on North Avenue. Then we head to Lincoln Park and find a spot to smoke a joint and toss a frisbee. It's one of those golden late-August days. A cool breeze is whistling through the trees and the first leaves are falling. It's just a rustle if your mind's elsewhere, but a warning if you stop to listen: Summer's ending. Get ready for change.

Nick feels it too. We stop tossing the frisbee, lie down in the shade of a tree, and finish the joint. "I hate this time of year," he says.

"I used to like it. There was something sweet about the last days of August, you know? Maybe because September brought so many demands and such crazy hope with it."

"Not for me."

He doesn't explain himself, so I'm left to wonder what he means. It must be hard when your friends go back to college and take the next steps in their lives, while you get left behind. "Yeah. This summer's different. I wanna be done with it, but I dread what's next."

"At least you can leave," Nick says.

What if I had to stay in the city and keep working at Bud's, hustling for tips, living for the seductions of the night, worrying every week that Terry would pressure me to hand out loaded bills one more time? "Why did you quit being the hot dog guy?" Nick eyes me like *who are you kidding?* "How did Terry let you out of it?"

"I just decided to start fucking up. Nothing major, just stupid shit. Asking the olive people if they wanted mustard instead of waiting for them to say it. Pestering Terry with questions. Acting stressed." He laughs. "Well, that wasn't an act."

"Maybe that's what I need to do. After Astrid's meltdown, it's way too risky. I've gotta find a way out."

"Isn't that the beauty of leaving? Two more weeks, and it's over."

I don't say anything for a while. I'm listening to that wind whispering in the trees. "That might not be soon enough."

Fitz picks me up outside Bud's in a blue Newport, a huge boat of a car—courtesy of his dad. Stu's sitting beside him. It doesn't seem right. They're oil and water. I guess it would've been weird for Stu to make Fitz drive him like a chauffeur. I figure he'll jump out and stick me with the front seat. But he just stares straight ahead.

I get in the back. "So, no Eddie, eh?"

"No Eddie," Fitz confirms.

"Weren't you saying he was going through something?"

"Hang on." Fitz speeds up to get through the light, and we're sailing along Division, on the way out of town.

"So what was it?"

"For shit's sake!" Stu snaps. "Let him get past this!" *Whoa.* Stu isn't usually so uptight, and he never takes Fitz's side.

"Got your door locked?" Fitz eyes me in the rearview mirror. Now I know why they're so tense. We're coming up to Cabrini Green.

Stu crouches in his seat. "Just look straight ahead."

"Don't be so obvious about it." Now it's Fitz who's all prickly.

A few weeks ago, I might've been, too, but now it seems comical. We pass under the El, and it dawns on me: These are the tracks that go Terry's apartments, the ones that face that wall with its cryptic graffiti. *Their* way of masking fear. I laugh.

"It's not funny!" Stu shouts.

"They don't give a shit about us," I tell them.

Fitz finally makes it to the highway. He and Stu let out big sighs. I want to point out how gutless they're being, but why bother? "So. About Eddie—"

"Eddie's got cancer." Fitz lays it out, just like that. He proceeds to tell me the details. Eddie has stage four Hodgkin's lymphoma. He's been going through chemotherapy. "There's a good chance he can beat it, but Eddie told me the five-year survival rate is fifty-fifty for what he has."

"Shit." Eddie's the last guy I imagine getting cancer—not that I expect anybody to get it. But Eddie… so full of life, so optimistic. You don't expect death to have a chance with him. Nobody says anything for a while. Finally, Stu pitches forward, groans, and buries his head in his hands. "Why is all this shit happening?!"

"Come on, Stu. Remember what Eddie told us?" Fitz finds me in the rearview mirror again. "We went to see him a week ago. I told him we were going to this game. He said he'd hate it if we wasted our time feeling sorry for him. Isn't that right, Stu?"

Stu lifts his head. "Yeah…"

"He said he'd be pissed if we didn't party hard. Said he'd be thinking of us when Harry sang for the seventh-inning stretch."

Now I'm getting choked up. We're all trying to keep it together. It goes on like that a while—stifled sobs, shaky sighs. Then— "Fuck, yes!" Stu yells. "That's the answer. That's the fucking answer! We gotta party. We gotta party so hard!"

And that's what we're thinking when we walk into Comiskey. Stu buys a round of beers. We find our seats off first base and start drinking. There's nobody around us, so we can stretch out. The Sox are just coming to bat in the top of the first. They go down one-two-three. And our beer's gone. Fitz gets up as soon as the inning's over. "I got this round." He heads off for the beer stand.

So it's just Stu and I, sitting next to each other. He's staring out across the field, and he's shaking his head ever so slightly, mouth open—catching flies, as Dad says. Whatever's bothering him won't go away. "Hey! You know what?" It suddenly occurs to me. "You're going to lose your mind over the stereo I got for our dorm room."

Stu works up a slow dreamy grin. "Losing my mind… Can't wait."

What do you say to that? Thankfully, the inning starts. Our talk dumbs down to swearing, cheering, grunts, and groans. Fitz gets back with the beers just as George Brett flies out to end the inning. They last until a vendor comes around in the bottom of the fourth. I do my part and buy another round.

"Hey, whatever happened to that chick you were going with at the end of last year?" Fitz asks out of the blue.

"Tara."

"Yeah. Her."

It never occurred to me that he might ask. "You were right. I should've dropped her the minute we left Ann Arbor."

"Why?" It's Stu who presses me.

"She's not coming back to Michigan. And I didn't try very hard to change her mind. So you had it pegged, Fitz. I thought I loved her, but I never really did."

Fitz sprays out a little of his beer. "That's bullshit."

"So now it's bullshit that I *didn't* love her?" Here we are again; in the same argument we had last spring. Only Fitz has completely flipped on me. *Fucking Fitz.* "You're the one who was telling me it was bullshit that I *did* love her."

"I was just playing with you, man," Fitz says.

"You were dead-on. I don't know what love is—fucking, friendship, infatuation, who knows? It's all just an illusion we call love."

"Jesus, Om." Stu's disgusted with me.

"No…" Fitz won't let it go. "You loved her. I could tell."

"Awright, Fitz. You know me better than I do."

"You were so sure," Stu says.

"Like all the other girls I thought I loved."

"But isn't that what love is?" Fitz says. "Just believing it enough?"

Is this shit really coming out of his mouth? "It's more than that," is all I say. I don't want to go another round with Fitz on the meaning of love. Okay, so maybe belief is what starts it, but it has to stand the test of time. Besides— "It takes two people to believe."

"Damn, Om…" Fitz shakes his head. "You're the last person I thought would turn into a cynic."

"It's fucking disappointing, is what it is," Stu mumbles.

Thank God for Eric Soderholm. Not five seconds later, he smacks a double. Fitz slaps me on the back. I throw my arm around Stu. We roar in each other's faces. The beer guy comes around again. Stu stops him. I shake my cup. There's still a third left. Fitz's is half full.

"You guys are pussies." Stu orders another round. *Fine.* If it takes one too many beers to get Stu out of his funk, pass me the cup.

We mow down the Royals in the top of the inning, and suddenly it's the seventh-inning stretch. Harry Caray starts shouting over the loudspeaker. The scoreboard puts up a Soxogram: *LET'S JOIN HARRY IN SINGING TAKE ME OUT TO THE BALLGAME.* Harry's booth lights up behind home plate. There he is, big glasses, silver hair, orange polo, leaning out over the balcony. He starts swinging his hand and singing. And we sing with him. And you can tell we're all thinking about Eddie. Stu's grinning ear to ear, tears streaming down his face. Fitz's beer is swaying in front of us, as if we're on a boat in rough waters. I've got my arms around the two of them, like they're what's keeping me from keeling over into the depths.

And now I'm good and drunk. We all are. The rest of the game goes by in a blur. I doze off. Fitz shakes me awake. And we've won. People are filing out all around us. "Where's Stu?" Fitz asks.

"I dunno."

"Shit, Om. He was right next to you."

"Yeah, and I was sleeping. Where the hell were you?"

"Maybe he snuck off to the bathroom." We go to the men's room near our section, check the troughs, call for Stu by the stalls. He isn't there. Now Fitz is worried. "I'm telling you," he says, as we're heading back to our seats in case he came back, "something's off. He's been weird from the second I picked him up. I asked how things were going with his job. Just harmless chit-chat. And you know what he said? He said, *what does it matter anymore?* All mopey and shit."

Stu seemed off to me, too, but Fitz's pointing it out gets me defending him. "Sounds like Stu. Probably just too much beer." Come to think of it, though, that was before he started drinking.

"I asked when he's going back to school. Know what he said?"

"What?"

"Maybe never."

"*Never?* Shit, I'm supposed to room with the guy."

We can see our seats now—no Stu. "Sounds to me like you need to have a talk with him."

We head back up the steps. "When are *you* going back to Ann Arbor?" I ask Fitz. If I could get into the dorm, I'd leave tomorrow.

"As early as I can. Maybe next week. The way things are with Eddie, we may need to find a new roommate."

There's barely anyone in the concourse now. Nothing to do but head to the car and hope he's there. I think about how edgy Stu was on the drive over, and I'm about to bring that up. But then I see him at the car. He's leaning against the driver's door, forehead against the glass, like he's pleading with someone to roll down the window.

"Stu!" Fitz calls out. He jerks upright. "What the hell?! Why didn't you tell us you were leaving?"

"I didn't wanna wake you."

"Where'd you get the beer?" Stu has an Old Style in his hand.

"The guys next to us had a few extra."

I see two crushed cans at his feet. Did Stu down those too?

There's hardly any traffic on the highway. Nobody says a word for a long time. Someone should say something… I lean my head up between Fitz and Stu. "Great fucking game. You ain't lived until you've sung with Harry."

"If Eddie coulda seen us," Stu says. "If he jus' coulda seen us."

We pull onto the Division exit. Stu breaks out into song. *"Tay me owtooda bawgay!"* It's either a terrible impression of Harry singing, or Stu really did finish off those three cans of Old Style.

We're driving back through Cabrini Green. It's dark and desolate. Stu rolls down his window and starts shouting out the song.

"Shut that damn thing!" Fitz yells. "What's wrong with you?"

Stu sticks his head out the window. *"I don' carefy never get back!* I don' care! I DON' CARE!" I reach up, grab him by the neck of his shirt, and try to pull him back in. He shrugs me off. "I'm not afraid to die!" he screams. "I'm not afraid! Eddie'll be there!"

We come to a stoplight. Now Fitz is trying to pull Stu back into the car. There's a huddle of men outside a liquor store. "Sox win!" Stu channels Harry. "Sox win! Eddie wins! ED-DIE, ED-DIE!"

"Fuck Eddie!" Somebody shouts. A beer bottle shatters across Fitz's Newport. He runs the stoplight.

"FUCK YOU!" Stu bawls.

They start running after us. Fitz is hemmed in by a car putzing along in front of him. I see the sign for Cleveland. I know that street. It's near Susie's place. "Turn left!" I tell Fitz. "Turn left!"

He wrenches the car off Division and speeds up the narrow lane. But there's a stop sign almost right away. He has to slam on the brakes. "Which way?" Fitz shouts over Stu.

He's still got his head out the window, and he's yelling back at the trouble we just escaped. "Fuck Eddie?! Fuck YOU!"

"Stu! Shut the hell up and get inside!" Now I'm hollering too.

"I'm going left," Fitz says.

"That's right." I can see that the other way loops back to Division.

Problem is, the way we're going suddenly hooks into the heart of Cabrini Green. "Where the hell are we, Om?"

It's Clybourn. It'll run into North Avenue. "Just keep going."

Stu's getting sick out the window now. *Great.* "Fuck!" Fitz barks.

"You'll be fine once you hit North Avenue," I tell him, but I'm not 100% sure on that. Everything seems turned around.

"But we're going away from Bud's," Fitz says.

Stu finally settles back in his seat. He's moaning, and I can smell the sharp tang of puke. "Just let me off here. I can walk home."

"From here? No way, man. You'll get jumped for sure."

"No, I've been here before," I lie. "That's Larrabee."

Stu goes from moaning to crying. "It's not right," he sobs out. "None of this is right!"

Fitz screeches to a stop. I glance behind us. All I can see out the rear window is the red glow of our brake lights. I open the door. It's dead quiet outside. I'll take my chances.

Before I get out, I tell Fitz, "Just stay on this road. North is two or three more blocks. Then go left."

"You sure?" Stu asks me, his bravado deflating.

"Owen knows this town," Fitz reassures him. I shut the door, and they drive off. I look around to get my bearings. This is nowhere I've ever been. There's nothing but brokenness around me—empty lots, crumbling buildings, dark voids nearby and darker distances. First chance I can, I turn to the lake. It's Blackhawk Street. Never heard of it. Still, it's what I have to do.

I wish *I* were a Blackhawk, gliding across the night, unseen and unreachable. I'll have to tell Susie about that one. That one, she can use. Instead, I'm the opposite. With the blue t-shirt and white shorts Terry bought, anyone on the street could see me. And with the rundown houses looming right off the sidewalks, they could reach me in seconds. I start to whistle. I'm not aware that it's "Take Me Out to the Ballgame" until I'm almost done with the song. Then I start singing it, low and slow, but strong, gazing straight ahead.

Harry would be an owl. With those big black glasses and that silver hair, he even looks like one. But he's not scowling at the world, like Jill's owl was. He's gazing at it wide-eyed, unflinching. *We are here together*, Harry's owl says, *and we don't need to be afraid.*

## Because the Night
*Because the night belongs to lovers. Because the night belongs to us.*
*- Patti Smith*


Susie and I worked Friday lunch to get out by six. She doesn't go on at Los Toros until nine, but she wants me to come to the Pie and give her advice on what she should wear. Her first outfit's this jazzy sundress with purple sequins and barely visible shoulder straps. It's nice. I wish the guys at work who say Susie's shlumpy could see her now. In her baggy white button-down and Bud's apron, you can't tell where the curves are. But in this dress… Wow. She's thinner at the waist than I knew, and that makes her top and bottom look bigger. Stunning; that's what she is. Nobody's going to listen to a word she says on stage.

"Too much?"

"Well… it isn't Saran Wrap."

Susie stares me down. "Stop gawking. You know what I look like."

"It was dark."

"Well, you shouldn't be doing it anyway."

"Hey, if I can't help it, how do you think the audience'll react? You'll have trouble talking over the catcalls."

"Yeah…"

"And if you're wearing that, the whole 'Hot Blooded' bit comes off a little disingenuous."

"So what you're saying is, men are pigs, so I can't look good."

"You can look good. Just not… distracting."

"Alright. Let me show you something else." She leaves and comes back wearing a white short-sleeve button-down, tucked into Calvin Klein jeans. The top two buttons of the shirt are open. "Better?"

It's more modest, but the open collar is still hard to ignore, and the jeans are skin-tight. I don't want to go another round, though, on the freedom of women versus the nature of men. "Better."

"You think I should button it up one?"

"Probably. If you want to be heard. But you still look great."

Susie snickers. "I'm learning something about you, Owen." I'm sure she thinks I'm like every other guy. But I just want her to do well.

I go back to my apartment for a quick nap. Nick's coming over at eight so we're sure to get a seat before the show. When I answer his knock, Garrett's with him. Susie didn't want anyone else from Bud's coming. Nick must sense my uneasiness; he comes right out with an explanation. "Garrett heard Susie and I talking about it and asked if he could come." I wonder if Garrett said anything to anyone else.

Los Toros is an out-of-the-way bar in the basement of an old building near Lincoln Park. The room's a big triangle like Susie's place, with the stage at the point, clamshell booths angling away on both sides, and a bunch of two-tops funneling in from the long bar in the back. That's where you come in. There are two entry doors back there, one from either street. The place is about half full, but the low ceiling makes it seem more crowded and noisier. We pull a couple tables together halfway to the stage and off to one side. The waitress is right there to take our orders. It's the kind of place to have cock-tails. I get a Manhattan, Garrett has an Old Fashioned, and Nick goes with the classic martini.

There's no sign of Susie. The pianist's doing a sound check on stage, and the drummer's tapping at his kit. It takes a while to get our drinks, so we order a second round as soon as the waitress brings our first. The musicians leave, we drink and talk for about 10 minutes, then this guy in a suit starts *one-twoing* into the mic. "Welcome, everyone, to Los Toros. We have a special treat tonight. Susie Starling is going to kick things off. She's an up-and-coming comedian, and this is her first time at Los Toros. So let's give her a warm welcome!"

There's a smattering of applause. Suddenly, I'm nervous for Susie. The clapping grows, and a chorus of whistling rises from the back of the bar. Susie's striding down the long run of booths behind me. Damned if she isn't wearing that sequin dress. She gives me a quick smile, then sashays past in a way I've never seen her walk before. It's all a come-on. When she gets to the stage, she takes a long step up, her dress parting at the side, hip showing. She pauses, looks over her shoulder, and lets the audience take her in. Then she bounces up to the microphone. More whistling. Howling. Catcalls. Just like I predicted. Are there *any* women in here? I look around the room—

Then I see her. Over my shoulder, two booths from the stage. Denise. The receptionist where Dad works. She's with someone, but I can't see around the shell of the booth. I know who it is, though, by the way her eyes lock onto mine. A hand comes out from behind the shell and grabs a glass. Now I see the back of his head as he leans in close to Denise.

*Dad.*

The crowd's finally obeying Susie's gestures to tamp down the howling. "You love me now. But wait until I'm done."

Denise comes walking my way. "We're going to leave," she whispers, slowing down as she squeezes between my chair and the table behind me. "If you're over by the far door, he won't see you when we go." I wait until she disappears into the back restroom. Susie's doing a mini-version of her city/country bit, complaining that she doesn't fit either place—too naïve for the city, too smartass for the country. I get up just as she's moving into her "Hot Blooded" routine. "The truth is, America's a tough place for any woman to be," I hear her say as I retreat to the back of the bar.

"Have you heard of these gentlemen?" Susie holds up the Foreigner album I got her. "They have the number one song in the country right now. It's called 'Hot Blooded.' Here's how it goes." She goes into her bit, wondering why any woman would get turned on by someone with a 103-degree temperature, why any man would think that's a good pick-up line. The crowd's laughing.

Denise hurries back to her seat. I can see Dad now, his profile shining in the stage light. He's nodding as Denise talks to him. When Susie starts going on about how the guy in the song is totally creeping on an underage girl, Dad and Denise start walking out.

"This is the top song in the country, people. Men actually fantasize about this happening." There's just the slightest edge of anger in her voice. "This is today's version of *I Wanna Hold Your Hand*. I'm sick as a dog. You're underage. How about a little statutory rape?"

The crowd laughs. Susie gazes into the lights, hand above her eyes. She points at Dad and Denise, skulking away. "Oops. Hit too close to home." The room erupts with laughter. Dad keeps walking. He has no idea he's being made fun of. Denise looks mortified. I feel bad for her.

I wait until Susie starts setting up her city critter joke before heading back to my seat. I'm halfway there when Terry and Jill come walking in the door Dad and Denise just exited. I wheel around and head back to the far end of the bar. Did they see me? I have no idea. Why am I hiding anyway? I was surprised. That's all.

Susie's killing it. When she points out the rat's powers of repulsiveness, a knowing murmur ripples through the crowd. "And a special bonus—I can have a garbage diet. Because… well… it's all garbage!" The room's howling again. Terry's clapping and beaming. Jill's scanning the tables. She knows we're here somewhere. Susie does the squirrel bit, and it works too. "Come on! What woman wouldn't want the powers of invisibility in this city?" she says to the kind of humming ascent you'd hear from a churchful of converts.

Jill and Terry are sitting down now with Nick and Garrett. I start heading back to my seat. I know Susie's routine. She's almost done. There's the monkey bit, a quick thank-you, and it's over.

"You know what's better than the power to go unseen, though? The power to see through others. I went out on my deck the other day—"

*Oh, fuck.* I turn around.

"—and there on the rail was a great horned owl." The owl story. With Jill sitting right there, knowing where it came from, wondering how much I told Susie. "You know the kind, right? Huge yellow eyes, steady scowl. Well, he stared at me. I stared at him. And we had ourselves a good two-minute standoff.

"Then, the strangest thing happened," Susie goes on. "I suddenly felt like that damned bird was peering into the depths of my soul, that it knew exactly what I was thinking. That's the kind of power I want: the power to see people as they truly are."

Susie stops. And she looks slowly around the room, staring at person after person. Just when the muttering starts, Susie shudders. "Nah. That's no fun. I'd rather be that chimp in the zoo flinging poop at everyone."

There's a second where it sounds like the silence got sucked out of the room. And then a roar. I can't explain how she's done it— timing, surprise, luck. But she's switched the crowd electric. She smiles humbly—there's the Susie I know—waves into the lights, says a quick thank you, and steps off the stage. Everyone stands and applauds, and they keeping standing the whole time as she strides away and disappears into the hallway behind the bar.

Susie wants to go to Burton Place to celebrate. Terry drove his Triumph, but it's a two-seater, so only one person can go with him. He insists on taking Susie. I've never seen Terry act any other way but dismissive with Susie. It's weird to watch him fawning over her now—and all because of a few good minutes on stage. As for Susie, she's drinking in the adoration. Laughing like she only laughs when we're alone, talking loudly, smiling at everyone. When she looks at me, though, she puts on this mask of coldness.

It's a 10-minute walk to Burton Place. I hang back and let Nick, Garrett, and Jill get a little way ahead. After a couple blocks, Jill drops back with me. "You told Susie about our owl."

"Jill—"

"And you knew she was going to use it. That's why you stayed away from the table at the bar."

"I just said I saw an owl. I didn't say I was with anyone."

"But I told Terry the same story."

"So I was over at your place. Why's that a problem?"

"I guess it isn't," she says. "He's had his flings too—with Astrid and Susie and who knows how many others."

"Wait. Susie?"

"They were a thing a couple winters back. You knew that."

"No. I didn't."

She stops walking. "Oh," is all she says for a moment. And then: "I get it. Owen's in love."

I had to think about who she meant for a second. "I'm worried for her. That's all."

Jill starts walking, faster than before. When I catch up, she says, "I can read Terry pretty well. If Susie told him where she got the owl story, and he's bothered by it, I'll know as soon as I see him."

"What are you two to each other?" I come right out with it.

"A mistake," Jill answers straight away. "A big mistake."

Terry and Susie already have a table at Burton Place. It's a round one in the far corner. The two of them are sitting next to each other against the back wall, leaning shoulders together and laughing, oblivious to everything around them. I sit next to Susie. Jill sits next to Terry. Nick and Garrett turn their chairs out to the crowd so they can watch the goings-on. Terry's already ordered a bottle of champagne, and the waitress has already opened it. Everyone gets a second drink anyway.

"Incredible! Just incredible!" Terry gushes as he pours the champagne. When we all have a glassful, he stands up. "How about this lady?" Nick and Garrett can't hear him. They're still turned to the crowd. And the jukebox's right next to us, blaring out that Patti Smith song, "Because the Night." Terry puts his hands on the table, leans in, and repeats himself. Louder. "Who knew we had a star in our midst?" He holds up his glass. "To Susie, and the beginning of something big."

We all drink. Susie starts holding court then. She tells us the owner of Los Toros wants her for the next three Fridays. She says someone from Second City invited her to audition. She tells us how strange it was being on stage and having everyone look at you. When she starts telling us about how different it is to tell jokes to the mirror than actual people, Jill quietly excuses herself. I watch her go.

Susie stops talking abruptly. I turn to her. She's looking at me. "Anyway. It was just five good minutes."

"Five *great* minutes," Terry chirps.

Our drinks come. Everyone gets busy drinking. Jill comes back but doesn't sit. She leans over and whispers in Terry's ear.

"No! Come on, stay!"

"I'm just not feeling great."

"Look! Here's your drink. Let's just have this, and we'll go."

"That's okay," Jill says. "Stay. Have fun. I'll get a cab." She gives the table a wave and leaves. Terry seems fine with it for a second. But then he gets up and hurries after Jill.

Susie turns to me. "So what happened to the mystery man?"

I don't know what she's talking about. "What mystery man?"

"I get up on stage, start my bit, then you head for the exits."

"It had nothing to do with you."

"I knew you'd be pissed about the dress, but you could've just sat through the act and at least pretended to support me."

"I do support you. You were great. Really."

"So, you loved it, but you just couldn't bear to watch it. Okay."

"That's not it."

"You." Her voice goes soft. "Of all people."

"All right." I couldn't take it anymore. "You wanna know why I got up and left? You know that couple you pointed out leaving?

"Yeah—"

"That was my dad. And it *wasn't* my mom."

"Oh." Susie rocks back. "*Fuck.*"

"She came over as soon as she saw me and said if I hid at the bar, she'd hustle him out before we had a scene."

"So you know her?"

"She's the receptionist where my dad works."

"Damn. I'm sorry, Owen. Bad timing."

"Great timing. They got up at the perfect time for 'Hot Blooded.'"

Susie laughs. It's a relief to hear her laugh. I wish I didn't have to stop her. "So you decided to use the owl."

Susie wags her finger. "See? I knew you wouldn't like that."

"It's done." I wave her off. "And I'm glad it worked. It's just—I don't want people knowing the story came from me."

"Why not?"

May as well just come out with it. "Because Jill told Terry she saw an owl on her balcony." Susie isn't getting it. "So if you told him it was me who saw the owl… he'll know we were together."

Susie thinks about it. "I might've said I got the idea from you, but I'm sure it slid right by. He was talking so much he barely heard me."

We go silent and drink our drinks. Jill and Terry are still up by the front door, standing close together, laughing.

"So you and Jill," Susie says beside me.

I was waiting for her to circle back to that. "And you and Terry."

We go on drinking and watching them across the bar. Then, at the same time, we look at each other. "For a few months," she says, "when I first moved to the city. I wish it never happened."

It would be easy for me to say that I didn't either, but it wasn't true. "I don't know how I feel about Jill."

She leaves the bar. Terry comes bustling back to us. He slides into his seat beside Susie and downs his whiskey in one big gulp. "I'm going to drive Jill home." He leans in close to Susie, says something, waves goodbye to everyone, and rushes away.

"What was that all about?" I ask Susie.

"He wants to go out tomorrow."

"Just the two of you?"

"I don't know. He said we didn't celebrate enough."

"What did you say?"

"I said okay."

I settle back, chewing that over, trying to make sense of it. I can't for the life of me figure out what it means. Between Susie blowing hot and cold over Terry, Jill and this owl thing, and my hot dog worries, I don't know how I should feel.

Right now, though, it isn't good.

## Bad Moon Rising

*Don't go around tonight. Well, it's bound to take your life.*
*- Creedence Clearwater Revival*

First thing every morning, I do the Bullworker. There's a mirror in the Fun Room. I taped the poster of exercises to it. And I go through all of them, no matter how hungover I am. It doesn't take long. Each exercise is 15 seconds. You squeeze the handles of the metal bars that slot together and hold. It's isometrics—pitting your strength against yourself, forcing it on your weakness. Over time, you get stronger. You can take more pressure. There's a gauge on one bar called the Powermeter. The first time I did the Bullworker, I couldn't get the Powermeter over the 100 mark. Now, I get to 150 on most exercises—with no sign of strain. My arms don't shake, my face doesn't contort. You can't even tell I'm struggling.

This morning, just as I'm finishing the last exercise, I hear scraping at my front door. I go and open it. No one's there. But now I see leaves, tumbling off the landing above. I go up my steps—and there's Bud. He's got a tiny rake, tinier because he's so big. He stops and looks at me. "Shit. I'm sorry. Did I wake you?"

"No, I was up."

"These damn things." He swings the rake across the concrete, whiffing on all but a handful of leaves. They float into my sunken entryway. "Here it is, August, and they're already coming down."

I remember the leaves whispering in the park. "Yeah…"

"I'm not ready for the fall."

I haven't seen Bud in weeks. Rumor is he's busy building a second Bud's on the river. He looks tired. What if he found out what was happening in his bar? What would he do? "I'm not ready either."

"How's everything been working out for you?" He perches his hands on top of the rake. It looks like a flimsy cane holding him up, bearing his weight. "I've been meaning to check in."

"It's great," I tell Bud, holding my smile like I do with the Bullworker. "I'm really grateful for all you've done."

"Bah!" He waves me off. "I haven't heard from your dad in a while. How's he doing?"

I think about Dad rushing out of Los Toros, clutching Denise's hand. I think about him telling me Mom was coming home. "I don't know." Bud tilts his head to study me. I could've told him he was doing great. But I didn't even try to lie.

"Well…" Bud shrugs. "Knowing Mikey, he's doing his best."

I laugh. Not hard. Not long. Just enough to get Bud to smile.

When I had just a handful of fives to give out, I'd put them in my front pants pocket, walk to Bud's, and transfer them into my apron there. I can't do that with 15 lumpy singles. Instead, I place them in a lunch sack, then put that in my gym bag. When I get to Bud's, I'll put five singles in each of my three apron pockets, one pocket per customer. No worries about separating bills on the spot.

It's 11. I have four hours to kill. The phone rings. It's Jill. "Just so you know, Terry figured out we were together."

*Shit.* This is the last thing I need. "What did he say?"

"He doesn't care what we did. He's just disappointed I wouldn't be honest with him."

"Well, it's not like you lied. You just didn't tell him."

"It's all the same to Terry."

"But it's not like he's going to do anything about, right?"

"I don't know," she says. "He's not impulsive, but he isn't afraid to do what thinks he needs to do."

I'm tempted to ask what that might be, but Jill doesn't know I've got more trouble with Terry than jealousy.

"When do you leave for school?" she asks then.

"A week or so. Sometime before Labor Day."

"Maybe you wanna leave now. You wouldn't be the first Bud's employee to just stop showing up."

*Holy shit.* "So you're telling me this could get bad."

"Like I say, I don't know. Just be careful. With everything."

"I will." If Jill knew about the drugs, she'd know I have to go through with tonight.

"If you need anything, just gimme a ring. I'll be here."

"Awright." Calling Jill would be a bad idea. "I gotta go."

"Wait. You don't even have my number."

"Oh. Right." There's a pen by the phone, but I can't find anything to write on. I take out my wallet; a dollar bill will do. Then I see that folded bar coaster. Jill tells me her number. I write it under the one Tara left me, beneath the ragged fold. I can't imagine why I'd call either number. Still, there's a comfort in having them. I write down Susie's number, too, above Tara's. I know it by heart. But one day, I might not. "Okay. See you soon."

"I guess I wasn't clear. I'm not coming in tonight."

"At all?" I don't remember a Saturday that Jill didn't work.

"No. I need a break. But I'm here all night."

She couldn't have picked a better shift to skip. It makes me wonder. Does she know more than she's letting on?

After I hang up, I make a PB and J sandwich. I'm running out of jam. Two more sandwiches and that's it. There's half a joint in the nightstand. If I smoke it now, I'll probably be fine by three. *Probably...* I don't smoke it. Tara's poetry anthology is in the same drawer. I stop on the first short poem I find: "Wants" by Philip Larkin. Two lines in, I'm lost. If I thought about it, I could figure it out. But I need to focus on what matters. The only line that sticks with me is the last one: *Beneath it all, desire of oblivion runs.* I can't sit here with that cluttering my head. I need to walk.

It's hot already. My only clean shirt is a red Izod, the kind of shirt Terry says brands you as Joe College. *Fuck it.* I'd give anything to be that person now. The shirt smells like cigarettes, but there aren't any stains on it. I've got one pair of shorts I haven't worn yet, my cut-offs. Funny. Last summer, I wore them almost every day. What would Terry call me with these on? *High School Harry.* They're so short, the front pockets poke out of the frayed bottom. If I sit down, you can see my underwear. Oh, well. I grab my gym bag and leave.

When I get on the street, I head for the park. If I go toward Division, I'll run out of things to do and get sucked into the Bud's vortex earlier than I want. It's been a while since I went to the zoo. Everyone knows about the shit-pitching chimps. But I've never actually seen them throwing crap at each other. Maybe they'll do it today. I could use a laugh.

In the Primate House, there are gorillas and chimpanzees. I see the gorillas first. A handful of little ones are running and swinging around in a big enclosure of ropes and logs and nets and platforms. It's like a grade school playground. The youngsters wrestle with each other, bare their teeth, and shriek while two bigger gorillas sit off to the side, watching the roughhousing.

"Those are the mothers," says a boy next to me with a Cubs hat, thick glasses, and a little notebook. "They try to keep everything calm around the silverback." He points to the huge gorilla sitting over at the far end. "He gets pretty mad at the juveniles."

As if on cue, one of the youngsters sneaks up beside the huge male and pokes him in the butt. The silverback lashes out, grabs the little gorilla by the arm, and hurls him against a log. Then he lifts his chin, looks up at the ceiling windows, closes his eyes, and holds still that way, like he's meditating. Peace after violence. Calm after chaos. The boy in the Cubs hat writes in his notebook.

A line of children presses against the window of the chimpanzee exhibit. I look over their heads as I pass. A trio of chimps is playing in the high netting. They're racing around, slapping, screaming, laughing with their inside-out lips. The kids laugh along, like they're watching the Three Stooges. I'm sure if I wait long enough, shit'll start flying. I keep going, though, out of the Primate House and into the blinding sunlight.

It's 12:30. I'm not hungry, but I know the closer I get to going to Bud's, the less I'll want to eat. I go to a food stand and get a cheeseburger, fries, and a Coke. I sit down at a picnic table. It feels good to get a break from carrying my bag. I've got a lot in it today—my work clothes and a change for after work plus a pair of shoes, a coat, a bunch of toiletries, and the bag of spiked singles. It isn't heavy, not even 10 pounds. But it's starting to feel heavier.

A few tables over, a young couple tries to pacify two kids. The mom rocks a baby in her stroller, while the dad waves tufts of cotton candy at a little girl spinning herself dizzy out of his reach. By the time I'm done eating, the girl's holding the cotton candy, brazenly eyeing me as she loads up on sugar. It's unsettling to be stared down by someone so young. I get up, toss out my garbage, and head for Oak Street Beach. I'll sit on one of those benches and spend my last hour before work being the one doing the watching.

"Excuse me!" The young dad is running my way. He has my gym bag. "You left this."

A shock of panic shudders through me. "Oh, man. I can't believe I did that. Thanks a lot."

"Don't thank me. Thank my four-year-old." I'm a good 20 yards away, but I can see the little girl staring at me, pouting now, her cotton candy gone. I wave. She doesn't wave back. I thank the man again and hurry away. The whole thing has me rattled. If that girl hadn't pointed out my bag to her dad, and I kept on walking, how long would it have been before it got taken? All the way across the park, I mull the prospects of losing the cocaine. There's no way that wouldn't have ended in disaster. I go down the stairs to the tunnel that runs under Lake Shore Drive. Cars rumble and squawk above me, monstrous birds in flight. If I lost this bag, I'd run. I'd hitch-hike my way out of the city, as far away as I could get.

People-watching at the beach doesn't help. There are still the same amusements and oddities. But they seem pointless against the magnitude of what I almost did and what I still have to do. The first time I came here, I was enthralled by the place, fascinated and ter-rified at the same time. Now, everything just seems sad. Those dark city creatures I imagined crawling out of Lake Michigan hold no power or mystery for me anymore. I've fallen in with real people who could be more dangerous.

It's quarter to two. How long do I have to sit on this bench and wait? I have to get there at three to start the dogs boiling. But I should get my apron in order with the singles before that. So, 2:30. And say it takes 20 minutes to walk from here to Bud's. Then 2:10. That's when I can go. That's when everything begins.

When I get to Bud's, I open the door to Moose. "You're early." He doesn't move, as if I'm not allowed in yet.

I'm so tired of this guy's bullshit. "Yep." I brush past him.

Kretch is in front of the door to the basement, gabbing with a regular about something. How does Kretch, of all people, not know what's going on in this bar—right under his nose? He glances at me and does a double take. "You need something?"

What's he so alarmed for? "I'm just trying to get downstairs."

"Ah." Kretch moves out of my way. "No rest for the hot dog man."

"Never." I smile until the door shuts. Then I bound down the stairs. I want things to happen fast now. I want to get my apron ready. I want to get the dogs boiling. I want my shift to start. I want to get rid of these singles. Then… then maybe I *do* leave, like Jill suggested. I split up the packs in the bathroom and put them in my apron pockets. I put my apron back in my locker. I go upstairs and start the pot boiling. I stock up the hot dog box. I go back down-stairs to get dressed for my shift. It's 20 to four. I lie down on the bench in front of my locker and start deep-breathing to calm my nerves. One thing after another; that's what this is all about. Do this, then that, then the next thing, and the next, until it's over.

The noise from the bar intrudes. Footsteps come down the stairs. I sit up. It's Terry. "There you are. All set?"

"Yep."

"Good. Great." He ambles over and stops beside me, really close. "And about this stuff with Jill…" Terry pauses to watch how I react. "It's okay with me."

"Terry, I didn't know—"

"It's fine." He sighs. "I guess we're all in this together now."

"All of us?"

"She knows what I'm doing. Hell, she got me into it."

"What do you mean?"

"Ah, that's a long story. Let's just focus on tonight." He looks at me like I'm the one who brought up Jill.

"Right…"

"Good." He nods with a sort of grudging approval, as if I've barely passed some crucial test. "In a few hours, this'll all be over."

Terry heads for the stairs. I get an idea: *what if I played dumb about Susie?* "Then after, let's go out and celebrate."

He stops, but he doesn't turn to me. "Yeah. Sure."

"Or maybe you've got something else to do."

"I'll let you know," he says, then he hurries back upstairs. Why wouldn't he just tell me about Susie? Why's that a big deal? And if he wanted me to stay focused on tonight, why would he announce that he knew about Jill and me? Why would he say that she's in-volved? That she's somehow to blame for him being in it? He thinks I'll lose my nerve and tell someone what's going on. That's what it is. He doesn't trust me to keep my mouth shut, and he's worried I'll give him up. That's why he brought Jill into it. He thinks I'll stay quiet to protect her, and I might not do the same for him. He's right, damnit. He's right. And there's no time now to think about it. That's why he waited so long to tell me. So I couldn't stop and think of a way out. Now, it's all just go and do. Go steam the buns. Go put the dogs in the box. Go strap the box on your shoulder. Go wade into the crowd. Go…

It isn't even five minutes, and the first customer hits me up back where Jill and I talk. It's that same guy who was so nervous the first time. Now, everything's clockwork: *Do you have olives? No. I'll take double mustard.* I make the dog. He gives me a twenty. I reach into my left apron pocket and give him the five singles. He walks away.

Hadley's here, at the round top in the front of the side room. When I spot him, he holds his eyes on me for just an instant. If I were keeping watch on the operation, that's where I'd sit too. He can see the whole side room and most of the main bar, except for up by the front window. Plus, he's out of Kretch's view. Meanwhile, I'm rarely out of his sight.

It's another half hour before I see the woman with the beehive hairdo and cat glasses. She's sitting alone by the jukebox. I'm not crazy about where she is. Kretch isn't even 20 feet away. When he looks across the bar from the front door, she's almost the first person he sees. I slow down as I come near. We make eye contact. "I'll have a hot dog," she says. Maybe she's not so crazy to sit here after all. The way she's angled, I have my back to Kretch. He can't see anything I'm doing. We get through the exchange, I turn—and I nearly bang the hot dog box into some guy at the jukebox. That gives me an idea. He leaves, and a Creedence Clearwater Revival tune starts up—bad moons and trouble and nasty weather. I press the code for "Paint it Black." When I turn away, Kretch is looking at me, thumb up, eyebrows raised. I return the thumbs-up. He breaks out a beaming smile.

I go into the side room—and there's the Professor, sitting with Hadley. This isn't in the plan. I've never seen these two together. Ever. I swing by them with my head down.

"Hey-hey-hey!" The Professor grabs my arm. "Can I get a hot dog?"

It takes a second to jump into my act. "Sure," I chirp, snaring a dog in my tongs. "You want one?" I ask Hadley, keeping up appearances. He shakes his head with a stony scowl.

"Say, you got any olives with that?"

What did my face do? I don't know, but it feels like everything inside me is draining out. "Olives? No…"

"Aw, come on. Surely somebody's asked you that before."

I make a show of trying to think about it. "I don't *think* so."

He turns to Hadley. "I wonder what Kretch would say about all this. Or Bud."

"You want mustard, ketchup, or both?" I jump in.

"Forget it," he says, eyes still on Hadley.

I walk into the kitchen and go back to the boiling pot, where I can hide. What's the next thing now? If someone asks for olives around the Professor, I can't hand them the singles. But what if he's in the other room? Should I go through with it then? If I don't get rid of this coke, and the Professor makes a scene with Kretch, I'm screwed. Then again, if I try to pass it now, and he catches me in the act, that's even worse.

"Hey Owen." I practically leap out of my skin. Terry's right behind me. "Someone's asking for a dog. One of our regulars."

"Did you see the Professor with Hadley?"

"Yeah. So?"

"He asked me for olives."

Terry's stunned. "What did you do?"

"I played dumb."

"And Hadley was sitting right there?"

"He was looking at Hadley the whole time."

Terry takes a while to think it over. "Take care of your last customer, and we're done."

I follow him out of the kitchen, expecting the guy to be in the bar area, but damned if he isn't already in the side room, standing just a feet away from the Professor. Terry speeds up ahead of me, like he's trying to outrun the problem. The guy holds up his hand to stop me. I act like I don't see him and hurry past. What the hell am I going to do? I go back to the alley door. I need to think things through. What I'd *like* to do is take off this box, slip out of the bar, and start running. Susie sees me while she's waiting for drinks and comes over. "Some guy in the side room was asking for a hot dog."

"Okay."

"Are you mad at me or something?"

"No."

"Is something wrong?"

Great. Now this. "Terry knows about Jill and me."

Susie's mouth falls open. *Shit.* All I wanted to do was change the subject. "Is he mad? What did you say?"

"I'll tell you later."

"I mean, should I still go out with him?"

"You can't cancel now."

"So, he isn't mad at me?" Susie wants to know.

"Why would he be mad at you?"

"I was the one who told the owl joke."

For the first time all shift, I laugh. "You didn't know," I say. "Put it this way: he'll be a lot madder if you stand him up."

"Yeah." She doesn't look convinced. "No, I'm sure you're right." She gives me a quick smile and heads back for her drinks.

I still don't know what to do. If I go back into the side room, that guy's going to be on me, and I'll be standing 10 feet away from the Professor. If I stay here, everyone—Hadley, Terry, Moose, the guy in the side room—they'll all start getting anxious.

"Paint it Black" is finally playing. Kretch is bobbing his head to the beat like he's about to break into Mick's rooster strut. A couple people want hot dogs by the front window. I turn to leave—and there's the Professor, slinking by me to get to his seat. "Sure you don't want one?" I ask innocently.

He barely glances at me. "No."

Now's my chance to finish this. I hurry into the side room. Hadley gets up and crosses right in front of me. "Let's talk," he whispers in passing. I watch him turn for the back of the main room.

"Hey!" My last customer is poking his head around the end of a booth. He throws up his hands at me, like *what's the hold-up?* I shake my head and walk away.

In the bathroom, I have to wait for a guy who's at the urinal next to Hadley. It's just the three of us, but it feels crowded. It doesn't help that I have to take off my box and set it on the floor. "Even the hot dog man has to pee," the guys jokes, edging past me to the sink.

"You got it," I say, filing in beside Hadley.

The door slams. Hadley looks over his shoulder. He flushes the urinal. "Shut it down. No more handoffs. Terry'll tell you what to do." With that, he goes to the sink, washes his hands, runs his fingers through his hair, and leaves. It hits me then. Hadley's haircut is a lot like Terry's. Did he go to Wendy too? Who went to her first?

I try to pee, but I can't. Still, I wait there. I have no idea what I'll be dealing with when I walk out that door. It's all happening so fast. All of it; not just this damned hot dog business, not just the bullshit between Terry and Jill and me, not just Terry's sudden interest in Susie and maybe hers with him, but everything, the whole summer—the wreck Dad's become, Mom leaving, Neil lost, Eddie sick, Tara gone. What did I do to deserve all this?

I strap on the box, take a deep breath, open the door… and nobody's waiting for me. I walk the whole place, past the jukebox, through the crush of people at the bar, up near the front window, into the side room. Then I backtrack and stop again by the alley door. I look out across the bar. Hadley's gone. The Professor's gone. My last buyer's gone. There's nothing to do now but sell hot dogs, make money, and wait to be told what to do.

Terry comes up to me near the basement door. "You're cut." He leans in close and lowers his voice. "Leave the singles in your locker, and we'll pick them up. What's your combo?"

I whisper the numbers. "I'll leave them in my apron." He nods. It clears out around us. "What's going to happen?" I ask.

Terry just shakes his head. That could mean anything. *I don't know. Don't ask. Nothing good.* I can't read him.

Regardless, I'm happy to be done. I go back to the kitchen, clean everything up, and count my money. With all the shit going down, I still came away with $263.

"How much did you make?" Susie's looking at me from the window where you wait for the cooks to put up your food.

"Better than usual." I don't want to say the amount in front of the kitchen guys. If they knew how much I made for three measly hours of work, they'd lose their minds. I go out into the hallway where Susie's standing. "How are you doing?" I'm not talking about her tips—and she doesn't take it that way.

"I'm okay." She's worried. I can tell. Maybe she *should* just cancel on Terry. With everything going on, he'd probably be happy if she did. It's hard to tell. All I want to do is make Susie feel better.

"If you need me for anything, give me a call." I realize as I'm saying it that Jill said the same thing to me. "I'll be in all night."

Susie gives me a wooden smile and nods. I wait for her to say something. *Okay. Thanks. I will.* Anything. But she turns away and watches the cook put the finishing touches on her food.

"Okay. Well… later." No reaction. I walk away.

"Hey!" She practically shouts. I stop just outside the kitchen, customers within feet of me. "I'm taking the owl out of my bit."

"Oh?" I go back to her.

"Get this." She's all animated now. "I was thinking it through on the way over, and out of nowhere, a squirrel skitters in front of me. Sure enough, he scrambles behind a tree and disappears, just like in the bit. But then, instead of giving up, I *keep* following him. I'm thinking, how long will he do this? You know the answer?"

The story's coming at me too quick. The answer to what? "No."

"Not very long. Turns out, squirrels don't try all that hard!" She's as amazed as if she just learned quantum physics. "This one didn't even go once around the tree. Then he stopped. It wasn't that hard to see him. I just had to try a little."

The cook puts Susie's food on the shelf. "That's when I realized, he was counting on my not trying." Susie starts picking up her plates. "That's what he'd learned about people—we don't try very hard. Observation: that's his real superpower."

"But it didn't work with you." I don't know why I'm prolonging this. I just want to go downstairs, dress, and get out of here.

Susie has her plates loaded now, two in each hand. "I read somewhere that if you feed squirrels regularly, they'll leave nuts at your doorstep. Give you a little gift. That's another thing they've learned; we have a soft spot for kindness."

"Why don't you just stick with the owl story? Nobody cares where that came from anymore."

"I don't know," Susie says "There was something about that squirrel. And that's a superpower I could actually do—just pay attention to people." She edges by, eyeing me the whole way past, like she's practicing her superpower on me. I wait until she's serving her table, then I hurry behind her and down into the basement.

No one's in the locker room. I open my locker, take out my gym bag, and change out of my clothes. I check my apron. The remaining singles are still there in the right pocket. I hang the apron on a hook so the pocket's upright and the bills won't fall out. Then I shut the door, close the lock, spin its dial, and give it a good tug. I take my bag, bound up the steps, and edge around the crowd to the front door. Kretch isn't there. Moose is checking an ID. And Terry? It takes a second to find him. He's over in the corner, by the front window, leaning against the wall next to the last barstool.

That's where Kretch is too. Both of them have their hands up to their mouths, and they're leaning in close to each other. I don't know if they see me, but I nod, just in case. Kretch gives me a little salute, unsmiling. Terry raises his hand but doesn't wave it. They saw me alright.

Were they talking about me?

## Tired Eyes

*He tried to do his best, but he could not.*
*- Neil Young*

I get a tuna melt at Bill's Diner and take it back to the basement. It's about eight. The sun seems to have already set. I can't tell for sure with all the buildings. But the sky's glowing like a distant smoky fire. Who knows? Maybe a storm's rolling in just beyond the city. For the first time all summer, I wish I was in Canada, on the shore of Lake Huron, where you could look across that great flat expanse of water and know exactly what the sun was doing, and the kind of weather that would be coming in the night.

Now that I've told Susie she can call, I have to stick by the phone. Fine. It's a relief to have nothing to do but wait. I hear footsteps crossing the ceiling above me. And there's a fluorescent tube buzzing in the hallway. Funny how just a little bit of noise can set you on edge. I flip through my shoebox of cassettes until I find Neil Young's *Decade*. It's one of the tapes I used to listen to with Tara. It's a double album. I like the second tape better. I pop it into my recorder. Angry guitars. Tin soldiers. Nixon coming. Four dead in Ohio. This isn't what I need right now. The topic's rough enough, but the sound makes it so much worse. The recorder's chintzy speaker buzzes so loudly it seems like part of the song. Before the summer, this crappy recorder was just fine. But not after I heard those Maggies. Which reminds me: I've got to get them out of the living room before Mom gets home. And I have that lunch with Dad on Monday. Am I still doing that? I don't want to think about it now.

I remember the money in my pocket: the $263 I made selling hot dogs. I go to the side of the bed, kneel down, and pull out a yellow envelope where I'm stashing my money now. I haven't counted it in a long time. I separate the bills into piles—twenties, tens, fives, and ones. It takes a good five minutes to count out everything. I knew I'd be close to $4,000, but I never thought I'd be pushing five. Altogether, I have a four-inch stack of bills worth $4,827. In my wildest dreams, I never thought I'd make so much money this summer—and come away with a bitching stereo to boot.

I tuck the stack back into the envelope. Then I roll it up tightly. There's a rubber band in the nightstand drawer. I take it out and wrap it around the envelope. The half-smoked joint is still in the nightstand. If I smoke it now, it might take the edge off. Then again, it could muddle things. No. Not now. Not yet.

I stuff the packet of money through a tear in the liner of the gym bag. Now: what to do with the bag? There's no good place to hide this in my apartment. I take it out to the Fun Room. There's a round table cluttered with chandelier parts. It has a skirt over it. I put the bag under there. Why go through all this trouble? No one's coming down here to rob me. It's just nerves. All the tension of the day, that need to keep doing the next thing—even though there isn't anything left to do.

Terry isn't going to follow through with taking Susie out. I'd bet everything in that envelope. Whoever's behind this coke dealing, whether it stops at Hadley or goes higher, is going to want answers from Terry. They'll want to plan out where to go from here. And they won't want to wait, not with the Professor threatening to expose what he knows. They're going to want to get a handle on this right away. Terry can't blow that off to take Susie out. He's hinted more than once that these aren't the sort of people you fuck around with.

Sooner or later, Susie's going to call. But it won't be a call for help. She'll be calling to say Terry bailed on her. She'll be calling to get together. *That's* the next thing. I feel better for thinking it through. *Now you can smoke your joint.* I go to the nightstand, take out the half-joint, and light up. I breathe deep after every hit, until the roach is too small to worry about.

Neil's singing a sad song, "Star of Bethlehem." *All your dreams and your lovers won't protect you. They're only passing through you in the end.* I don't want to be the kind of lover who just passes through. That's what's happening, though. Maybe I just need to accept that...

The phone rings me out of a daze. I lurch down the hallway to the Fun Room. "Owen?" It's Susie.

"Yeah."

"You're sleeping."

"No. I'm here."

"I had to tell you something."

I hear laughing in the background and a piano. "Where are you?"

"Someplace called Lupos," she says. "It doesn't matter. I have to do this quick—"

"Why?"

"Terry thinks I'm just going to the bathroom."

The tension in her voice shakes me. "Okay. Tell me."

"I was leaving work, passing the guy's locker room, and I happened to glance in there. Moose was in your locker."

It takes a second to get how Susie might react to seeing something like that. And not much longer to come up with a lie. "Oh. Yeah. I found a diamond earring in the bar, put it in my apron, and forgot about it. The woman showed up, so they needed my combination."

"Shit."

"Don't worry about it. Moose got the earring out of my apron, and the lady was relieved. Everything's fine."

"I shouldn't have gotten in his face." That stops me cold. "Oh, well. Just one more reason for Moose to think I'm a bitch."

"So what did he say when you got after him?

"I gotta go—" Susie says. "Terry's coming."

"Wait! Does he know about your fight with Moose?"

Too late. She's gone. What if Terry *did* know? Susie mouthing off about something to do with our dealing wouldn't sit well. He wouldn't blow it off. The risks are high enough already. Whether he'd yell or threaten or smooth-talk his way out of it, he'd make clear to Susie why Moose getting into my locker wasn't her concern. My guess is he'd go the smooth-talk route. He'd come up with a lie. But it would be a different one than mine. Susie would know someone's lying. What would happen then?

Lupos. That's where she said they were. Where's Lupos? There's a Yellow Pages book on a table by the phone in the Fun Room. I look up the address. It's on Wells, the street where Second City is, and where Terry turned down a side road to get to those apartments backing up to that big graffiti wall. I call the number and ask the hostess for better directions. It's not that far away. Should I go there and make sure Susie's okay—take her away if it comes to that? Or should I stay by the phone? She wouldn't dream of trying to call again, at least not while they were there. Maybe later, though, somewhere else, she'd find a way to sneak off. If I'm going to go, it has to be now.

The music's still bleating out of my tinny recorder. *He tried to do his best, but he could not.* What a terrible thought. What a helpless feeling. *Please take my advice. Please take my advice. Open up the tired eyes.* They're open. I'm trying. And I still don't know what to do.

I hit the STOP button.

## We'll Meet Again

*We'll meet again, don't know where, don't know when.*
*- Vera Lynn*

It takes 10 minutes to get to Lupos. I'm glad I decided to come. It's a quiet Italian restaurant. The place is so small I can see the whole dining room just walking in. Terry and Susie aren't here. There's a stand-up bar off to the side, barely big enough for three empty stools. I go up to the bartender. He's busy making martinis.

"Good evening, sir." He looks up just long enough to come off as courteous, then focuses back on the drinks. "Have a seat, please. I'll be with you in a moment."

I'd rather just ask the guy about Terry and Susie. But with all his formality—he's got a white shirt and a bowtie on—acting anything but polite will slow me down. So I sit. And I swivel my chair enough to see out across the dining room. My first thought, honestly? This is the sort of place where Pacino whacked those guys in *The Godfather*. Would I think that if fear wasn't what brought me here? I don't know. It could be the weed too.

One thing that's different from the movie: there's a piano player off in the corner, an old black guy with a tight salt-and-pepper afro and a blood red sportscoat. He's playing and singing so lightly you have to strain to hear him over the hushed table conversations. *We'll meet again, don't know where, don't know when. But I know we'll meet again some sunny day.* I shudder. Even a song as soft and sweet as this seems ominous. I've got to get my mind right. Am I just being paranoid?

The song ends, and the bartender's in front of me now. "What can I get you, sir?" he asks, stiff but smooth.

"I'm just looking for someone. My sister. She's got short, blonde hair, big curl on one side. And she was with this guy. He's—"

The bartender cuts me off as politely as you can interrupt someone. "I'm sorry, sir. We can't give out information about our patrons."

I lean in and wave for him to huddle with me. He bends over just enough to appear reasonable. "My mother got in a car accident, and I need to get a hold of my sister. I know they came here for dinner. I just need to know when they left."

The bartender stares me down and, in the first sign of decorum slipping, let's out a long breath with the slightest rattle in it.

"For God's sake, Tod. Just tell him." It's the piano player. When did the walk over?

"But Frank said not to—"

"I'll take care of it." He turns to me. "What are you drinking?"

"Nothing."

"Well, I can see that. What are you *about* to drink?"

Is this the price for information? Fine. "I'll have Jack on the rocks."

"Make that two, Tod." He holds out his hand for me to shake. "Oscar Llewellyn."

"Owen Maloney."

Oscar lights up a cigarette. The drinks come. He raises his glass. I clink it with mine. "Your friends left ten minutes ago."

"The girl. Did she have sort of a Marilyn Monroe bob haircut?"

"Your sister?"

"Yeah. My sister."

He cracks a half-smile. He doesn't buy it for a second. "It was them."

"Was she…" I don't know how to put it delicately, "doing okay?"

"That's what I thought you should know." Oscar takes a draw on his cigarette and blows the smoke aside. "She was fairly drunk."

"Drunk?" That isn't like Susie.

"Not falling down. But tipsy. And too loud for a place like this."

"Did you hear what she said? Any idea where they were going?"

"All I heard her say what that she was sorry." Oscar swirls his glass. "She just kept saying that."

I down my drink. I don't need to hear anything else. "Well… thanks for helping me out."

"When they left, he was tugging her hand. She didn't want to go."

Even worse. I take out a ten and put it on the bar. I feel like I'm paying him now to *quit* talking, quit working me up. He picks up the ten and hands it back to me. "That's the one great perk of this gig. They let me get people drinks for free."

I put the ten back down on the bar. "Then that's for the music."

"You're not supposed to notice the music." He laughs. "It's just supposed to wash over you. That's what they told me. They said, *if people notice you playing, then you ain't playing right.*"

"Well, I noticed. And it made an impression." I get up and leave.

Where to now? If Susie had her way, she'd go to Old Town. From what Oscar said, though, she wasn't having her way. Still, it's a five-minute walk. I'd be kicking myself if she was there, and I didn't go a few extra blocks. I start heading to North Avenue. Then again, I told Susie I'd be by the phone. So every minute I'm not at home, there's that much more of a chance I'll miss a call. I come up on Burton Place, where we celebrated last night. Would he bring her back again? Hell, I'm right here. May as well check.

I'm in and out in a minute. They aren't there. I head off for Old Town. Then I stop myself. What's more important: taking a shot in the dark that Terry took her to her favorite place, or waiting by the phone in case she needs my help anywhere else? I cut down the alley beside Burton Place. It goes all the way to Dearborn. I'm back at the door of my apartment just over half an hour after I left.

The phone's ringing. I fumble for the key. I can't get the damn thing in the lock, what with the bad lighting. Another ring. I get in. I feel my way through the dark to the phone. I pick it up. Nothing but a dial tone. *Damn.* If I just would've come straight home from Lupos… I don't know that it was Susie. But who else would it be so late? Maybe she'll call back. Maybe she was calling from home to say everything was okay. Maybe *I* should call *her*. I try her number. No answer. Now I'm worried. And I know I won't stop worrying until I see Susie the next morning at Sunday brunch.

Usually, I turn the hallway light off when I go to bed. Tonight, I keep it on. And I push the waste basket against my door so it's wide open, and the light slants like a beacon across my bed. If another call comes, I want to be up and out to the phone as fast as possible.

I'm not going to be able to sleep. I know it. There's no point in trying. I lie down on top of the blanket and prop my head up on the three pillows. I don't even take off my shoes. I need to be ready…

I wake to noise. A thump. Now another. Panic seizes my chest. I stagger into the hall. My legs don't want to work. There it is again: that thump. It's out in the Fun Room. I rush down the lit hallway and into the dark. My eyes aren't ready. I can't see a thing. The sound comes again. It's at the door. A shadow's moving across the windowpanes. I trip on my way across the room and nearly fall. I open the door. Nobody's there.

I hear footsteps on the sidewalk above me. I bound up the stairs. Someone's running away. A hulking figure, a mane of wild hair in silhouette. "I see you, Moose!" My words chase him down the street and come echoing back. I shouldn't have said anything. Now Moose knows I saw him trying to break in. Did Terry put him up to it? I go back down my steps.

That's when I see Susie. She's slumped in the corner of my stairwell, and she isn't moving. The streetlight isn't illuminating much, but I can see that her hair's a tangled mess. Her white blouse is torn at the shoulder. And there's a cut on her arm that's bloody.

*Jesus.* My worst fear. I kneel beside her, push the hair out of her face. It's wet and puffy, like she's been crying. And there's a cut on her upper lip. Something's smeared around her mouth and nose too. Something that makes her look ghostly. *No way.* She'd never get this messed up by herself.

A light comes on above me. Bud's front door creaks open. "Hello?"

"Down here." Before Bud gets to us, I try to shake Susie awake. It doesn't work, but she leaks out a wisp of air.

"What the hell happened?" Bud's looming over me on the steps, hands on hips, the streetlight a blanket of bright needles outlining his massive black form.

"Somebody left her here." I didn't say it was Moose.

"Is that Susie?" He comes down to me. Bud takes Susie's jaw in his hand and gently tilts her face into the dim light.

"She wouldn't do this to herself," I say.

Bud wipes away the remnants of blood and cocaine from around her mouth. He puts his arm under her head. "Help me get her upstairs." We lift her as gently as we can. Bud's doing most of the work, cradling her while I keep her legs from hitting anything. After we get her through Bud's door, he guides me to a parlor off to the side, and we lay Susie down on a couch. Then he switches on a nearby lamp. That's when the horror of what happened hits me. Her face is pale and bloated. Even after Bud takes out his handkerchief and wipes away the smear of coke, her skin stays waxy. And now I see the full damage to her upper lip… the depth of the cut… the marring of those beautiful lips. Susie's blouse is stained brown under the neck—more a reckless pour than a careless spill—and she reeks of whiskey.

I want to cry, but I can't break down in front of Bud. He's trying to wake Susie. She rouses and moans but never regains consciousness. "Who would do this?" Bud's on the verge of crying himself.

"What's going on?" A woman is in the doorway, arms crossed over a thick robe, like it's a cold night. She must be Bud's wife. I've heard talk of her at the bar, but we've never met.

"Someone got hurt outside, honey." Bud looks over to her, starts to say more, then shakes his head and turns back to Susie. There aren't any words to describe how awful it is.

"Should I call nine-one-one?" she asks.

"Yeah… And could you get me a cold rag?"

She looks at me. "You must be Owen. I'm sorry we're meeting like this."

I can't think of anything to say to that. She turns and leaves. "Me too," I whisper, far too late. She reminds me of my mom. And for the first time all summer, I truly miss her.

"Who the hell?" Bud seethes again.

I break. "I think it was Moose." I'm not sure he hears me—and half-hope he doesn't.

"Moose?"

"I saw someone running away. I'm sure it was him."

"Why would he do something like *this*?"

I take a deep breath… Then I tell Bud everything.
*Everything.*

## Heroes
*We can beat them, just for one day. We can be heroes, just for one day.*
*- David Bowie*

The ambulance comes around four a.m. Kretch shows up minutes later. I tell him what I told Bud. About dealing coke. About using hot dog night as cover. About Hadley and Terry and Moose. How they got spooked and shut the operation down. How I left coke in my locker for Moose to pick up, and Susie caught him getting it. The whole time I talk, sitting now beside Bud on the couch where Susie had been, Kretch stands, arms folded, staring stone-faced at the floor.

"So would Moose pay her back like *this*?" Bud prompts his manager after I fall silent.

Kretch shakes his head. "It's more than that. If he just wanted to get back at her, he wouldn't dump her here."

"True."

"She was out with Terry tonight." I forgot to tell them that. "She was worried about it. I told her to call if she had any trouble."

"With Terry?" The notion seems preposterous to Bud.

"She called me from this restaurant. Lupos. That's when she told me about Moose. But then Terry saw her at the phone, and she hung up fast. So I went to the restaurant. It's not far."

"I know the place. Frank Fortuna owns it," Bud tells Kretch.

His eyes go wide, like *uh-oh, bad news*. "What happened?"

"They were gone. A guy there, the piano player, he said they had some sort of spat and left. That's when I got worried."

And now I start to cry. Because I was too late to Lupos. And because I was too late coming home to get her next call. And because I fell asleep and couldn't keep Susie from getting hurt.

"It's okay." Bud pats my knee. "We're going to take care of this. What do you think, Dan?"

I hadn't heard Kretch's first name since we were introduced. Arms still folded, jaw still clenched, he's nodding slowly, like it's all coming to him. "This is about shifting blame. Susie's got her head screwed on too tight to get this out of control. They get her drunk. Maybe spike her drink. Wait until she passes out. Then they make it look like she was snorting coke, drop her off outside Owen's door, and let the rest take care of itself."

Bud nods now. I'm the only one who doesn't get it. "The rest?"

"Something like this," Kretch explains, "people are going to wonder, why at your door? They're going to have suspicions, whether it's Bud or me or the police. And they're going to want answers."

"I told you what I did. I handed out the coke, but that's it. I swear."

"We believe you." Bud pats my knee again. That calms me a little, but I'm still confused. Why would Terry do this to me?

"I bet there's still coke in my apron," I realize suddenly.

"Yeah." Kretch has already concluded that himself. "This isn't just about blaming Susie."

"Damn." Bud shakes his head. "Never in a million years."

"Well—" Kretch starts to say.

"I know, I know. You told me."

"It was just a hunch. I didn't have anything solid. But when the Professor's au pair made that scene…"

"We should've stepped in then," Bud says. "*I* should've."

"No use beating yourself up now."

*Wait.* I'm trying to catch up. "You knew?"

Kretch and Bud look at each other. Finally, Kretch decides to answer. "We had our suspicions. We—"

"You didn't think I'd know what was going on in my *own bar*?!" Bud cuts him off with an anger I've never heard before. "That kid's like a son to me."

It takes a second to get who he's talking about: Terry, who started at Bud's in his teens like me and lived where I live now.

"I'm sorry," is all I can think to say.

"You got used." Kretch's voice is softer. "Happens all the time."

"Why don't you step outside a minute." Bud's anger has gone cold. I leave and go down into my stairwell. I sit facing the door to my apartment and the corner where Moose dumped Susie. Kretch was right. This was all Terry. When did he decide that I'd be the one to blame if things went south?

A phone's ringing. Faintly. I can't tell if it's mine or Bud's. If I open my door, I'll know. I get up. Bud's door opens above me.

"Owen?" It's Kretch.

"Down here." I meet him halfway. We sit on my steps. He lets out a big sigh and wipes his forehead. He's sweating. I can see the sheen on his face, even with the streetlight behind him. He looks almost as bad as Susie. But it's just the toll life has taken on him.

"Okay. Here's the deal. You're not coming in tomorrow. Or ever again. This is from Bud." He takes an envelope out of his back pocket. "It's a thousand dollars. First thing tomorrow, pack up and leave. You don't want to be around here when the shit goes down."

I take the envelope. "What kind of shit?"

"That's not your concern. Right now, though, you've got some desperate people who are about to be very unhappy."

"Kretch…" I want him to know how sorry I am. I want to explain how I got into this so deep. I want him to see I'm not as bad as all this looks. I can't bring myself to say any of that.

"You're a good kid." He slaps my back. "You'll learn from this." His words come off encouraging and demanding at the same time. *You better figure out who you are*, he seems to be saying. But I have no idea what sort of lesson I should draw from this. I can't think beyond what's right in front of me.

"What'll people think when I don't show up in the morning?"

"I'll be honest. You aren't coming out of this looking very good. At least not in the eyes of your fellow workers. But we've got to protect the interest of the business. Bottom line: you're not going to get in any legal trouble."

"So I'm taking the blame, just like Terry wanted."

"Not with the people who matter," Kretch says. "Not with me or Bud. And not with your dad. He doesn't even have to know."

"But they get away with it."

"Trust me, they're not getting away with this. The police won't be involved, but heads are gonna roll." Kretch slaps his thighs and stands up with a long groan. "So get out of here as soon as you can. Before anyone finds out you came to us." He holds out his meaty hand. I shake it, half-expecting he'll crush my fingers. But his palm is soft and warm. He turns and plods up the stairs.

"You said this happens all the time."

Kretch stops and looks back at me. "A few years ago, we had to fire an entire crew. Somebody was stealing money. We were pretty sure who it was, but we didn't know if the problem was bigger. So we got rid of everybody."

"Everybody?"

"Except the old timers, yeah. That's why I try not to make friends with you guys. You never know."

"I guess not."

"I'll miss having someone to play 'Paint it Black,' though."

"Somebody'll do it."

"Probably a brown noser." I laugh. He points at me with both hands, like he always did when I punched the song into the jukebox. Then he walks down the sidewalk, whistling that Stones tune.

I go inside and start packing. It's nearly 4:30. I'm not going to be able to take everything. All I have is my gym bag. So I'll have to toss some stuff out. I start separating my belongings into piles; take, toss, and wait to see how much room's left.

The Bullworker's a maybe. After all the effort I put into getting stronger, it'd be a shame to let myself go. The Manson book—a definite no. The poetry books… They're the only things I have to remind me of Tara. I gotta take them. My tape player and cassettes… I'm not going to have the room. It's a shitty recorder anyway.

Now… all the clothes—

The phone rings. It startles me. I rush down the hallway and pick it up. Jill's talking before I get it to my ear. "Where have you been?"

"Jill. Thank God."

"You've got to get out of there."

"I am." How does she know what happened? "Kretch told me."

"Kretch told you? Told you what?"

"After Moose dumped Susie here—"

"What?!"

"—I told Bud everything, and he called Kretch."

"What's everything?"

"It's a long story. I don't have time."

"Is it about the coke?"

"I had to," I tell her. "You should've seen what they did to Susie."

"What do you mean?" She sounds panicked.

"They got her all drugged up and left her at my door. She had to go to the hospital."

"Shit! SHIT!" She's practically shrieking. "Fucking Hadley."

"Hadley? No, this was Terry. This was all Terry."

"Terry doesn't do anything without Hadley telling him."

How does Jill know all this? Terry said she was involved. But how much? Damnit. I can't figure anything out. It's all too fucked up. I have to stop thinking. Go back to doing one thing after another. "I'm getting on a train in the morning."

"No. You need to leave now. Are you packed?"

"Pretty much."

"How soon can you get to my place?"

"Maybe fifteen minutes."

"All right," Jill says. "I'll take you where you need to go."

"I don't know where that is." I feel myself choking up.

She doesn't notice—or care. It's all suddenly business. "Figure it out on the way. And don't walk down Dearborn. They could be watching. Come a different way, a way you'd never think to go."

She hangs up. For a few seconds, I'm frozen in the Fun Room. Then I lurch into action. I can't take all my clothes. I've got two bags full. I put my work stuff in the pile to toss. Everything but the Bud's tie, with his cartoon leprechaun likeness. It barely takes up any space, and I should keep at least one memento of my time in Chicago. As for Terry's clothes, fuck them. He was probably playing me all the way back when he bought them for me. And the Joe College crap, that ought to go, too. I'm not the smooth operator Terry dressed me to be. But I'm not the naïve prep boy either. I don't know what I am.

Before I put everything into the gym bag, I take the envelope Bud gave me and tuck it into the tear of that liner where the rest of my money is. I find a garbage bag in the Fun Room and stuff everything I can't take in there. That includes the Bullworker. It's not going to fit. I'll have to stay strong some other way.

It's quarter to five. Time to go. I leave the key on the nightstand. Jill said not to go down Dearborn, that they'd be watching for me there. If that's true, aren't I taking a risk going outside at all? I creep into the stairwell, pulling the bags behind me. Then I reach back and quietly shut myself out. The door locks. If I've forgotten anything, it's too late now. There's an iron fence between my stairwell and the corridor that cuts along Bud's house to the alley. I swing the bags over the fence and climb it. If you were right across the street, you'd see me. But any farther away and I'm blocked from sight. When I get to the back alley, I turn right and sneak between a gauntlet of dumpsters. I drop the garbage bag in one near the end. It clangs and clatters in the metal container. *Damn.* I've got to stop screwing up.

If you didn't know the dawn was coming, you'd think it was night. Dark clouds press down so close to the city, they glow with the lights they're snuffing out. You can't see the top of skyscrapers; it's like they've dissolved in a sulfurous mist. I try to stay off the crossroads—Burton and Schiller and Goethe—then I take back alleys that parallel Dearborn. I know when I see the Hancock Building I'll be close. But this low mist might obliterate my view.

I run out of alleys to take, and I can't find the sign for the crossroad. I turn left to the lake, my one reliable guide. The headlights on Lake Shore Drive worm their way toward me, yellow-needled eyes of giant snakes. Everything about my escape seems sinister, doomed to failure. A dark figure comes down the sidewalk in front of me. I step into a bus shelter. He passes silently.

Finally, I see the sign for Division. I know where I am. I start to run. Jill's street is deserted, and the entry to her building is still brightly lit for the night. But you never know. If they were keeping an eye on places I might turn up, Jill's apartment would be at the top of the list. I take it slow, watching every shadow—

Headlights blind me. A car growls and lunges. It's Terry's red Triumph. *Shit.* It screeches to a stop. I rush for Jill's entryway—

"Owen!" It's Jill. She scurries around to the back of the car and opens the trunk. "Put your bag here." I can't see inside the car. The top is up, the windows tinted. Am I getting into a trap?

"Why do you have Terry's car?"

"This isn't Terry's car. Now put the bag in and let's go."

I do it, but I'm afraid right up to the instant I open the passenger door. No one's there. Jill roars off and turns on Lake Shore Drive.

"Terry drove me around in this." We swerve in front of the misty monstrosity of the Hancock Building.

"Yeah," Jill says. "He takes it out more than I do, but it's mine. Well, Hadley's really. He gave it to me."

"Hadley *gave* you this?"

"It was a long time ago." For a moment, she seems wistful about it. "I keep waiting for him to take it back. It's going to be any day now. Probably today, after last night."

I'll be damned. Terry wasn't bullshitting after all. "So you're involved in this." I put it to Jill just like that. Point-blank.

She ignores me. "Are we going to Wheaton?"

"No."

"Then where?"

"Back to college." Why does that feel like such a surrender to me? "Just get me out to the highway, and I'll hitchhike from there."

"You're not hitchhiking. I'll take you there."

"It's five hours to Ann Arbor. Then five back."

"Do you want a ride or not?" I don't argue. We drive in silence, past Lake Point Tower, where Terry dreamed of living, then over the river. I look upstream. The water mirrors those glowing clouds. It slithers toward us. The silhouette of the Wrigley Building flashes by and is gone. I wonder: where's Dad now? Is he with Denise?

Jill loads a cassette into the player and turns up the volume. The music squawks, lurches, and grinds. She's done talking. She just wants to drive. Problem is, she doesn't seem to know where she's going. She cranes her neck to take in the signs we pass.

"If you get to ninety-four, it'll take you all the way there."

"I know where I'm going. I grew up in Battle Creek."

Funny. I never asked Jill where she was from. I never even considered that she was once younger than me. What was she like? What did she dream of? Has she got what she wanted, or is she as lost as I am? I want to talk more. I want to ask her these things. I want to know how she's involved with Terry and Hadley. But the music's too loud, and now the singer's singing. "Is this Bowie?"

"Yeah." She hands me the case. "It's pretty new."

I look down at a moody black-and-white close-up of Bowie. His face is a pale mask, but he's pulling his hand away from it like he just removed a different mask. And he's clutching something to his chest. Another mask? How many will he take off before he's himself?

"So Hadley just *gave* you his car?"

"It wasn't exactly for free." I'm surprised Jill answers. "I had to—" She cuts herself off, veering across two lanes to make the exit for the Dan Ryan. There isn't much traffic, but we still get some honking. Jill doesn't react at all. She's put on a mask of her own.

A song I've heard comes on—a dreamy, soaring howl. Bowie, fatalistic yet hopeful: *Though nothing will drive them away, we can beat them, just for one day.* Taking consolation in a momentary victory: *We can be heroes, just for one day.* What about every other day? Are we cowards? Villains? What about me? Getting sucked into what I knew was wrong, letting Terry use me, seeing the damage it did to Astrid— and still doing nothing, putting Susie—my best friend, the person I care about most—in harm's way. Am I a hero, just because, after all that, I finally summoned the decency to confess to Bud and Kretch? And what about Jill? Would she think she was a hero now for helping me escape this trouble—trouble she knew about in the first place? How *was* she involved? Was she still?

Chicago's behind us now. The mist has lifted, and the sky shows a strange uncertain light; it could be the beginning or end of night. The sign for I-94 is all the way to the right. Jill changes lanes, and we drive under it.

"I got a couple thousand dollars just to hand out tiny packs of coke," I say. "You got a car. What did *you* do?" Jill keeps the mask on, stays silent. "Okay, I guess I'll just assume the worst."

Finally, she takes a deep breath and looks at me—for the first time, really, since I got in the car. Her eyes are sad, haunted. Maybe they've always been, and I never noticed.

"I got people involved," she says.

## Late for the Sky

*The words had all been spoken, and somehow the feeling still wasn't right.*
*- Jackson Brown*

Jane turns down the music. "I was younger than you when I came to Chicago." That's all she says for a while. The sun's rising now, and we're driving into it. I put down my visor. Jill finds Terry's sunglasses in the side door pocket and puts them on. She starts talking again, as if hiding her eyes makes it easier. "When you grow up in Battle Creek, and your parents don't have money, your dreams are pretty simple. You want to go somewhere bigger, because you know there's more to life. For the kids I grew up with, Chicago was the dream. I wasn't afraid of going off on my own. I knew I could get a job, waiting tables or answering phones. And I knew I could attract a man." She says it matter-of-factly, like it's just another necessity. "I left for Chicago the day after graduation. And within two days, I was working at Bud's."

"That was what?" I know that she's 25 now. "Seven years ago?"

"God. When you say it like that." She shakes her head. "Two years later, I met Hadley." An older man. A younger woman—a girl, really, growing up too fast. He was to Jill what Jill is to me. "He was the charming guy you see on backgammon night," Jill defends him. "Before I even knew he was faking his sophistication, I was going out with him. He was an exotic car salesman—Porsches and Bentleys and Lamborghinis. Triumphs. Within a month, I moved in with him, into the apartment where I am today."

"How old is Hadley?"

"Mid-thirties, I guess. I never asked, and he never said."

"Did you love him?"

"I thought so." She gets quieter. "I really did."

"And he loved you…"

"Hadley can't love anyone. It took me way too long to learn that."

"But you're still in his apartment."

She doesn't answer directly. "A few years ago, he asked me to do him a favor. This guy was coming to Bud's, and he wanted me to give him an envelope. He said it was paperwork for a car the guy bought, and I'd be getting an envelope back for the money he owed."

"Let me guess. He had a reason why he couldn't do it himself."

Jill laughs; a bitter laugh. "He said he couldn't be there that night. I didn't think anything of it until the guy came in, we exchanged envelopes, and he opened his. He wasn't very careful about it. And I saw a baggie of powder."

"How big?"

"A lot bigger than what you give out. I was pissed off. I told Hadley, *never again*. He came clean about what he was doing and how much he was making—more than he made selling cars. He said he had more buyers than ways to get the stuff to them. *Too bad*, I said. *That's your problem*. Then I told him we were through."

"But you weren't."

"We were. And we weren't. We broke up. But he offered me a deal: if I found someone who'd help get the coke to his customers, I could stay in the apartment and he'd move out. I wasn't going to do it. Then Terry showed up. That was maybe four years ago.

"He was a city kid—street-smart, hungry. I told Hadley about him. He asked if I'd help… persuade Terry to work with him. That's how the hot dog thing started. It didn't seem like that bad a thing to do. I mean, I liked Terry. He was a lot like me. His future wasn't mapped out, like the kids from the burbs Bud always hired. And he was willing to take a small risk for a big reward."

"Like me."

"You're different."

"I don't see how. Except it was Terry who brought me in."

"He had to. Terry started selling in Cabrini Green. He told Hadley he could make more money there, so he wanted to stop the hot dog gig. Hadley put his foot down, said he had to find a replacement. His clients didn't want to go to the ghetto for drugs, and if we didn't supply them, a shitstorm was going to come down on all of us. That's right around when you started working."

"Okay, I get it. Terry needed to find somebody. And he decided I was the one. Because he saw something… vulnerable in me."

"That's not true," Jill says. "Terry didn't think you were right for it. He said you didn't have enough to gain—and no reason not to confess if you got caught."

"Well, he must've changed his mind pretty quick. He was after me practically from day one."

"Not until Hadley found out about your dad's friendship with Bud. You got approached because of Hadley. He thought if Bud found out you were involved, he'd keep it quiet. He'd feel obligated to protect you. And it sounds like that's what's happening."

"Come on, Jill. Terry wouldn't've come after me if he didn't think I was impressionable enough to do it. He knew I wouldn't be strong enough to say no."

"And yet you did."

"Only after Susie got hurt."

"Damnit, Owen!" She slams her palms against the steering wheel. "Stop beating yourself up! This isn't about being strong. Will you just listen? You wanted to know how I was involved."

"You told me."

"Not everything. Not how I helped with you."

"With me?"

"Terry still didn't want to use you. He liked you too much. He thought you were too good a kid to keep quiet if thing's started going bad. That's why he tried Nick first."

It seems like more dodging. "Then he tried me."

"Not until he found—what did he call it?—*insurance* to keep you quiet." She glances at me. I see sadness in her eyes. And shame. It's just for a second, then her eyes are back on the road.

"You."

"I didn't have to do what I did. Terry just asked me to be a friend."

"Wait a minute. Are you saying that night you came out with us to O'Banion's and we got together, that was all just *being a friend?*"

"No! That's what I was trying to tell you. I didn't *have* to do that. I *wanted* to… even before Terry asked me to help."

Jill has to know I'm looking at her. I'm leaning forward, my face a foot away from hers. Still, she holds her gaze on the road. It's a test of wills: can she keep that straight face longer than I can hold onto my anger? Maybe she's telling the truth, maybe she isn't. But she's here now, driving me all this way. Still, there's a bitter taste in my mouth. "You lied to me back then. You could be lying now."

"I wish I was." She looks over and gives me the weakest smile. "Terry didn't count on *me* being the one to fall for *you.*"

"We fell for each other." It feels like I'm trying to cheer her up. Did I ever love Jill? Not really. I loved being with her… I loved that someone like her wanted to be with me… but I didn't love her. No use saying it was more than it was to spare her feelings. She's giving me plenty of silence, though, to question myself. Who knows? Maybe I could've loved her. Maybe love takes root slowly rather than striking like a bolt of wonder.

The silence builds and builds on itself. I wait for it to settle into acceptance, or at least indifference. But it just feels heavier. "Did you know what was going to happen last night?"

"I knew things went bad. And I knew Hadley and Terry were looking for a way out." She looks over at me. And this time, it's not a glance. Her eyes are off the road long enough to worry. "That was enough," she says, before looking forward again.

"Enough to give me your number to call."

"Enough to warn you. I was worried enough to do that. I just wasn't brave enough to tell you what I was worried about."

"That Terry would hurt Susie?"

"No…" She vents three quick breaths. "I thought you might be."

"Well, if that's why you're beating yourself up, don't. I got that message loud and clear."

"I guess I'm just sad," Jill slumps back. That's when I realize: All this time, she's been on the edge of her seat… and only now is she resting. "I knew this would unravel sooner or later. That something bad would happen. And I didn't do a thing about it."

"Well, you are now. And I'm grateful for it."

Maybe it's the angle of the sun, but her eyes are gleaming like she's about to cry. "A little late. That's me, always a little late." A tear falls onto her lap. One drop.

I look out my window. "I know the feeling. All these chances I had along the way. To get myself out of it. To keep Susie from getting hurt. And I didn't take any of them."

Jill sighs for me. "The worst part of regret is knowing that if you could replay things, you'd do it all the same again. Sometimes, we just aren't ready to do what we need to do. That should make us go easier on ourselves. But, somehow, it makes us go harder."

"If Susie's really hurt…" Then what? What'll I do? Will I go back and fight for her? Will I take revenge? No… "Then I'd just feel sadder. I wouldn't do a thing."

"She's the one you love," Jill ambushes me with that. "I always thought so, but I knew it after Los Toros."

"Yeah, but I didn't know it."

"Maybe you were just beginning to."

"I'm afraid I'll never know when I'm in love." It feels like I'm voicing a secret I've held all summer. "And because of that, I'll always be looking for something better, something else."

Jill doesn't try to argue the point. I'm thinking, *she must agree with me*. But then she says, "Being afraid that you won't find love, that's nothing to be sad about. It means you're open to it."

Maybe she's right. Maybe you need to want love bad enough to be afraid. "Okay. But I still don't know what the fuck love *is*."

Jill bursts out laughing. It reminds me of how we used to talk at the back of Bud's across the bar rail, when the place was empty and there was nothing to do but keep each other company.

"Me neither," she says, "but I'm getting closer."

I'm not sure what she means, but it makes me feel like I should say that I could've loved her. Is there anything worse than hearing that, though? Jill slaps my knee. It startles me. "So we keep trying." She grins with a hard jaw—her brave face.

"We do," I agree, like we're making a pact.

Now I'm the one who slumps in his seat. I didn't realize *I* was still so tense. I've gotten used to feeling on edge. For how long? Before I escaped to Jill's. Before I told Bud and Kretch what was going on. Before I found Susie outside my door. Before I missed her call for help. Before Hadley shut down the hot dog scheme. Before. Before. Before. How far back could I unwind this nagging fear?

I need to sleep. And it's just the start of the day. At least the sky is obliging. The clouds that hung so ominously over Chicago have followed us all this way, and now as we're crossing through the farmland of western Michigan, they've overtaken us. Where they felt sinister in the city, here they come as a comfort, snuffing out the day just as it's starting, rolling the darkness back over us, like a big blanket. This trip isn't the beginning of something; it's only the end.

Jill rummages through Terry's cassette box, pulls one out seemingly at random, and swaps it in for the Bowie tape. The new music is sad, slow, dirge-like. I can't place the singer. "Who's this?"

"Jackson Browne," Jill tells me. "*Late for the Sky*."

Sounds about right.

## Slip Slidin' Away

*The nearer your destination, the more you're slip slidin' away.*
*- Paul Simon*

I wake to rumbling. The Triumph's off the road, crossing the gravel shoulder on my side, bouncing toward a steep ditch. Now the car jerks back onto the highway. Jill's blinking her eyes wide. "Oh my God! Oh my *GOD!*"

She's flustered, going way too slow now. Cars flash by us. "Maybe we should stop," I say. "Get a cup of coffee."

"I'm okay now. It's just this music. It's so drowsy."

"I have to pee anyway," I tell her. I don't really. But why not take a break? Get a jolt of caffeine so this doesn't happen again. In a few minutes, we take the exit for Mattawan. There's a truck stop right there. Jill starts to turn in then speeds up and continues on.

"It was open."

"Too close to the highway. You can see the whole parking lot."

It takes a second to get her meaning. "You think they'd follow us?"

"I do."

We find a diner a mile or so away, on the outskirts of town. "Can you get the coffees to go?" she asks after we park.

I check my wallet. Three dollars. "Can I borrow a five? I've got money, but it's in the trunk."

Jill gets her purse out of the side door and takes out a five.

"Cream with your coffee, right?"

"It doesn't matter," Jill says.

I get her cream anyway. She's pulled the car in front of the entry and pushed my door open. That's thoughtful. Still, I go around to her side. I don't want to try getting into that low seat with two coffees. She's gazing through the windshield at the eastern sky. That cloud front has turned the morning purple. I knock on her window. She shudders and covers her face with one hand, like she's trying to hide from me. Then she opens her window. "Here's your coffee." I hold out the cup.

She takes it and quickly turns away. Is that a bruise on her cheek? I go around to my side and get in. She gets on the road back to I-94. I go to open my coffee top. My hand's shaking. "Did he hit you?"

"Just last night," Jill exhales like she's been holding it in forever. "For the first time."

For a second, I'm relieved that it was just the first time. Then it hits me: what does that matter? Terry's shown that it's in him to be violent. And with everything about to explode at Bud's, he'll be more volatile than ever. "You can't go back."

"I have to."

"Just leave! You're right near Battle Creek. You can go home!"

"Home… Ha! *You* could've gone home too."

She's right. I could've. But it wasn't home anymore—and I hadn't been gone a year. It's been seven years since Jill left. "You have to go somewhere. I have money. You could go up north. Get a room on a beach. Stay there for a week or so."

"If I'm not back by tonight, a week's only going to make it worse."

We drive through a long stretch of silence, me stewing over Jill's predicament, her sipping her coffee. Kalamazoo comes and goes. We pass the exit for Battle Creek. And now we see the first sign for Ann Arbor, 72 miles away.

"I don't want you to call me," Jill says. "Ever. There's no point in it for either of us." She pokes on the radio. Short translation: *We're done talking.* She turns the knob, trying for something clear in this no-man's land between what we're escaping and what's ahead. It's just AM radio, but she manages to find a soft rock station. They're playing Paul Simon, and we're slip slidin' away.

We come up on Jackson, 40 minutes from Ann Arbor. Billy Joel's promising that he'll take his lover just the way she is. I want to turn the radio off. I want to talk. I want to make sure I say everything there is to say before we leave each other. I want to tell Jill she doesn't have to stay trapped in that apartment. She was brave once—she left home and made a life for herself when she was a lot more vulnerable than she is now.

Jill turns down the volume, like she's trying to hear me think. "What?" I'm not letting her get away with it.

"Nothing."

"I thought you wanted to say something."

"I'm going to look after Susie, alright?" Jill says, like I've been badgering her about it. "You don't have to worry."

I'm speechless, touched. "Thanks," is all I can manage.

We pass Chelsea and start seeing exit signs for Ann Arbor. "Where am I going?"

"My dorm. Take the State Street exit."

I don't know why I thought there'd be more students on campus. Classes don't start for another week or so. Maybe it's because I've never been here when school's on break. Still, the sidewalks are more crowded than you'd see around Bud's at this time of day. Almost all students, striding purposefully here and there, showing their maize and blue colors, weighed down by bulging backpacks and mini fridges. Jill putters along, taking in all the funky stores—the head shop, Pinball Pete's, the Brown Jug bar, Middle Earth novelties. It occurs to me: she never had a chance to live this, to be among the legion of eager innocents—frat boys and clustered coeds, hippie posers, would-be academics—streaming in single files through their new home away from home.

"God, they're all just kids," Jill marvels. I don't know what she expected. Maybe she thought she'd be more like them. Knowing what she's been through, though, how could they *not* seem like kids to her? What I can't figure out is why everyone looks so young to *me*. Had I gotten that much older in one summer?

We wind around the edge of campus, up to the Hill dorms. There's hardly anyone around. Where are the freshmen? Where's the traffic? All the parents dropping off their children to a new life—and ending another? We turn on the road to Markley, my dorm. The last time I was here, I said goodbye to Tara. And I looked down this road out the back window of Fitz's Cordoba to watch her disappear. There's no one at the entry, no cars parked in the lot across the street.

"This doesn't look open," Jill says.

"No, it doesn't." A guy comes out the front of Markley and props open a door with a milk crate full of albums. I recognize him. He was the R.A. on the floor above us. "Let me talk to that guy."

Jill stops. I get out, jog across the street, and meet the guy at the propped door. "Not open," he spouts before looking up. Then our eyes meet, and he must recognize me, because he drops the official act. "Sorry. I can't let you in. Not until at least Thursday."

"Shit. Where am I gonna go?"

The guy glances at the Triumph then shifts his eyes back to me. "When my parents dropped me off a couple years ago, they stayed at the Bell Tower Hotel. You know Burton Tower?"

"Yeah." Everybody who goes to Michigan knows Burton Tower. It's the limestone monolith in the middle of campus, with the four clock faces and the giant bells that chime every 15 minutes.

"This place is right across the street from it," the guy says. "If you didn't know it was there, you'd walk right by. But that's where rock stars stay when they're in town."

Once we drive away from the Hill dorms, Burton Tower comes into view—the Hancock Building of Ann Arbor. It takes a while to wend our way through the streets to get there. We circle the block twice before Jill spots a small awning with the Bell Tower Hotel's name on it. She stops in front of the entry. A bellhop hustles out and asks if we want valet parking. Jill tells him no. "It'll be tough to find a spot close by," he warns.

"I'm not going to be long." She turns to me. "Well…"

This is it? She's just going to drop me off and drive away? "Can you wait a sec? I don't even know if they have a vacancy."

I know her plan: I'm going to go inside, and she's going to take off. I get out anyway. It's a small lobby. There's just me, the bellhop, and a woman at the front desk. "Do you have a vacancy for the next few nights?" I can see Jill through the smoky panes of the entry door. Sure enough, she's putting my bag on the curb.

"We have rooms available until Tuesday," the desk clerk says.

Now Jill's hurrying back around to the driver's door. I rush outside and catch her ducking into the car. "Were you just going to leave?"

She stands up slowly. "There's no point in a long goodbye."

"Any goodbye would be nice."

Jill holds her ground. I start to come around to her. "Don't."

"We'll never see each other again."

I'm on her side now, inching closer. "I'm serious about not calling," she says. "I want you to throw away my number."

"Okay."

"Promise?"

Now I'm in front of her, close enough to whisper. "I promise."

She seizes me in a sudden hug. It's so hard, I lose my breath. She won't let go. I try to loosen her embrace, enough to look at her, but she clings to me more fiercely. Her lips touch my ear, like she wants to say something. But she doesn't.

When we let go of each other, I see that she's crying again. Her cheeks are smeared in tears. And the bruise from Terry's blow, red on her left cheek, purple under that eye, is more pronounced. I reach for Jill's face. She lets me touch her. Then she gives me a timid smile, turns, and folds herself into the car.

And now she's driving off. Something flushes through me—the magnitude of the moment? Gratitude for her kindness? Regret that I forgot to thank her? Fear that I'm alone again? All of that and more. Jill turns at the end of the road and is gone.

I pick up my bag and go inside. The desk clerk signs me in for the room. "Is there a card you'll be putting this on?"

"I'll just do cash." I dig into the tear in the liner of my bag and take out the envelope Bud gave me. "How much is it?" I pull out a fistful of twenties.

The clerk's eyes go wide. You'd think a drug dealer just walked up to the counter. It's not that far from the truth. She regains her composure. "Tuesday checkout? Three hundred twelve." I count out the twenties and stack them in front of her. She double-checks my count. "You gave me an extra one. And I owe you eight dollars."

"That's for you," I say with a smile. "I was wondering if there was a room looking out the front of the hotel, down onto the street."

"I think we can make that happen," she says. That's one thing I learned this summer: the power of money. It can get you whatever you want. I also learned that it can't take away all your problems.

Before I slide the envelope with Bud's cash back in the torn liner, I take out five more twenties and put them in my wallet. There I find the folded coaster with the phone numbers for Susie, Tara, and Jill. I tear it in half. If I keep Jill's number, I'll always be tempted to call. I put the half with Susie's and Tara's numbers back in my wallet, and hand the other half to the clerk.

"Can you throw this out for me?"

And, just like that, Jill is out of my life forever.

## Who Are You
*Who, who, who, who?*
*- The Who*


Abell gongs. Again. And again. The jolts resuscitate me. *Oh yeah.* I'm beneath Burton Tower. How many times has it rung? I turn over in bed, crane my neck for the clock. It's five. Six hours gone in a blink. I go to the window and crack open the drapes. The clerk put me right above the hotel's awning. If a car was under it, I wouldn't know. I open the drapes all the way to get more light. Not much comes in. The clouds that followed us here have hunkered down, and I'm facing east, in the shadow of the building.

It's a cramped room. There's a desk chair beside the window, but no desk. I sit down. What now? After Tuesday, I'll have nowhere to stay. All my clothes are dirty. I can't stop worrying about Susie and Jill. And who knows how long I'm going to feel on edge? To think, I had such big dreams about starting up school again, dreams of Tara and I together. Everything's changed.

At least I have money. I can pay to stay somewhere else until my dorm opens. I can buy clothes. Eat at restaurants. Make long-distance calls. There's a notepad and pen on the nightstand. I need to write things down. Number one: call Dad. He needs to know I've left Chicago. If he can't get a hold of me, he'll call Bud. I don't want to put Bud on the spot. Two: buy new clothes. Three: wash old ones. Then what? Then call Susie. Find out if she made it home, how she's doing. Explain why I'm not there for her.

I put the pen down, tear off the sheet, fold it up, and put it in my pocket. That's enough for tonight. The phone's right there on the nightstand. I read the instructions for long-distance calls and dial home. I'm surprised when Dad answers after the first ring. "We're still on for the Billy Goat tomorrow, right?"

I forgot all about that. "I'm not going to be able to make it. I decided to get to school a few days early, and there was this guy who was driving here today."

"Wait. So you're in Ann Arbor?"

"Yeah."

"What about all your stuff?"

"I had all I needed with me at Bud's."

"Well, you don't have this stereo."

Damn. I forgot about that. "I'll get Stu to come pick it up."

"Stu?"

"Yeah. I'm rooming with him again. Remember?"

"He's not going back," Dad says.

"What?"

"His dad called. Stu's taking a year off. I thought you knew."

"No. Why?"

"Sounds like he's having some personal issues."

"Wow." I knew Stu was having troubles. All that shit when we went to the Sox game. But dropping out of school?

"Your mother is not going to want this stereo in the house," Dad circles back. "Not even in the basement."

"I'll find someone to get it." If Fitz can't pick it up, I'm screwed. Damn stereo. I spent all that money on it, couldn't wait to show it off in the dorm, and it's just become a giant pain in the ass.

"I'm not happy with this," Dad says. "You gave me your word."

*Your word.* That does it. "Are you going to stop seeing Denise?" Silence. "Because if you aren't, you should tell Mom."

"What are you talking about?" Figures he'd try to bullshit me.

"Don't make Mom live with your lie."

He drops the act. "How do you know about that?"

"Ask Denise." I hang up. I don't want to hear his excuses.

The only place I've bought clothes in Ann Arbor was Van Boven, the pricey men's store by Nickels Arcade, and Dad got them for me. Argyle socks, sweater vests, creased slacks. Everything designed to stand out. That's the last thing I want. I want to blend in. Same goes for the trendy stuff Terry pushed on me. I don't want to be somebody anymore. I want to be nobody.

"Where's a good place to buy cheap clothes?" I ask the desk clerk.

"What kind of style?"

"No style."

"The army surplus store's got basic clothes," the bellhop chimes in behind me. Basic. That's what I'm shooting for.

Harry's Army Surplus is all the way downtown, in a part of Ann Arbor where I've never been. I get a pair of used cargo pants, a couple black t-shirts, a bag of underwear, and, thinking ahead to the fall, a heavy sweater. All for less than 35 bucks.

I find a diner around the corner called Coffee Cup. It reminds me of Bill's Diner. Same setup with the lunch counter and the little stools screwed into the floor. Same assortment of misfits, old-timers, and down-and-outers. Funny: I feel more at home with them than all the high-strung students I've been passing on the streets. There's even a tinny radio playing in the background, some song I never heard before, the singer asking over and over, "Who are you? Who, who? Who, who?" It's Roger Daltrey. I get the joke.

The guy behind the counter seems annoyed that I'm there. "We close in fifteen minutes," he says. I take a seat among the line of loners. The guy rattles off a bunch of items that it's too late to order. I settle for a bowl of tomato soup and a grilled cheese sandwich.

"You're not missing much," grumbles a hippie relic next to me.

My soup comes right away. While I'm eating it, I go over my to-do list. Called Dad. Bought clothes. Now there's just finding a laundromat and calling Susie. "Excuse me," I say to the hippie. "You wouldn't happen to know if there's a laundromat nearby?'

The guy stops eating and turns to me. "If you're looking to sleep," he lowers his voice, "the one on Maynard's good."

"I just want to clean my clothes."

"Then I'd go to South U. They fix their machines faster."

What about me says I need a place to sleep? I sneak a whiff of my armpit. A shower should've been number one on my list.

My sandwich comes. I wolf it down. It's been a while since I ate. Maybe that's why this guy thinks I'm a bum; probably knows a hungry look when he sees one.

I pay the bill and head back to the hotel. It's nearly 7:30. I'll call Susie right after I get clean. I don't realize how ritzy the Bell Tower Hotel is until I'm taking my shower. The soap's wrapped up like a little gift. The shampoo and conditioner have French names. I get out, take a towel off a heated rack, and find a plush white robe beneath it. There are even matching slippers in the closet. All this luxury feels wrong. I get my wallet and take out the split coaster with Susie's and Tara's numbers. I dial Susie. The phone starts ringing.

Terry answers.

"You son of a bitch." I couldn't help it. He caught me off guard.

"I *knew* it," Terry shouts. His voice gets distant. "Guess who, Jill?"

Jill? And Terry? At Susie's place? "Is Susie there?"

"Here?" Terry laughs. His voice gets muffled again. "Is that what you promised your boyfriend—that you'd take care of her *here*?"

Oh, *shit*. I threw away Susie's number and called Jill's!

"Lemme talk to Jill. If you hurt her—"

"If I hurt her, what?" Terry snaps. "You'll come back for me? Don't tempt me, Owen."

*I'll kill you.* That's what I want to say. "If you hurt her, Bud'll know. Everyone'll know."

There's a catch in his breath. I can hear Jill pleading in the background. "Nobody's hurting anybody," he says, subdued.

I got his attention. "What about Susie?"

"Nick took her home this afternoon."

"I want this to be over."

"Well, it's a long way from over. Bud's cleaning house tomorrow."

"I mean, the punishing."

His answer is a sigh. "Damnit, Owen. I like you. I do. But you shouldn't've told Bud. It's putting me in a bad spot."

"Weren't you in a bad spot already?"

"Maybe." He's so quiet I can barely hear him.

"So think of it as a chance to get out."

Terry laughs slowly, bitterly—a chuckle of doom. "That's what I like about you, Owen. Naïve enough to waltz into trouble, smart enough to talk your way out of it. Too bad it won't work."

"What *will* work, Terry? Tell me. How do we get past it?"

"You mean, how can you go back to not feeling bad that people got hurt? I can't give you that. Sorry."

It comes to me suddenly. Susie's squirrel giving away nuts. "Maybe I can give you something for all the trouble I caused."

"There's nothing you can give me for this, other than shitloads of money. The kind of money you don't have."

"No, this is just a gift." I start softening my approach. "I know things ended bad between us, but I learned a lot from you, Terry."

"Don't fuck with me, Owen." There's more hurt than hate in the way he says it. That's my opening.

"It's not a big deal." Time to undersell it. "It's just—you know that new stereo I told you about with the Tympani Three Maggies?"

"Yeah…"

"I had to leave it at my dad's in Wheaton. He told me if I didn't have it out of the house in three days, he was going to trash it."

"No fucking way." He's hooked now.

"Maybe you could drive over there and get it," I say, like I'm asking for a favor. "And you might as well keep it. My dorm room's way too small for Maggies. I don't know what I was thinking."

"Maggies take some planning," Terry concedes.

And I have him. He agrees to pick up the stereo on Tuesday night and thanks me. Grudgingly, but a thanks all the same. I get off the phone as quick as I can and call Dad. "Owen!" he says as soon as I speak. "Thank God you called back. I talked to Denise—"

"I don't want to talk about that."

"Well, now, let me explain—"

"Don't try to win me over. Okay? Just don't hurt Mom." He starts to protest. I shut him down. "About the stereo—"

"Wait. There's just one thing you have to understand—"

"A guy's coming to pick it up Tuesday at six. Can you be there?"

"Yeah, yeah. But hang on. Hear me out. Please, Owen. Please?"

He's on the verge of crying. "Fine. Just don't bullshit me."

"First off, it's over. And as to why it happened, it was all my problems—the insecurities, the work failures, the drinking, needing to feel like I was worth something. It had nothing to do with Mom."

"But it does."

"I know…" Dad's breath rattles through the phone. "She knew about the affair. She knew about the drinking—obviously. But she didn't know what was going on in my head. I kept that from her. And that was the mistake that brought on everything else."

"You should tell her that."

"As soon as she gets home."

There's a long silence. "Okay. Well… I hope you can work it out." I'm about to say more, but I resist the urge. We say our goodbyes, then the call's over. I'm glad I decided to listen. I'm still not happy with Dad. But at least everything's out in the open. Who knows how things'll go with Mom. That's between them. They have their lives—and I have mine. I'm having enough trouble keeping that under control.

It was good talking to Terry too—even if it was a colossal fuck-up. I'm more relieved now. God knows why. I don't know if he hit

Jill again. And I don't know how Susie's doing either. Terry said she's home, but is she injured? Is she alone? Scared? What's she going to do? I can't believe I threw her number away. I thought I knew it by heart, but I can't for the life of me remember it. Maybe I should call down to the front desk and see if it's still in their trash.

*Wait.* Terry said Nick took her home. He'd know Susie's number. What was his last name? Bianchi. And he lived on La Salle. I dial the operator and give her the details.

"I have a Frank Bianchi at fourteen-fourteen North La Salle. Would you like me to connect you?"

"Can I just have the number?" It's late. His parents could be sleeping. I write the number down on the notepad. Under that, I start a new list. One: Get Susie's number from Nick. Two: Call Susie. Three: Wash clothes. Four: Find out when Fitz is coming. Five… five… Go back to the dorm. Find out what happens now that Stu's dropped out.

What classes am I signed up for, anyway? I don't even remember. I did it back in the spring on that call with Dad, planning out my future. *My future*… there's a laugh. One of the classes was Econ—that's right. And Dad had me sign up for Accounting too; a prerequisite to get into business school. That was his plan for me after I bagged on dentistry. *His* plan. But I went along with it, like I'd been doing my whole life, like I did with Terry.

Six: Find out what classes you're taking—and change them. Decide what *you* want to do.

This is your life now.

## Have it Your Way

*- Burger King Jingle*

It's an hour earlier in Chicago—eight in the morning. Nick's mom calls him to the phone. By the sounds of it, he's picked up in another room. "Owen, holy shit…"

"How is she?"

"She was coming around last night. They pumped her full of fluids, gave her a couple stitches for a cut on her lip, seven on her knee. They treated it like a rough night of partying."

"Did she tell you what happened?"

"She thinks she was drugged because she blacked out."

"She called me," I admit. "From the restaurant where Terry took her. She was drunk, but not *that* drunk."

Nick's voice lowers, like he's cupped his hand to the phone. "Rumor is they found her outside your door."

"Yeah. I caught Moose dumping her there."

"There's a Bud's meeting today. Everyone knows about the coke. A lot of people think you're… in the middle of it, since you didn't come in yesterday, and Kretch was calling around to fill your shifts."

Bud said this would happen, that I'd have to take the blame: his price for getting me out of trouble. "You don't believe that, do you?"

"That this is all on you? Of course, not. But… you *were* involved."

*So were you.* I catch myself before I say it. "I'm getting what I deserve." Maybe I shouldn't have said that either.

"Well." Nick weighs the point. "You *did* get to walk away."

"This isn't something you walk away from."

"But you're keeping the money." I can accept outsiders blaming me, but Nick? Do I really have to defend myself to him?

"I made mistakes. Mistakes I'll never forgive myself for. But I did finally tell Bud what was going on. I stopped it."

Nick huffs. "I figured that."

"That has to count for something."

"I guess. Hell, I didn't have the balls to do it."

Now that I've got his agreement, I realize how meaningless it is. *Count for something.* Who am I kidding? There's no accounting for this sort of calamity. "I need her number. I want to talk to her."

"She's not going to pick up. She doesn't want to talk to anybody."

"Come on, Nick. You know how much I cared for her."

He gives me her number, I thank him, and he hangs up, doesn't even say goodbye. It's too early to call Susie. Might as well do my laundry. By the time I get to the laundromat on South U, it's 10:30. There are signs everywhere telling you to stay with your clothes. I leave anyway.

I go to the Bagel Factory. They have this thing called a Fragel. It's a deep-fried raisin bagel coated in cinnamon sugar. You haven't lived until you've had a Fragel. I order one. There's a sign on the back of the register: *HELP WANTED. BAKER*. "How much does that pay?" I ask the guy taking my money.

He squints at me. "Shift goes from four in the morning to noon."

Is he trying to scare me off? "That's not what I asked."

"Are you really interested?"

"How much?"

"Five dollars an hour," he says.

"I could do that." I'm just thinking out loud. But now that I've said it, I think, *Why not? Throw yourself into something new.*

"Can you be in this Friday at four a.m.?"

"Sure."

He gives me my Fragel. "I'm Dave, by the way. The manager."

I should've known. He's too old to be a student, probably closer in age to Kretch. Come to think of it, he looks like Kretch. Barrel-chested, Bryl-creemed hair. His short-sleeve shirt's buttoned up nearly to the collar. He looks like a misplaced NASA engineer.

"Owen."

"Ever worked in the food industry, Owen?"

"I just got done working in a bar in Chicago."

"Oh? Which one?"

"Bud's."

"Ah!" Dave smiles. "The Irish pub next to Mama's, right?"

"That's the one."

He nods, impressed by my Bud's credentials. Good thing he didn't ask for a reference.

I still have half an hour to kill before the washer's done. I walk to the Diag and sit down on one of the benches that surround the main square. There's a crazy guy standing on a garbage can across the way. Doctor Diag, they call him. He looms over students crossing campus and screams out the Greek alphabet. That's his deal. I sit there, waiting for him to get to one particular letter: omicron. He never fails to shout it at the top of his lungs. Once, when Tara and I were passing by, he roared "Omicron!" so loud she lurched back and nearly fell. I was mad and ready to go after the guy, but Tara just laughed it off and kept walking. That was her way.

Doctor Diag finally gets to omicron. When he shouts it out, though, it isn't nearly as menacing as I remember. Maybe he's losing whatever fury the letter provoked in him. Maybe he's shouting just as savagely as always, and it doesn't shock me anymore.

I'm just thinking it's time to go when this guy comes up to me. He's older than a student, maybe Hadley's age—clean cut, white shirt, loafers. "Can you read this?" He holds out a business card.

I have no prayer of pronouncing the words on the card. Plus, why is this guy asking me to read it? "Sorry, I can't."

"It's *nam myoho renge kyo*," he tells me. "Can you say that?" He repeats it slowly, "*Nam. Myoho. Renge. Kyo. Nam. Myoho. Renge. Kyo.*"

"I'm not going to do that." The guy's some sort of religious nut. I stand up and start to walk away.

"It's a mantra," he says, following me. "By chanting it, you can change your karma and overcome all your obstacles to happiness."

I stop and look at the guy. Then I laugh. "Right…"

He has a sad look on his face but manages a tranquil little smile. "Maybe you want to keep the card, just in case you need it."

"No, thanks." I hurry away.

After I finish washing my clothes, I go back to the hotel and call Susie. She doesn't answer. It's almost one Chicago time. She might still be asleep. The notepad with my list is beside the phone. What's left? Finding out when Fitz comes… figuring out my classes… sorting out the Stu problem. I call around about that. After trying three different numbers and getting transferred twice, I finally find someone who can give me an answer. "Yes, we do have a record of Stuart Sheldon withdrawing his room reservation," she confirms.

"Do you know who my new roommate is?"

"We have a waitlist. The space is filled in the order of that list."

"What if I don't want him?" I ask like I'm being assigned a pet dog.

"You can withdraw your reservation. And you won't have to pay a penalty, since you've had a change in rooming arrangements."

I hang up wondering, what else would I do? Find somewhere new to live? Quit school? Then what?

These are the questions running through my head when I walk to CRISP, the place where they have your course picks in a big computer. It's a new system. I've never done it before. The line's out the door when I get there, and it's 20 minutes before I talk to anyone. I want to pick all new classes. A woman behind a table tells me I have to know the names and numbers of the courses I want. I thought all that was on the computer. "No." She shuts me down with an official smile. "Use this guide to read up on the classes and fill out this card with the classes you pick—name and number."

I take the guide and the card from her. "Do you have a pen?"

"No pens," she says, looking past me to the next face.

Now I'm retreating past the snaking line and out the door. I need to sit and go through this guide. Damn, it's thick. There are some steps off to the side, where a few other students are figuring out their schedules. I ask a guy sitting alone if he has a pen I can borrow. "I've just got this one," he says.

"I've got an extra one." This girl is sitting with two friends a couple steps up. She's already holding the pen out to me. She's cute. What can I say? I wish it wasn't the first thing I noticed. I mean, she has this sunny, on-the-ball disposition like life was never anything but great. I notice that too. But that's only after being taken with her bright eyes and pretty smile.

I take the pen from her. "I'm going to need it back." She's so serious I think she's joking. But she isn't. I look down at the pen to hide my smile. You'd think it would be one of those gold graduation pens for the fuss she made over it, but it's just a regular old Bic.

I start flipping through the guide. Last spring, when Tara found out what classes Dad talked me into, she got after me. "Do you really want any of these?" A few days later, she gave me the poetry books. "You have a gift with words. Don't lose it." I find the write-up for Creative Writing 240 and dog-ear the page. I do the same for Intro to Poetry. Beyond that, I have no idea.

"You should take Philosophy of Logic," one of the girls says behind me. Not the cheery pen nut. She's the one getting the advice.

"I don't want a cake course."

"It's not. It's supposed to be a good pre-law course."

"What grade did you get?" asks the Bic Queen.

"A B-minus."

"I'll take it. That puts all my classes on Tuesday and Thursday."

Shit. I forgot about timing. Writing and poetry are on Monday, Wednesday, and Friday. I should be looking for classes on those days.

Still, just out of curiosity, I check out Philosophy of Logic. It sounds dull. In the end, I go with Shakespeare and Greek Tragedy.

I give the sharp girl her pen and get back in the CRISP line. This time, I get steered toward an old man at terminal 12. I see the sign for terminal 27 two rows over. All these terminals, occupied with kids determining their future. The old guy's white beard tapers Santa-style to the top of his belly. I give him my card, filled in just the way they instructed. He asks for my student ID, too, and types in my name. "Looks like you already have four courses."

"Yeah. I want to drop all of them and add these."

"Oh." His fingers stop clicking away like he got unplugged. "Dropping and adding is a different process."

"What do you mean?"

"You have to fill out a different card."

"But that's the card they gave me."

He steeples his fingers on his stomach and taps the tips together. Santa has a problem. "We really need that card."

"Please can you just do it? I've been in line twice already." He wobbles his head, leans up, and resumes his typing.

The girl who lent me the pen crosses behind him and takes a seat right around the snaking maze at terminal 16.

"Creative writing's open," he reports. Seconds later: "So's poetry."

I can hear Miss Most Likely to Hoard Pens through all the swirling chatter. She's leaning into the terminal operator and pointing to his computer as if she's teaching him how to use it. Figures.

"Shakespeare's good, but Greek Tragedy's full."

I don't skip a beat. "Try Philosophy of Logic."

Back at the hotel, I call Susie again. Same story. I get Fitz's parents' number from the operator and try that. No answer there either. I fall back on the bed. It seems like I've been on the run forever. I want to stop, but I still don't feel like I can relax. Will I ever?

*I'm running. Terry's with me. My dorm's burning, students streaming out. They're chasing us. We jump an iron fence. Now we're in the alley behind Bud's townhouse, only it's a cemetery. "Everything's wrong," I say. Terry holds out the card that guy in the Diag showed me. "Say this."*

It's dim and grey, color bled out of the room, an arrangement of ashy shadows. I imagine that if I touch them, they'll disintegrate in powdery heaps. I prop myself up on the headboard, turn on the nightstand light. My list for the day's there. No contact with Susie or Fitz. No answers on how I'm going to live. Limbo.

It's seven. I haven't eaten since the Fragel. Burger King's a few blocks away. There's a line when I get there. They should open the second register. Some drunk knucklehead decides to take matters into his own hands. He goes to that register, climbs over the counter, and grabs the microphone workers use to call out orders. "Big Mac," he deadpans. "I'd like my Whopper to be a Big Mac." His jackass friends start giggling. A girl behind the counter pleads with him to stop. He starts singing the "Have it Your Way" jingle. "Hold the pickles, hold the lettuce. Special orders don't—"

"Get the fuck in line!" *Did I say that? Did that come out of* me?

The guy stops, hand still holding the mic. "What's your problem?"

"You're my problem." Now I'm coming toward him.

"What the fuck're you gonna do about it?"

I get to the counter, right across from him. "Let's find out." I glare at him. I'm ready to fight. I *want* to fight.

"Let us order," someone pleads behind me.

One of the guy's friends leans in. "Let's get out of here, Jake."

Jake shakes a finger at me. Then he breaks our stare-down and swings back over onto the customer side of the counter. I don't let him out of my sight. You never know. His friends are right there to usher him away. He gives me one last look. "Fuck you," he says.

"I'm right here." I hold out my hands. Jake stomps off, his buddies hurrying to catch up. I don't take a deep breath or anything. I don't feel relief. Nobody says anything to me. I just get back in line, order my meal, sit down, and eat. It feels good to stand up and not back down. If I'm going to stop feeling bad about what I did, this is who I need to be. Doing what's right, speaking up, confronting things head on.

The most popular bar in town is right next door to Burger King. It's called Dooley's. It's like a Bud's with training wheels—same Irish pub motif, same wood interior, even a leprechaun logo, but where Bud's seems personable, this one's generic, cartoonish—a Saturday morning TV leprechaun. And that's the whole problem with this place. It's gimmicky, inauthentic, the Monkees of Bud's.

The bar's bigger, louder, and rowdier than Bud's was on the worst tourist night. The bouncer asks for my ID. He's a hulking football type, but not nearly as menacing as Moose. Moose had this hard-eyed way of going about his job. He knew violence was coming, and he didn't care. This guy's on edge, eyes darting around, sweat on his forehead. "Everything okay?" I meant is everything okay with him. But he thinks I'm questioning why he's taking so long with my ID. That prompts him to examine the card more closely. When he hands it back to me, he puts on this overdone scowl, a bad Clint Eastwood impression. I try not to smile.

I find a seat at the end of the U-shaped bar. This is where I'd talk to Jill at Bud's. The girl in front of me is too busy for chit-chat. She's got two pitchers going while she pours a line of shots. She doesn't even ask what I want, just points at me. I order a Miller. The crowd's three deep around the bar. There's so much yelling you can't hear yourself think. God, they all look so young. It's hard to believe I was one of them a year ago. I feel old, removed, cast out. The guy beside me spills his beer and doesn't even know it. It streaks across the bar, laps up against the lip of the rail, and heads for my mug. Just as I reach to lift my beer, the bartender swipes a rag across the counter and intercepts the stream.

"Just in the nick of time," I joke.

"Another Miller?" She can't hear me.

"Sure." I'm not even halfway done with my first one. What the hell. I chug it down, like all the kids around me, thirsty to devour their youth. It makes me sad. I laugh, nothing more than a defeated huff, really. I laugh because I realize that I'm like one of those old drunks that sat at the bar at Bud's and looked so… unhappy. I used to think, *why are they even here if they're miserable*? What was the mantra that guy in the Diag repeated? I should've taken his card.

The next beer comes. I chug that down too. Some kid starts chanting "Chug-chug-chug!" Nobody joins in. I pound the empty mug on the bar, get a twenty out of my wallet, and fling it down. Then I walk out. I don't have to be here. Ever again.

Drinking two jumbo beers that fast was a bad idea. My head's spinning by the time I get back to the hotel. I've never seen the lobby so crowded. Four older couples pack the tiny space. Parents, here to see their children off to college. That's right: I have to be out tomorrow. And I have nowhere to go.

Back in my room, I try Susie again. Again, no answer. I call Fitz. Ring and ring—and then— "Hello?" It's Mr. Fitzgerald.

"Hi, is… um… is…" *What the hell's his first name?* "Is Mike there?" *That's it.* "This is Owen Maloney. I go to school with him."

"Oh, yeah. Hi Owen. No, he left for school yesterday."

"Yesterday? So he's here? Now?"

"If here is Ann Arbor."

"Do you have an address for him? I want to go say hi."

Mr. Fitzgerald gives me the address. It's 915 Oakland. "He'll be happy to hear from you," he says. "He could use a friend."

"Oh yeah?" I want to ask why, but I can't think of a less direct way to do it. Finally: "Is everything okay?" I'm too late. He's hung up.

I pack up everything but my toiletries, a pair of underwear, and the clothes I've worn all day. I take a shower. Tomorrow, I'll try

Susie one more time. Check out of the hotel. Get something to eat. Then go find Fitz. Ask if I can stay with him a couple nights. Be the friend he needs, the way I need one now.

When I lay down and turn off the light, the room starts to swirl. It's not as bad as it was on the walk from Dooley's, though. If I look at something long enough, like the strip of streetlight cutting open my drapes, my mind clicks back into focus. But after a while, it drifts again, and I have to find something else to concentrate on.

Have I done everything? Is there someone to call? Dad? Jill? Maybe Terry isn't there anymore. I turn on the light and get the broken coaster out of my wallet. I pick up the phone… *But Jill said never to call*. I'm still holding the coaster. I look at Tara's number. I dial it. A woman answers. I can't tell if it's Tara or not. Have I already forgotten her voice?

"Is this Tara?"

"Can I say who's calling?"

"Tell her it's Owen."

There's muffled talk now, rustling, scraping, a sigh. "Owen."

"Tara."

"I didn't think I'd hear from you again."

"I didn't either." I wait for her to talk. She doesn't. This is up to me. "But I kept the number you left at Bud's."

"I saw you there. And you saw me. But you turned away."

"I know. I'm sorry. I just—I couldn't do it. I was still hurting. But I'm better now." I'm saying it *for her*. I don't know if it's true for me. There's still pain here, but nothing compared to all my other afflictions. It's a pain I desperately need to feel tender, one I want to make easier for both of us to carry. I can't do that for Susie or Jill. "Really. It's okay. That's why I called—to tell you that. I didn't want you thinking back with… with…"

"Regret?"

"Bitterness."

"I'm not bitter," she says. "But I do regret. I *want* to regret. Otherwise, it didn't matter at all."

"Well, like I say, I'm over it—"

"We were about to be in love, weren't we?" Tara takes me by surprise. It sounds like the poem I wrote, the one I never sent to her.

Was it true? I don't know. But she's insisting it was. She needs me to say yes. "I thought so." It's the best I can do.

"Then we were."

"Then we were," I whisper likes it's our secret.

"Take care of yourself, Owen. Stay sweet."

"I will," I promise, wincing. Then it comes to me what I was going to tell her: "I'm taking a writing class, like you said I should."

No answer. Tara's gone. Maybe it's better that way. Maybe that's something I shouldn't think of doing for her sake.

I hang up and turn off the light.

The room isn't spinning anymore.

## Carry That Weight
*You're going to carry that weight, carry that weight a long time.*
*- The Beatles*

I stay in my room right up to checkout time. I set my bag in front of the door and try again to call Susie. There's an ominous tone, then an automated voice says, "The number you have reached is not in service. Please check the number and dial again." I hang up and dial the number slower. Same message.

The house on Oakland looks like a crumbling Victorian castle; a patchwork of miscolored red bricks, gables, pillars, dormers, even a vaulting spire-topped tower. It's like they took one of those townhouses on Dearborn, set it off on a hill by itself, and let it grow wild. I go up a long stairway to a cement porch and try the door. It's locked. There's a panel with buzzers and names taped beside them. Fitz's name is with four others. Eddie's name is there, too, but it's crossed out. Was he still going through chemo? Did he drop out like Stu? I press the buzzer. No one answers.

There's a beat-up couch at one end of the porch, red party cups scattered around it. I don't want to leave and miss Fitz again. I sit down to think. What is there left to do? No way to call anybody. Nowhere to go. Nothing to look forward to. It's all just looking back now, shouldering memories. People come and go, most ignoring me, one giving me a suspicious glance. A girl asks if I need to get inside. I've seen her before but can't place where. I say no.

When Fitz finally shows, he's with three guys I don't know. He and another guy have their arms full of grocery bags, one's carrying a couple cases of beer, and the last guy's wheeling along a shopping cart with a keg in it.

"Maloney!" Fitz shouts from the street. He sets his bags down on the steps, rushes up, and charges toward me. I barely have time to stand before he has a hold of me and he's hugging fiercely. "Poor Eddie," he cries. "Did you hear?"

Now I know: Eddie's worse than sick. I hug him back. Fitz's roommates wait at the bottom of the stairway for us to be done. When we finally separate, I ask, "How?"

"It was fast," Fitz says. "They tried over and over to bring him around, but the cancer overwhelmed him." He gasps so hard I think he might be sick. I put my arm around his shoulder. He leans against me and settles himself.

I help Fitz and his roommates take everything inside. Their apartment is the entire top floor of the castle. They're getting ready for a party. They've invited all the other people in the building.

"You should see the foxes on the first floor," one of the roommates says as he taps the keg.

Fitz is busy wiring the speakers in the living room to the stereo in his bedroom. It's the same one he had in the dorm last year.

"I got a new system—" I catch myself. I can't believe I forgot; Terry's due to pick that up from Dad later today. I shift gears and tell him about Stu.

"I heard that," Fitz says.

"I don't know if I'll even stay in the dorm."

Fitz stops fiddling with the wires. "Wanna stay here?" There's no enthusiasm in his voice. It's like he's only asking out of obligation. I get it. We never did get along. But now that it's just he and I, maybe we should.

"Thanks, Fitz. I could use a room for a few nights. But everything's up in the air after that." I don't want to answer him one way or another. This gives me the excuse to say no when the time's right.

Fitz gets the music going. We open all the windows, take the keg out onto the big balcony, and stand drinking beer, hovering over the street like puppet masters. Al Green croons behind us. This isn't Fitz's music. "Eddie loved Al Green," I say to him.

"He put his albums with mine last year when we packed up. 'No use splitting them,' he said. 'They're just gonna be back together.'"

What do you say to that? "He was the one who kept *us* together," is the best I can do.

People are showing up now. First, the guys in the place below us. Then, some girls who are friends with Fitz's roommates. Now, more people from the apartments below. It's too crowded on the balcony. I go inside. It's better here, but there's a clump of people by the front door. Before long, the whole place will be shoulder to shoulder.

I find Fitz closed off in his room, flipping through records. He's holding *Abbey Road* in his hands. "Remember that time we had the snowstorm, and we played Yahtzee all day? Eddie must've turned this record over ten times."

"He loved that album."

"And he knew all those clues on the sleeve—the preacher, pall-bearer, gravedigger. The shoeless corpse; the 28IF license plate; three Beatles. All to say, Paul is dead."

"Yeah…"

"But he wasn't. And now Eddie is." Fitz puts on the record. "I'm just gonna keep playing this over and over. My farewell to Eddie."

"It's fitting." Eddie goes out with the Beatles… the end of holding hands and loving you yeah-yeah-yeah and something in the way she moves. Someone as purely good as Eddie shouldn't have to know what comes after that.

"I talked to the guys," Fitz says. "If you want to take Eddie's place, they're cool with it. It's three hundred a month."

"I don't know, Fitz."

"I'm going to be a lot less of an asshole," he vows.

I realize then: it isn't Fitz that's stopping me from saying yes. "I just don't know if I can deal with *this* all the time." I put up my hands and go silent. The music and the yelling and the laughing take over.

"I don't know if I can either. Why do you think I'm in my room?"

"So, what you're saying is that you could use an ally?"

"I could use an ally."

"Let me think about it." I turn for the door. "You coming?"

"Gimme a minute."

I open the door into the party. Then I step out and close it on a narrowing strip of Fitz, still pondering that *Abbey Road* cover.

I wend my way into the front room. It's already getting hard to cross. And the balcony is worse than before. Last year, there was a story about a balcony collapsing during a college party and three kids dying. I see now how that could happen. But that's where the keg is. Of course, there's a line, and it's not very orderly. People sway and shove and stagger against the crush of partiers around them. I squeeze in at what looks like the end of the line.

And there she is, huddled with the girls she sat beside trying to figure out her classes. And one of her friends is the girl who asked me if I wanted to come in when I was waiting on the couch for Fitz. That's where I'd seen her before—outside CRISP.

"Philosophy of Logic." They're so close to me, I'm almost in their conversation already.

She looks at me with those bright, lively eyes. "The man without a pen," she replies, smiling that pretty smile.

We get jostled together. "You make it sound like a character flaw."

She shrugs. "You needed a pen. I had one."

So serious. It's almost laughable. "And you needed it back."

"I don't like to lose pens."

"Who does?"

Some guy in front of us is passing back cups of beer. He makes a point of giving the Bic Queen one. "So… did you take it?" she asks.

"I gave it right back to you."

"I mean the class. Philosophy of Logic."

"Oh." I laugh. "Yeah."

"We could use a little philosophy of logic now." She rolls her eyes around at the lunacy surging everywhere.

"That's for sure," I agree. Then—I don't know why—the senselessness of everything overtakes me. Not just the shaking balcony and the desperate revelry, but Eddie dying. And Stu struggling. And Jill captive. And Susie wounded. And my brother outcast. And my dad lying. And my mom deceived. "See you in class." I turn to go.

"I'm sure I'll see you before that. I'm on the first floor."

"I'm in Markley, up on the hill." I really have to leave. I feel like I'm hyperventilating.

"Oh. My roommate said you lived up here."

"No."

"Are you okay?" She's cocking her head now.

"Yeah, I'm good." My smile starts trembling. I turn and push my way back inside. It's as bad as the balcony now, people packed tight, some sitting on the kitchen counters, a few standing on the couches. It's worse than a rowdy night at Bud's. Just a bunch of reckless kids. They don't know how fast you can get into trouble. How are they different from all those lost kids who followed Manson? Take away privilege and family ties, add the temptations of sex and drugs, then leave them with a manipulative sociopath. And what do you get?

It takes a while to get to Fitz's room. That's where I left my bag. I'm out of here. I don't know where I'll go, but anywhere else is better. Ringo keeps extoling the virtues of an octopus's garden, but you can barely hear him. No one's listening anyway. Fitz's door is locked. I knock. When he doesn't come, I pound on the thing. Can't he hear me? I shout his name and beat on the door again. Still, nothing.

There's a dormer window next to Fitz's door, a little alcove you have to crouch down to get into. It's the only place where no one is.

I sit down there. A red light's glowing outside the window. I look to see what it is. I can't find the source, but I see a metal-grated landing. It's the fire escape. There's a handle on the side of the window. I turn and push it. Then I climb onto the landing and shut myself out there. Fitz's window is within arm's reach of the landing's rail. I lean over as far as I can—enough to see Fitz's head, bobbing to the music. Good. He's just ignoring me. I was starting to worry.

The red light is a bare bulb above the window. Maybe that's how you show firemen where the fire escape is. I don't know. One thing's for sure. It's a hell of a lot more peaceful out here than in there. A narrow metal staircase angles steeply to a lower landing, then doubles back and drops to the ground. I go down a few steps and sit. The roofline's at my shoulder. I can reach out and touch the gutter.

The sun's almost down. I can only see it in the treetops, bright yellow leaves jittering in the breeze. I think of that day in the park, when I heard something in the trees' rustling. A warning of what was to come. These leaves shudder like it just got here.

How will I go on? What sort of illusion can I possibly cling to that will get me through this? Is there a Bullworker that strengthens your soul? Can I write enough lists to propel myself from hour to hour, day after day? Maybe I should chant what that guy said. *Nam-myoho-renge-kyo.* That's what it was. Maybe there's a poem—

The music is suddenly clearer. *Boy, you're gonna carry that weight, carry that weight a long time.* It comes with the force of prophecy. And now the music's muffled again...

"What are you doing out here?" It's the Philosophy of Logic girl. She's on the landing, looking down at me.

"I just needed a little quiet."

"Oh, I'm sorry." She steps back. I can't see her now. But then her face reappears. "It's just... I wanted to make sure you were okay."

*It's fine. I'm good. It's nothing.* I run all those through my head. None of them are true. "I don't think so," I finally just tell the truth.

"Maybe it would help, you know, to have someone with you."

"Maybe."

She comes down the steps and sits next to me. "My name's May."

"Hey."

"And you're Owen," she says, after waiting for me to tell her that.

I laugh at myself. "Sorry. I do that all the time."

"I know your name because I asked." May smiles.

"Sorry. I'm not going to be much fun tonight."

"That's okay. Life isn't supposed to be fun all the time."

Something strikes me about that. I turn to face her head on. Who *is* this? She just goes on smiling. Gently, easily. "What?" she asks. I must be looking at her funny.

"Why would you smile at that?"

She shrugs. "You just have to be real about life."

"That's it?"

May considers the question, then nods, her mind made up. "That's it." How can you not love such young wisdom, such cheerful faith? You'd be lucky to love someone like that.

May studies my face; she's not sure I understand what she means. "Put it this way. Sometimes you don't get your pen back. But sometimes you do."

I rock back to take her fully in. A gust of laughter blows out of me. "You're a hoot.

"*You're* the hoot."

She nudges my shoulder. One last laugh dislodges. And now I'm gutted, empty, thoroughly lost. I start to cry. And I can't stop. I lean against May's shoulder. She doesn't move away.

## EPILOGUE: Come Away With Me
*Come away with me, and I'll never stop loving you.*
*- Norah Jones*

She's out by the side door of the bakery, crying. Owen can't just leave her, not after all these years of not knowing, of never quite forgetting. "Just a minute," he says to May, and he hurries off, down a path between the scrub trees that guard a mountain stream and the side of the bakery.

Owen will have to explain himself to May. He can't walk away from his wife to a crying woman. How will she take it? He should've told her long ago. Now it's 47 years later. The accumulated weight of that secrecy might be too much to bear.

Still, Owen has to do this. He has to go to her. He has to know she's okay. He's nearly in front of her now, just on the other side of a dumpster, yet she goes on sobbing, unaware that he's there. He shuffles his feet over the gravel to signal his approach. Her face stays hidden in her hand. There's nothing to do but speak.

"Susie."

She seizes up like he's a ghost. She looks past him to the road. She looks the other way to a rusty fence blocking her in. She steps back to the door. Then, finally, she accepts that she can't avoid this. "I'm sorry. I wasn't ready for that," Susie says, feeling the need to apologize.

"Me neither." Owen stops a couple steps in front of her.

"Was that your wife?"

"Yeah."

"Does she know about Chicago?"

"Not really." Owen glances behind him. "But after this…"

When he turns back, Susie's staring at him. It's a sunny day. Her face is in the light. The last time Owen saw her she was lying on Bud's couch. He sees a faint scar on her upper lip. A song comes to mind, the song that piano player sang at Lupos. *We'll meet again.* It's not the first time he's thought of it. A strand of hair falls across Susie's eye. She puffs it off her face, like she used to at Bud's.

"How have you been?" She cocks her head to study him.

Owen takes a deep breath, holds it for a second, then lets it go. "Better than I was back then." No point in wasting time. "I called. Over and over. Until the number was disconnected."

"I didn't want to talk to anybody. I just wanted to leave."

"Chicago?"

"Yeah. I went back home to Indiana."

Owen figured that's what Susie did, but the confirmation still brings a sting of defeat. "What about the audition at Second City?"

She laughs, surprised, like she'd forgotten all about it. But the memory quickly settles into sadness. "I never went."

"You would've gotten that job," Owen says. "I still remember that night at Los Toros, how funny you were… how happy."

"I was," she says. "But it didn't even last a day."

"I went to that restaurant. Lupos. I went right after you called. I knew something bad was going to happen."

"When he saw me on the phone, he got me out of there fast."

"Did you try to call me later?" Owen asks. It's a question that still haunts him.

"I don't know," Susie says. "That whole night's a blur. The last thing I remember is fighting with Terry and Moose while they tried to force me into a car. Next thing I knew, I was in an ambulance."

"They left you at Bud's house, just outside my door." It never occurred to Owen that she might not know that. "They did it so people would think I was the one dealing coke out of the bar. The only one, I mean."

"Nick told me. He told me everything."

"I'm sorry, Susie. I should've told you back then. I'll never forgive myself for that. It might've changed things."

Susie waves him off. "It was a long time ago."

"Nothing you still think about is that long ago," Owen says. "Time and memory are two different things."

"That's why I try not to think about it."

Owen feels like he's about to choke up. He changes subjects. "Do you still keep in touch with Nick?"

"Not for a while. Last time we talked was maybe ten years ago."

"Did he ever start his breakfast diner?"

"No. He's an EMT in Naperville, or at least he was."

"What about Terry?" Owen asks. "Whatever happened to him?"

Susie shakes her head. "You'd hope someone like that would have to pay for what he did. Turns out, Terry's just one of those people who always lands on his feet."

"Where'd he end up?"

"Bud opened a new bar down on the river, and he made Terry the Kretch of the place."

"He kept working for Bud?" Owen's aghast. "But I told him what he did. I told him he was behind the drug dealing."

"Bud always had a soft spot in his heart for Terry. He did fire Moose, though. And he banned Hadley and a bunch of others."

Owen thinks about how Bud said Terry was the son he never had, how Terry used to shadow Kretch. How long had Bud been grooming him to get into the business? "So that's it?" Owen says. "That's all that became of him, just a manager of a bar?"

"Oh, no. No, Terry's big into Chicago politics."

Owen shakes his head. Neither of them speaks. Finally, Owen whispers what he's been wondering since he asked about Nick. "And Jill?"

"I don't know."

"Nick didn't say anything about her?" Susie clamps her mouth. She blinks and blinks. "Come on, Susie. What did he tell you?"

"She died a few years after that summer." Susie can't hold it any longer. "Twenty-eight years old."

Owen goes numb. "How?"

"A car accident on Lake Shore Drive. Her three-year-old boy didn't have a scratch. That was the saving grace."

"She had a son?" The news staggers him.

Susie hangs her head and nods. "Kretch told Nick she swerved to save him. They could tell by the skid marks."

"Three years old." Owen gasps, suddenly overcome.

Susie knows what he's thinking. "Everyone figured it was Terry's since he helped take care of him."

Owen doubles over. He looks like he's about to lose his balance. Susie puts a hand on his shoulder to brace him. "So did he get custody?" Owen asks, hands on his knees.

"No. He went to live with Jill's parents."

"Battle Creek…" Owen says under his breath. *Forty-seven years. And now everyone has their own life. What would be the point in knowing?* He straightens up with a sigh. "Tell me about you."

Susie isn't ready for the question. "I… I run this bakery."

"Are you married?"

"I was," she says. "He passed away two years ago."

"Oh, I'm sorry."

"It was the best thing at the time. He was in a lot of pain."

"I see…" Owen can't think of what else to say.

Now it's Susie who moves things along. "Do you have children?"

"A boy and a girl. They're in their thirties now. I still can't believe that. What about you?"

"One son. John. He turned forty this year, took over my parents' farm in Indiana." Owen smiles to think of Susie with a son so old, so many years removed from the night when she was left battered outside his door. He feels like he's gotten past something, that they both have. They could be any old friends catching up now.

"They died." Susie looks off at the mountains. "Five days apart."

It takes Owen a second to realize who she's talking about. "My mom just died a month ago. My dad's at a total loss without her."

"So they stayed together, after that night at Los Toros? Your dad stopped…" Susie doesn't know how to put it.

Owen knows what she means. He told her about his father being with another woman. "Apparently. I never saw them anything but happy after that. And now he's crushed."

"That's what time will do to love," Susie says.

The notion strikes Owen like an epiphany. "Exactly."

"And in the end, that's all you hope for in life."

Owen knows what he wants to ask, but he doesn't know if he should. He has to know, though. "So, in the end… all in all…"

"All in all?"

"Have you had a happy life?"

Susie takes a long moment to consider the question. "I have."

Owen's relief is immediate, liberating. "I bet you're still funny."

Susie laughs, that tough, tender laugh of hers, preserved through all the years. "I have my moments."

"I could have loved you," he suddenly declares.

"Me too," Susie admits. "I don't regret that it didn't happen, though. That's life. I still think… fondly about that time."

"So do I," Owen agrees.

Susie opens her arms to him. He steps in. They embrace. Not long. Not hard. But enough. Then they let each other go.

Owen doesn't notice that May moved the car until he can't find it through the trees lining the stream. By then, he's almost to the sidewalk. That's when he sees May across the street, watching him approach. He hurries over and gets in the driver's seat.

May's holding his phone out to him. "My turn to play something."

A woman's singing. Owen's heard the song before, but it's not off his trip playlist. "Who's this?" he asks, pulling out.

"You have to guess," May says.

"Where are we going if I win?"

"Where do you want to go?"

The woman keeps imploring, "Come away with me." Owen should know this, but the voice is almost too familiar. They ease up to the only light in town. Flatlands stretch from every corner of the intersection. Owen thinks of that night he walked from Bud's, past all those dark alleys, to the train station where so many lost souls huddled. The mountains seem small in the distance compared to the skyscrapers that loomed over him back then.

"Let's go to Chicago," he says. But he doesn't guess the singer. Instead, he tells her everything that happened that summer before they met—how it started with a woman he thought he loved and ended with the one he knew he'd love forever… all because of two others who taught him the difference.

## AUTHOR'S NOTE

I finished my freshman year at the University of Michigan in 1978 and left Ann Arbor that spring thinking that my future was with one girl. Within weeks of returning in September, I met Michelle, and we married less than two years later. How could one summer change my life so dramatically? I never asked myself that question until I started writing this book.

All my novels have elements of autobiography to them. I've taken pains, however, to disguise the facts under layers of fiction. *Once in Chicago* is no different in that respect, but the layers are more transparent. This is the most personal story I ever written— about one of the most formative periods of my life.

For the record, I did work the summer of '78 in a Chicago bar. It wasn't Bud McGee's. It was, as some may surmise, Butch McGuire's. The bar's still there, hauntingly similar to the place I remember nearly half a century later. And Butch was indeed my dad's good friend and roommate at Michigan. I even spent the summer living in his basement. Many of the Bud's employees you meet are also based on real people—Jill and Susie; Terry, Nick, and Garrett; even Kretch and Moose. I never saw any of them again. I want to make clear, however, that the illicit activities that go on at Bud's have nothing to do with Butch's. They're based on my experience working at Bennigan's in Ann Arbor, where several employees were caught selling cocaine out of the bar. (I should mention, though, that I *was* the "hot dog man" at Butch's—as good a gig as described!)

The summer of 1978 was also when I began to notice the cracks in my parents' marriage, though they weren't as extreme as depicted here. My father also had his first cancer scare that summer.

And much to his chagrin, I really did spend a good chunk of my Butch's earnings on a high-end stereo. I even tried to sell my dad on its virtues by playing it for him at high volume—but the album I chose to blow his mind was Jethro Tull's *Thick as a Brick*. (That said, he did love Ravel's 'Bolero.')

Music was a big part of that summer, as you can tell from the chapter titles. Like a lot of teenagers back then, my album collection was a valuable, albeit faulty, source of wisdom. The Rolling Stones' *Some Girls* came out just after I started working at Butch's, and I must've heard "Miss You" 300 times that summer. It was on the bar's jukebox—as was "Paint it Black." It's no lie that our floor manager Dave loved that song and could be softened up if you played it. Fittingly, 1978 was a big year of change in music. I was more tempted by the lure of punk's rebellion than disco's conformity. We went to O'Banion's often; we only went to Faces once.

Some of my college friends will recognize Fitz and Eddie and Stu as former roommates of mine. Sadly, they all passed away much too soon. As for Tara and a few of the girls Owen and Fitz argue about, they're also based, more or less, on real people.

The toughest part of writing a book this personal was sharing it with my wife Michelle. I couldn't very well avoid it; she is, after all, my editor. I realized as she read the first draft that, like Owen, I didn't exactly tell her everything that went on during that summer in Chicago. It made for some interesting discussions. However, I think it also gave Michelle a better understanding of why I broke down and cried one night shortly after we met. No, we weren't on a fire escape, but it was at the top of a stairwell in our dorm.

Everyone has a time in their life when they must reckon with what love is and what it means to them. I think that's true, but I'm not sure. Anyway, this was my time. Revisiting it has given me a greater appreciation for the journey that Michelle and I have taken for the last 47 years since that fateful summer.

**ALSO BY PETER TIERNAN**

History of the House Next Door
Boiler Beach
Family Trees
Unopened